Mike Grist is the British/American author of the Chris Wren thrillers. Born and brought up in the UK, he has lived and worked in the USA, Japan and Korea as a teacher, photographer, writer and adventurer. He currently lives in London.

HAVE YOU READ EVERY CHRIS WREN THRILLER?

Saint Justice
They stole his truck. Big mistake.

No Mercy
Hackers came for his kids. There can be no mercy.

Make Them Pay
The latest reality TV show: execute the rich.

False Flag
They framed him for murder. He'll kill to clear his name.

Firestorm
Wren's father is back. The storm is coming.

Enemy of the People
Lies are drowning America. Can the country survive?

Backlash
He just wanted to go home. They got in the way...

Never Forgive
His home in ashes. Vengeance never forgives.

War of Choice
They came for his team. This time it's war.

Learn more at www.shotgunbooks.com

HAVE YOU READ EVERY GIRL 0 THRILLER?

<u>Girl Zero</u>
They stole her little sister. Now they'll pay.

<u>Zero Day</u>
The criminal world is out for revenge. So is she.

Learn more at www.shotgunbooks.com

HAVE YOU READ THE LAST MAYOR THRILLERS?

The Last Mayor series - Books 1-9

When the zombie apocalypse devastates the world overnight, Amo is the last man left alive.

Or is he?

Learn more at www.shotgunbooks.com

FIRESTORM

A CHRISTOPHER WREN THRILLER

MIKE GRIST

SHOTGUN
BOOKS

SHOTGUN BOOKS

www.shotgunbooks.com

Paperback ISBN - 9781739951153

For Su

1

RACHEL

Sitting at the wheel of her parked Chevrolet Impala, Rachel Day's heart hammered against her ribs like a trapped bird in a cage. Sweat ran down the back of her neck and it felt like her skin was burning, tingling as her clothes shifted.

Everything was coming to a head now.

She swallowed and turned off the engine. The Impala wound down, the engine juddering like the bird wheezing its last under the hood. She sat for a moment looking out at the other people in the lot like they were citizens of a different world.

Mall of the USA. Downtown Cincinnati. She'd been here hundreds of times before, with her kids, on dates with her husband, as a college kid herself. Four floors, a cinema, an indoor theme park, a bowling alley and over five hundred shops, all within an aircraft carrier-sized glass and plaster structure. Familiar brand names danced before her eyes, summoning happy memories. Slurpees with the girls. Canoodling with the boys.

She opened the door and stepped out. The Impala's engine ticked in the heat; too hot out to cool. 11:25am on a Saturday, prime time shopping, and she watched people pouring across the baking blacktop lot toward the air-conditioned comfort inside.

The door slammed. She moved around to pop the trunk. The heat of the car's bodywork sizzled the sweat off her fingertips.

The bag was inside: gray canvas, nondescript and heavy, a thick zipper down the middle affixed with a big yellow zip tie. Easy to open. Even in a rush, you could grab that zip tie. She pulled the zip an inch, the teeth peeling loudly and opening a dark hole to the interior, then pulled it back and hoisted the bag over her shoulder.

"Can I help you with that, ma'am?"

She turned. Some young guy wearing the Mall of the USA's helper outfit. Rachel saw a blur of fuzzy hair, bright young eyes, apron, smile. Aiming for tips, she figured. Her husband John had looked much like this on their earliest dates back in junior high. She felt her collar pull painfully tight on her neck, turned at an awkward angle to hide the bag.

"I'm fine," she said.

"I'm happy to carry it for you," the young guy said.

"I'm fine," she repeated. "Really. Thank you."

"Yes ma'am," he said and started away. She watched him striding off like a missionary, then turned and slammed the trunk shut. The click of the latch was final. The weight of the bag dug into her shoulder.

The lot passed by under her feet. The automatic doors slid open at her approach. Cold air blasted her, chilling the sweat down her temples. 11:51. An old greeter smiled at her, said hello. Rachel nodded back and pressed on.

Faces passed her by, young parents pushing strollers, kids on leash lines babbling happily, old folks power-walking in uniformed troops, sales staff out front hawking their latest deals. A shoe salesman stepped in her path, handed her a leaflet.

"Specials on Jimmy Choo."

She hurried past.

Every eye was a window. He lurked within them all.

She circled the ground floor, glancing into all the shops she'd once cared so much for, all the places she'd giggled with her friends, clutched the arms of whatever boy she'd been dating, the restaurants she'd eaten at with her kids. On the second floor she circled, third floor, up to the cinema on the fourth.

"Today," the man had said. An hour earlier at her front porch, dressed as a mail man. Handing her a package. Going through the process of signing.

She'd stared up at him. His face was different every time.

"Noon," he'd said, "Mall of the USA food court. Stand by." Then he was gone. Down her drive, turning right, heading for his next delivery like he hadn't just torn a hole in everything.

She rode the escalators down into the food court on the ground floor. It was as big as a football field around her, with four tiers of shopping stacked around it like the layers on a wedding cake. People clustered at long red plastic tables: gangs of teens laughing too loud, kids bawling in their high chairs with parents trying to persuade them to eat a few more limp noodles, old folks setting down their canvas bags and smiling at the load off, all divided into cliques like high school.

A server glanced at her. An old guy smiled. All different faces, all suffering in ways they couldn't even imagine.

She was here to set them free.

She bought pho noodles and a coke and sat down in the center of the food court, at the edge of a table of diverse-looking young people, as wholesome as the cast of Friends.

Her heart raced. Her phone rang in her back pocket, but she ignored it. Her husband, calling.

She forced herself to eat. The noodles were slippery and hot. Pouring food down her throat like a waste disposal.

11:58 and her hand shook against the table. Sweat puddled from her palm. Maybe she was crying.

"Lady, are you OK?"

One of the Friends. She could barely see them through her watery vision, sucking hungry little gulps of air. He was tall, wore a college JV jacket in red. The faces of the others were like smudged ovals all staring at her. How much were they all suffering right now?

11:59.

"I don't feel well," she said, and the words felt like vomit pulled up from the soup of noodles and broth in her belly. Barely a human now. A cog in some grander machine.

"We can call someone, if you like?" the boy said.

A good boy.

12:00.

She stood.

"I'll be fine, thank you."

She walked away, barely restraining the panic. Standby, he'd said, and she'd stood. Her bag lay behind, tucked underneath the table close enough to the Friends that no one in security would think anything of it.

She pushed back through the crowd; noisy, laughing, living on the surface. They hadn't fallen through the cracks yet. They hadn't looked through the window.

Through the mall she went, headed for the lot. Her Impala and the dream of a past life. Maybe it was all in her head. Their faces in the flames. Maybe, maybe…

She was at the automatic doors before she saw him.

The young guy from before, wearing his Mall of USA

helper's outfit. The same, but different. She knew it by looking into his his eyes.

"Fear is a portal," he said.

His voice. Not his voice.

Then he was gone.

She stood locked in the automatic doors, caught in the mechanism as they tried to close then shuddered open again to either side. Cool air washing out, hot air pouring in, standing in the mall's purgatory as his words reverberated, driving her back underwater just when she'd been so close to the surface. Seconds passed, minutes. Then the greeter was there at her side.

An old guy, navy cardigan, holding a bucket for donations. She hadn't noticed that before. For a second he stood by her side, leaning in like he was going to ask if she was OK.

"Pain is a doorway," he said. No more, no less, then he was moving on, already past her.

Her mind shut down. It was too much.

She turned around, started walking with no sense of direction. The bag was gone, she knew that much. Her Impala was far behind with no path of return. Her life trailed in her wake like a wedding train. Everything she'd made, all the people she'd loved, stretched out on the tracks.

Fear was a portal. Pain was a doorway.

She couldn't think. Then he was there again.

"Walk in the fire," he said. In passing. Barely enough to catch a glimpse of his eyes. The shoe salesman from before. Pushing his deals on Jimmy Choo. The phrase came like a lash. A terrible responsibility. She wanted to seize his arm and demand answers, demand certainty, but he drifted smoothly away through the crowds, leaving her alone.

The certainty was there. She'd seen the evidence. It was

all she'd thought about for months. Now it was time to be brave.

She turned. Her feet knew the way. There were no words but the mantra she'd drilled into herself.

Fear was a portal. Pain was a doorway.

The food court was waiting. The Friends were still at their table, watching her approach, their faces just masks concealing the truth inside.

Pain. Suffering. Agony like nothing you could imagine.

One of them spoke. She felt very far away as she hooked the bag from under the table, worked the zip tie and the zipper ripped open like pulled teeth, reached inside. One of the Friends gasped.

She'd practiced what followed exhaustively in the garage. He'd told her to drill until it came like clockwork, automatic as day follows night. Her fingers curled around the handle of the red five gallon jug. Her right hand lifted. Her left hand unscrewed the black cap.

"What the-" one of the young people began, but she gave them no time.

The acrid smell of gasoline hit as she lifted the jug high and poured the thin liquid over her head. It gulped down like a flooding storm drain, burning her eyes, getting in her nose, this holiest of baptisms splashing down to the floor.

All five gallons.

The Friends were on their feet now, falling over themselves trying to get away.

He'd told her it would be hard. Only the bravest could do what had to be done. But she'd seen through the portal, and knew it wasn't bravery but a mother's responsibility. There really was no choice.

She pulled the lighter from her back pocket and dragged her thumb across the striker wheel. It caught on the flint and sparked.

They were all screaming now, and that was right and true. The worlds were conjoining, and soon they'd understand. She paused for a second, just long enough to think of what grace her children would feel when she finally rescued them from their suffering, then she pressed the lighter to her throat and the fire took hold.

Flames rushed up over her cheeks and into her hair, down her arms and legs to lap out across the food court's marble floor like ravening tongues chasing the spilled lake of gas. For the first second it felt like everything he'd promised: a bracing plunge into deep cool waters, and she had long enough to see the Friends' faces shift in horror, finally seeing through to the same truth that had forever changed her life.

Fear was a portal. Pain was a doorway.

Walk in the fire.

Then the pain hit. As soon as that happened, she stopped being a person and became a machine existing only to scream.

2

KELLER

C hristopher Wren watched from the wings of the stage as President-elect David Keller drew riotous cheers from the crowd. They were out in the middle of rural Kansas, the fifteenth stop on Keller's post-election victory tour, and the crowds only seemed to be getting bigger and louder.

Now they stretched back and back on a patchwork blanket of blue and red mats covering some ten acres of land.

Keller dominated them all.

Speakers pumped out his firebrand speech like the voice of God. The big screen behind him displayed his face for all to see.

The mood in the air was ferocious. People wept and roared, high on the bright new hope they saw in David Keller.

Wren saw only danger.

Just three weeks back David Keller had shared his election night stage in Washington D.C. with the Apex himself. Wren's father. A death cult leader and killer on a vast scale, not seen since his 'death' twenty-five years ago, now right up close with the next President of the United States.

Wren had been drunk when he saw the moment on TV. In

a diner somewhere, out in the Midwest. It had sobered him up on the spot.

"He's toying with us," Wren said, knuckles tight.

CIA agent Sally Rogers grunted by his side. "It's not much of a game, Chris. He has all the cards. We've just got your word on who that old guy on the stage was."

Wren turned to face Rogers. She was in her early thirties, hair tight back in a blond ponytail, with an aquiline nose and sharp green eyes, wearing a navy letterman jacket rounded out by muscle. She was no slouch when it came to lifting. Bench two-fifty, Wren knew, putting her head and shoulders above most men.

"Do you think I'm wrong?"

She met his eyes but didn't say anything for a moment. She'd grown tougher in the time he'd known her. "We're lucky Keller even agreed to see us. He doesn't have to. So, we take what we can get. We ask our questions. If he lets something slip, that's great. I don't think he will."

Wren said nothing. She wasn't wrong about that.

On the stage, Keller was closing up his speech. His arms were spread wide, the crowd responding. Unity, was his promise. An end to the division. It was a smart political move.

"There's been so much pain in the last year," Keller boomed. "Our country has come under attack from within again and again. Now we're seeing ourselves in ways we never imagined possible, and I know that is terrifying. But we are strong, and our strength has allowed new heroes to rise up from the masses. Heroes like Christopher Wren!"

The giant screens behind Keller flashed to life, illuminating the stage as a medley of Christopher Wren's greatest hits began to thumping rock music: Wren jumping a tiny, hot pink Sart Fortwo microcar into the Los Angeles river; Wren at the head of the protests in front of the Wilshire

Building, standing before a crowd that moments earlier had been rioting, now all on one knee.

The crowd went berserk.

"He's playing your song," Rogers said. "Isn't it great?"

Wren grimaced.

"We can all learn from these heroes," Keller boomed, then stepped aside from the lectern. "If we just have the courage to stare unflinching into the dark, and the wisdom to listen, and humility to learn."

Keller dropped to one knee. It was a perfect mirror of a giant version of Christopher Wren on the screen behind him, dropping to one knee at the LA riot.

The crowd went nuts.

"You've got to admit, that is pretty cool," Rogers said. "What a way to culturally appropriate you, right?"

"I'll be in the green room," Wren said, and stalked away.

Three Secret Service agents peeled off to follow him.

The green room was a boxy pre-fab space little better than an interrogation cell, with a sofa, a platter of fruits carved into the shape of flowers on a dark wood coffee table, along with various biscuits, drinks, tea and coffee.

Wren sat on the sofa and the Secret Service agents fanned around him. He reached out, picked up a pineapple carved like a rose.

"That's not for you," one of the agents said.

Wren chewed.

President-elect David Keller arrived five minutes later, followed by Sally Rogers.

He was beaming and glowing, pumped off the adoration of the crowd. Hollywood handsome, maybe as tall as Wren and powerfully built, with a strong chin and a solid neck. His dark hair was cropped short, looking younger than his forty-eight years, impeccably dressed and groomed.

"Mr. Wren!" he boomed, immediately dominating the

room, easily bypassing his own security to stretch one hand out to Wren. "It is an honor to finally meet you."

Wren didn't get up. He didn't offer his hand. He'd been close to Keller before, back in the California governor's mansion in Sacramento, but Keller had been close to burning alive back then; seated in a paddling pool of napalm, naked with a black bag over his head, held hostage by a a mad ex-CIA officer called Anais Kiefer.

Keller owed his life to Wren. He'd wasted no time in rushing to the front of the mansion once Wren had negated Kiefer. In front of the media circus, he'd burnished his own image by generously applauding Wren and all the emergency services.

They hadn't spoke then, though. Wren didn't trust him at all.

"The Apex was on your stage," he said, cutting any attempt at niceties short. "A mass serial killer, and you looked him right in the eye. The man responsible for all the attacks you're talking about in your speeches. You looked right at him, and you really had no idea?"

Keller sidestepped smoothly, like none of this was an insult. He pulled his hand back easily, looked down at his empty plate, looked back at Wren and smiled.

"I see you ate all my fruit."

He had a deep baritone voice, reassuring and effortlessly confident, with a slight Southern lilt. The kind of man who could move between worlds with ease, from California to Idaho right through to New York.

"The eyeline's clear," Wren pressed. "It's unmistakable."

"The pineapples shaped like corkscrews are my favorite," Keller said pleasantly, like nothing mattered so much as fruit.

Wren stood up. He knew from experience it would get all the agents on edge, maybe even disconcert Keller too. Wren was a big guy, after all, with a big reputation. Two-hundred-forty pounds of agile, man-killing mass rising to six foot three in height. Not an ounce of fat on him. A DELTA operator, later CIA black ops specialist, nicknamed 'Saint Justice' for the sheer number of terrorists he'd set on the straight and narrow, often permanently, with a bullet.

If anything Keller seemed amused. "I must admit, after seeing you projected twenty feet tall on the stage screen, you do seem smaller in person."

Wren almost laughed. "That's only natural. I'm afraid none of us lives up to our legend."

Keller's grin spread. "The people love you, Mr. Wren. I make no bones about it, I have ridden your coat-tails somewhat. I'd be happy to welcome you on stage in the flesh, should you ever wish to join the party you started."

"Impossible," Wren said. "I voted for the other guy."

Keller's grin didn't dim a bit. "We both know that's not true. I actually had my team check the rolls, for the purposes of the speech, you understand. You're not registered to vote anywhere in any state in this great country, and you never have been."

"There are other ways to vote, Mr. President-elect. I'd be happy to discuss them with you further."

The moment got hot and stretched on. One of the Secret Service agents took a step forward.

"Mr. President-elect," Rogers intervened. "About the man on your acceptance speech stage. If you could please account for that."

Keller blinked and turned to her, adopting an entirely different tone.

"Agent Rogers? A pleasure. The truth is, as my team has told your people multiple times, I've never seen that man before." He looked at Wren then back to Rogers. "You know I've already fired my entire security team from that day. You know I agree that it is imperative we hunt this man down."

He paused a moment, as if considering something. "To that end, you have all the resources at my disposal to help find him."

Wren just stared. Keller turned and matched his gaze.

"You looked right at him," Wren said. "Right in his eyes. You looked proud."

Keller didn't budge. "Appearances can be deceiving, Mr. Wren. We see what we want to see. You're a student of psychology, I think. You should know that."

"It goes two ways, Mr. President-elect," Wren countered. "You look at me, and you see a brand image you want to co-opt. You put me in your campaign ads like I endorsed you. But I don't endorse you. I don't trust you. I think you're lying to me right now."

Rogers' eyes flared wide.

Keller handled it with a slick grin. "I understand you might be angry at me. Everything we've done here builds on your work. I hope our use of your image doesn't offend you too much. In fact, I hope that you're proud of our message. Only time will tell, of course, but I'm not lying about my campaign promises. I am here to unite the country. So any time you'd like to call me, I will listen."

Wren searched Keller's eyes, but found nothing except his own reflection bouncing back. "And kneel," he said.

That almost put a crack in his façade. "Excuse me?"

"And kneel," Wren repeated. "It was right there in your speech. Stare unflinching into the darkness. Seek out wisdom. Kneel."

Keller's smile shifted. For a moment Wren glimpsed something lurking beneath the glossy sheen of his eyes, but didn't know what it meant. "Speeches. You understand." He reached into a pocket, held out a card. "My number. A direct line to me. I want you to call the moment you learn anything about the identity of this man, Mr. Wren. I may not be

President yet, but I will bend the rules for you, at least as much as I can."

Wren said nothing. Keller was transparently fake, like a pane of one-way glass, but so were most politicians. From one angle you saw straight through. From another, all the dark secrets reflected back.

He just needed to find the right angle.

"I'll call," Wren said. Took the card. "And stop using my footage in your campaign."

Keller gave a wan smile. "The campaign's over, Mr. Wren. We won. And that footage belongs to the people now. I'm afraid I can't control it."

Wren smiled back. "So bend the rules. At least as much as you can."

Keller's façade almost cracked. He gave a nod to Rogers, then strode out of the room just as a replacement platter of carved fruit arrived.

3

ANAIS KIEFER

"Well that was worthless," Rogers said afterward, sitting opposite Wren in the back of a large black Escalade SUV, heading north toward the nearest airstrip. "You feel happy that you ate all his fruit, though?"

"He's lying," Wren said.

"Right, well, good luck getting him to admit it. If you're right, it is terrifying. The Apex on a stage with the next President?" She shuddered. "If you're wrong, though, then you'll be harassing the most powerful person in the world."

"Doesn't phase me," Wren said.

Rogers frowned. "You want to go back to your black site? Be imprisoned again?"

Wren flashed her a rare smile. The last time he'd been in a black site prison, it was because Sally Rogers had put him there. They'd come a long way since then, now working together under the auspices of a special FBI/CIA confab, which gave them license to investigate foreign threats on both international and domestic soil.

"I only went to prison for you, Sally."

She snorted. "Like you had a choice."

Wren said nothing, just looked out of the window. Ever since he'd seen that footage of the man with sparkling blue eyes on Keller's election stage, he'd done everything he could to hunt him down.

There'd been nothing.

"Let's get a helicopter," Wren said.

"You're in a rush?"

"I'm thinking about black sites again. Maybe time to revisit mine."

Rogers seemed perplexed for a moment, then she shook her head. "No. Absolutely not."

"He's the only lead we've got left. The only confirmed person we know who actually met the Apex."

"You're talking about Anais Kiefer, yes? He may be a lead, but he's never said a word about the Apex except to gloat. He's also a psychopath who tried to burn me alive. He actually burned three other law officers down; one of them was a member of our old task force. He tried to kill you, Keller himself, and about a dozen other agents who had narrow escapes. It's a bad idea, Chris."

Wren said nothing, just looked at her.

"No," she said again.

"It'll be good for you. Face him down."

She laughed. "Anais Kiefer. The Ghost. Of course. Thanks, Chris. Yeah, we're doing this for me."

In twelve hours, they were there.

Their Sikorsky UH-60 Black Hawk put down in the depths of the Sonoran Desert in Mexico, a landscape of orange dust scattered with sand-scoured boulders, creeping low creosote bushes and large concrete berms. A largely abandoned compound in the middle of nowhere, once a nuclear fallout shelter for the US government. Now it housed an underground black site for off-book CIA detainees.

Wren had been here for three months as punishment for

one too many off-book executions, getting tortured every day for the names of his fellow 'domestic terrorists'. Now it housed Anais Kiefer, a genuine terrorist with the kill count to prove it.

They stepped out of the Black Hawk as the rotors wound down. The downdraft blew hot, scurrying desert sand in vaporous wafts, like spray off ocean breakers.

The sun beat down on Wren's bare head. He'd shaved all his hair off the day everything changed, when he saw the Apex on David Keller's stage. He'd stopped drinking and bent everything he had to the task.

"He'll have been looking forward to this," Rogers said, joining him as they walked toward the nearest berm, a low and rounded structure that could almost be a sandy mound in the earth; the better to proof it against bunker-busting cluster bombs. "He's that much of a psycho."

"Me too," Wren said.

Rogers snorted. "You're not a psycho. You're just deranged by choice."

A rusted red door opened in the side of the berm and a guard led them in. They passed down several flights of stairs and through several heavy blast doors, each bolted in triplicate, then came upon a familiar corridor. The same place they'd detained Wren.

"In his cell?" Wren asked.

"In the interrogation room," the guard said, and led them over to an observation room. Wren remembered it well.

It was dark inside the obs room. On the other side of the glass hulked Anais Kiefer. The 'Ghost'. An ex-colleague of Wren's in the CIA, they'd gone undercover in Afghanistan with IS-K, an offshoot of ISIS, together for three months, until they'd been sold out. The person who'd sold them out had been David Keller; Kiefer's ultimate target at the end of his burning spree.

Keller had never yet had to pay for that corruption. If anything, he'd been rewarded.

Wren studied Kiefer.

He was built like a bull, bigger than Wren at 6' 7", with a neat haircut and a clean-shaven chin. The cuffs on his wrists and ankles didn't look nearly strong enough to contain him.

"He thinks he broke us both," Rogers said, standing at Wren's side. "He thinks we're desperate."

"He's right, we are."

Kiefer stared right back at them through the glass. It seemed like somehow he knew they were there.

"I'll go in alone," Wren said.

Rogers raised a thick brown eyebrow. "No good cop, bad cop?"

"We're all good cops to him."

Rogers snorted. She'd been around Wren long enough to know how he operated. "If you hurt him, you're going down for it alone."

"I'm already down," Wren said. "Just lock the door on your way out."

He opened the door. It was brighter in the interrogation room, a ten-foot square white cube. White LEDs recessed into the ceiling allowed no shadows, no respite. Kiefer looked even bigger up close, a man mountain.

"Chris," he said, grinning. "I thought I smelled your perfume. What's that line, 'I love the smell of napalm on the morning?'"

Wren said nothing. He closed the door and stood looking at Kiefer for maybe ten seconds. It seemed to amuse Kiefer.

"Is this a psyche out?" he asked, and looked over at the one-way mirror. "Am I being punked? Who's in there, it's someone famous, right? Let me guess. Tom Hardy wants to play me in the movie. They've sent you to negotiate the rights. Only if he gets to wear a mask, though, and speak unintelligibly. Put that in the contract."

Wren pulled out the chair, legs rasping on the concrete floor, and sat. The metal flexed under his weight.

"The Apex," he said. "We need to know what you know."

Kiefer smiled and raised one eyebrow. "We've been through this once. You've come for a second round?"

"We never finished the first round," Wren said softly. "You surrendered, remember?"

Kiefer laughed. "There you are. With a classic Chris Wren judo move. Trying to reframe things. What really happened was I refused to burn myself alive, even if it meant taking you and that bastard Keller along with me. But there's more now, isn't there?" He looked over to the one-way glass, then back at Wren. "She's here, isn't she? The woman. Rogers."

Wren gave nothing away. Kiefer took that as confirmation and smiled, settled back in his chair like the smug fool he was.

"Sally Rogers. The bitch that got away." He seemed to luxuriate in the insult. "What have you brought her out here for, Chris? Prove some kind of macho point, that you can man me down?" He studied Wren. "We could arm wrestle, I guess, but I don't think it'll go your way. You've lost mass, frankly. Hardly the man you once were, but I guess that's the failure setting in."

"Only one failure, from where I'm sitting," Wren said.

Kiefer leaped on that. "You sad old man. Nothing I liked better than taking the shine off you, Chris. All-American my ass. I like the new hair, by the way. Nothing says mid-life crisis better than a middle-aged man with a buzzcut." He took a breath. "So, you're hunting the Apex. Getting nowhere, I expect. There are things I could tell you, but I don't know why I would."

"So don't tell me. Tell the woman you tried to burn alive."

Kiefer laughed. "You'd put her in here?"

"Not up to me. I imagine she'd like to rearrange your face. But yes, I would. Because I, unlike you, still have some faith in your principles, Anais. They call you a psycho, and you did burn innocents, but we both know you're not at ease with that. Your heart bled for the corruption you saw, right? That's a hunger for justice if ever I saw one. You know the Apex is a wild dog that needs taking out. So help us take him out."

Kiefer eyed him. "What are you doing, Chris? Playing to my better angels?"

Wren shrugged. "I think you have them. Rogers is watching. Maybe you'll tell her. Make up for the injustice you did her."

Kiefer's eyes narrowed. "Sally Rogers," he said. "Woman of the hour. Kicked me right in the head, and you don't get a lot of that, pushing seven foot tall."

"You're barely six and a half."

"Six seven, and OK, let's get her in here." Kiefer threw his arms wide, like he didn't think for a second it was going to happen. "We'll reminisce."

"Deal."

Wren got up, went to the door and turned to the one way glass. "Come on in, Sally," he called.

It took a second. For a moment he feared nothing would happen. Maybe she'd left, deciding this wasn't for her. Maybe she couldn't face it. Then the door opened and Sally Rogers came in. There was a quizzical look in her eyes, like she hadn't expected any of this.

Kiefer stared, suddenly stony-eyed, his bravado gone.

"You wanna call her a bitch again?" Wren asked. "You go ahead. But think about who you're performing for. Nobody's watching now. Does it amuse you that much?"

Kiefer just stared. Not at Rogers. At Wren. Really angry now. Ready to pop.

"Or you can tell her you're sorry," Wren said. "Spill your heart at her feet and hope she doesn't knock your head off your shoulders. I can't promise you'll get forgiveness. Maybe you won't survive. But I think she'll listen. She was there too. She knows what my father can do."

"She'll do more than knock his head off," Sally muttered.

"She may," Wren cautioned, "but perhaps she'll listen, too. Perhaps she'll help you do something good with your life."

Kiefer grunted. "Nice speech."

"Glad you like it. Did it work?"

"None of your business. Now get out of here."

Wren looked at Rogers. Rogers nodded. "Go ahead, Boss."

He smiled. So maybe he was the good cop after all. He walked out without looking back.

4
———

THE RQ

Wren sat on a rock beside one of the large concrete berms in the beating sun, playing a game on his phone. It wasn't much of a game, something about plants and zombies, but it was addictive.

Some thirty minutes later the door to the black site opened then swung closed with a distant clang, and Sally Rogers came over to stand in front of him.

"He sang like a songbird," she said.

Wren's pulse leaped. "Seriously?"

"It seems six months in solitary has given him time to reflect on what he did." Rogers sighed and sat down beside Wren. "He admits he went too far. He regrets he didn't just kill Keller and be done with it. He really regrets that Keller's now going to be President."

Wren laughed. It wouldn't bring back the friends he'd lost to Anais Kiefer's ruthless crusade. It wasn't much, any way you looked at it.

"Oh, and he asked if he could join your Foundation."

That got his attention. "He did what?"

Rogers shrugged. "Yeah. He seemed sincere."

That silenced Wren. He really hadn't expected it and

didn't know what to think. Join the Foundation, his private support and rehab group for ex-addicts, cons, intelligence workers and paramilitary operatives? He couldn't quite imagine it. It would mean he'd forgiven Kiefer, on some level, that he thought there was some route back for him.

Was there?

"I'll let you dwell on that," Rogers said. "In the meantime, he gave us some real intel."

Wren's gaze snapped up. "What intel?"

"Four different locations he claims he met the Apex," she went on. "Dates stretching back four years. Says your father led some kind of 'roving franchisee conference for death cult leader wannabes'." She paused, looking disgusted. "His words. It sounds like total BS to me."

Wren struggled to absorb that. "Roving what?"

"His words. Maybe it's nonsense, but like I say, he seemed sincere."

Wren rose to his feet. He had nowhere to go, but he couldn't sit anymore. "Where?"

Rogers squeezed the bridge of her nose, took a moment like she was resetting herself. "OK. So, Jib-jab. You remember that?"

Wren frowned, wracked his memory and came up sixes. "That's the cover operation the Order of the Saints were using?" Rogers nodded. "In Minneapolis. An online shopping service, big warehouse fulfillment center, where Richard Acker held me prisoner. Why?"

Rogers winced. "Kiefer says that's the main place they met. Not just him and the Apex, but all of them, like a who's who of the last four major terror attacks on American soil." She held up a hand, started counting off fingers. "Richard Acker from the Order of the Saints. Somchai Theeravit, AKA Pythagoras, from the Blue Fairy. Yumiko Harkness from the #Reparations. Anais Kiefer, our Ghost, and some others.

Apparently they got together in the board room over grape soda and candied pecans to calmly plot the end of America."

Wren blinked. Grape soda and pecans? He tried to picture it, conference table laid out, the Apex at the front with a laser pointer while giving a slideshow, the rest sitting politely in business attire, raising their hands to speak.

"That does sound like bullshit."

"Right?" Rogers asked, and kicked at the sand in frustration. "I just sent the audio recording over to your hackers and Director Humphreys, they can run analyses, but I don't know what to make of it."

Wren sucked his teeth. "What else?"

"He talked a lot about data. Said the Apex had all these graphs and tables packed with death count projections. Apparently it all builds toward a number he invented, the RQ."

Wren leaned in. "What's the RQ?"

"Revolution Quotient. It's a number he built off numerous indices of public unrest, like suicide rates, domestic violence, hate crimes? It's supposed to represent the cumulative effect of successive attacks on the American people. Kiefer even drew an RQ graph for me, climbing over time as national stress levels rise." She sketched a shallow incline followed by a sudden, steep rise in the sand at their feet. "A hockey stick curve, they call it. At a certain point, the RQ rises exponentially. To hit that point, his goal is to make life so unbearable that people turn on each other and we devolve into murderous anarchy."

Wren grunted. It seemed to sync with the Apex's general life goals. "That checks out."

"I guess," Rogers said. "Your father sure loves him some civil war. Except every time he tries to foment one, he fails."

"True." Wren chewed on that, working the angles for a long moment. "But are they failing?"

Rogers snorted. "Of course they are. He tosses them up, we smack them down. He's 4 for 0 right now, top of the ninth, what's left to say?"

Wren grunted. It wasn't the first time he'd thought like this, but maybe the first to talk about it. The Apex was nothing if not patient, and this 'RQ' seemed to play into that. All his 'child' cults meeting together meant something.

"Look at it this way," he said. "Did the Apex really expect Acker's Saints would start a national civil war?"

"They tried hard," Rogers said. "From what I saw it was only you that stopped it."

"Forget me," said Wren. "Even if I'd done nothing, if the Saints had pulled off the scale of attack they were aiming for, would we really have seen outright revolution in the streets? Neighbors killing neighbors, government collapsing, mass indiscriminate slaughter?"

Rogers made a face. "Maybe not that far."

"Exactly, but that is his end goal, right?"

Rogers allowed a noncommittal shrug.

"The Apex isn't stupid. If we can see that, then he could too. He knows our values and institutions are too strong to break with one crisis." Wren spun that forward, trying to lay out the whole chess board. "Think about it. It would explain why he had the Blue Fairy lined up so fast, only four months after the Saints failed, and then the Reparations right after, and Kiefer too?" It unfolded before him. "They were all rungs on this 'RQ' curve, leading up to true chaos."

Rogers' eyes narrowed. "So you buy the candied pecans?"

Wren was already gaming it through. Maybe he did buy it. Flipping everything on its head.

"I do buy it." He thought for a second, searching for evidence. "Look, there's no doubting that this 'RQ' is high right now, is there? It's thick in the air. Everywhere you go, people are on edge. They're afraid." He paused a second. "I was on the road for three months before Keller was elected, Rogers. Getting drunk and running away, whatever, and I saw it in people's eyes. It's gotten into the mainstream." He cast his thoughts back to TVs glimpsed in motel rooms, with pundits at all hours questioning the very tenets of the country, the doctrine of exceptionalism, the moral contribution of the Founding Fathers, the American Dream itself. "I think we're looking at a prolonged, systematic attack on our way of life. There's multiple stages. It's cult indoctrination on a massive scale."

Rogers frowned. "Indoctrinating the whole country?"

"Exactly. It's been done before; look at Nazi Germany. A whole country turned against scapegoats and the world." His projections took a dark turn. "The Apex made Steven Gruber *want* to kill himself in just three days, Rogers. He did it to a thousand people in the Pyramid. He got all my brothers and sisters to choose asphyxiation in one of his pits. Mass death is always his endgame, and on those scores he's 3 for 0." He paused a moment. On some level he'd known it the second he'd seen the Apex on David Keller's stage. They were coming toward the grand finale of the Apex's magnum opus. "Keller. That's it."

"That's what?"

"David Keller's linked to the next attack. He has to be. With the Presidency in his pocket, the Apex could bury America in dead bodies. Start a war with Russia, that'd do it. America's a radioactive wasteland for ten generations." He took a breath. "Whatever it is, it's coming soon."

Rogers eyed him doubtfully. "You've got no evidence for any of that."

Wren stood. "Then let's find some. You said Kiefer listed four locations? Where were the others?"

5

TRUST

"I'm not hopeful on that score," Sally Rogers said.

"Why not?" Wren countered.

"OK." She took a breath. "So location number two was Yumiko Harkness' silicon chip fabrication plant. Remember that place, where they had the billionaire arena? It got completely leveled after our teams were done with it. There's nothing left! Number three was the abandoned school where Gruber tried to burn himself down. There's nothing left of it, either. The whole thing burned to the ground."

Wren frowned. "What about the fourth?"

"The fourth is useless. It was Kiefer's first time, and the Apex's men blindfolded him. Maybe there was a flight to get there, he said, maybe some driving, then there was a concrete hall with tiered seating and an open glass roof. He has no idea where or what it was. All he remembers is the stench in the air."

"Stench?"

"Like rotten eggs, he said, but overpowering. Maybe that means it was near some kind of waste plant, or in Yellowstone Park near the bacterial blooms, or anywhere, Chris. It's a non-lead."

Wren's mind spun. "It's the only lead we've got. Did he mention any other attendees at this location?"

"I asked. He said Yumiko Harkness was there; but she's dead now, isn't she? Richard Acker was there, but he's dead too. One other man was there, Kiefer thought he was Indian from his looks, but he never spoke, so he never caught an accent."

Wren snapped his fingers. "There's our target. An Indian man. We'll get Kiefer working with a sketch artist. We'll find this guy."

Rogers opened her mouth to say something, seemed to think better of it, then let out a slow breath. "Yeah. We can do that."

"He's likely attached to another cult," Wren went on, rounding out the profile. "One he leads. We can cross-reference the sketch to known cult leaders. Maybe it'll lead us to him, and that'll give us the jump on the Apex."

Rogers didn't look too convinced. "It's thin, but possible."

"Possible's good," Wren said. "How many Indian cult leaders are operating in the continental United States?"

"We don't know it was in the continental United States. He caught a plane, yes? He didn't specify how long."

Wren waved a hand. "Whatever. I know plenty of cult experts in the US and around the world; we'll circulate his sketch and someone will recognize him."

Rogers grunted. "I admire your optimism. Now shall we-"

Wren's phone rang, cutting her off. He brought it up. No number showed, rather there was a single line of text where the numbers should be: HELLION

He sighed. Hellion was a member of his Foundation, a black-hat hacker who'd used her incredible keyboard warrior skills to extract millions from companies and smaller nation states via blackmail attacks, at least until Wren had gotten involved. His interference in her life, and the life of her hacking partner B4cksl4cker, had turned them both around and set them to work for the Foundation, often stepping in as his operator when he was involved in violent action.

She could be quite irreverent, often calling him randomly to share puns and jokes she'd thought up, and Wren wasn't really in the mood for her now. He killed the line and looked back at Rogers.

"Now what?" he prompted.

The phone rang again. Again he squeezed the red icon to kill the call, but this time it didn't work. She'd hacked his phone; not a difficult task for someone of her calibre. He tried to lower the ringer volume but was overridden. A second later the call answered by itself and Hellion's voice came through the speaker, her Bulgarian accent underwritten with the familiar sound of keyboard keys clacking.

"Christopher, there has been attack you will be interested in. Woman just burned herself alive in shopping mall. Footage of this is everywhere, probably is related to your father. I am sending to you."

A link came through. A video began to auto play.

6

MALL OF THE USA

Wren studied the CCTV footage of a woman walking through a large mall.

The shot was grainy and from high up, shifting cameras as she passed along, easily lost in the crowd. News anchors talked over the feed in jerky snippets, clearly a stitched-together job Hellion had prepared herself, but Wren ignored them.

She was early thirties with blond hair, wearing mom jeans and a fashionable-looking cardigan, and carrying a large bag. She walked with her head down, barely looking where she was going, like she was lost in her own world but with a purpose.

A banner along the bottom of the screen gave the ending away:

WOMAN BURNS SELF ALIVE IN CINCINNATI MALL

That was highly evocative for Wren. Burning alive had always been the Apex's way of killing his cult members. He watched through to the gory end, until the screams finally abated, then looked up at Rogers. She was watching the same video, with the final screams repeating from her own device.

"This is it," Wren said. "The next attack."

Rogers looked up. She seemed traumatized. It was only a few months ago that she'd watched Jessica Grimes burn alive right by her side. At least that had been done by someone else. To burn yourself alive took an incredible degree of brainwashing.

"To what end?" Rogers asked.

"The RQ," Wren said. "A video like this, it's like dropping a bomb into the national psyche. Everyone in that mall will be forever scarred. Everyone who sees this video will be scarred. Murder is bad, but suicide? It's deeply corrosive."

"I'm getting details from my team," Rogers said, studying her phone. "Apparently she was a mother of two, happily married, good salaries, healthy children, no obvious risk factors of suicide at all. Why would she do this?"

"That's what he wants everyone thinking," Wren said, already feeling an adrenaline boost pump in his system. "That's what it was always about. Sow doubt and despair. He loves that."

"Then he's a sick puppy, your father."

"He's evil," Wren said. The truth was, he'd grown up with this kind of thing every day as a child in the Apex's Pyramid cult, where babies were routinely locked into cages to scream for hours, where adults drowned and boiled to death in vats, where children were brainwashed into burying themselves alive as an. act of the greatest faith.

Wren had tried back then to fit in, to enjoy being at his father;'s absolute mercy, but it had never worked. It was wrong, and you either let it grind you down or you found a way to transmute it into something you could use.

He punched buttons on his phone screen and raised it to his ear. Sometimes you had to lay down a marker. The phone rang and his heart pounded. The guy had said to call anytime, after all.

"Mr. Wren."

Straight through, as promised. Genteel, sophisticated, that same rich baritone. David Keller, President-elect.

"Have you seen the video?" Wren asked.

A second passed. Feigning confusion, maybe. "I take it you're talking about the video of the young woman burning?"

Wren gritted his teeth. "You promised to help. I need you to do something for me."

"Anything. No, it's all right. I'll take this call." Wren pictured Keller standing in his den, waving off staffers and maybe moving out to the porch for privacy. "What can I do?"

"Put a candle in your window," Wren said. "Tell that bastard I'm coming."

He hung up.

Rogers was staring at him. "Tell me that wasn't the President-elect."

"He did ask me to call," Wren said, and started toward the Black Hawk. "Let's get out of here. Those leads aren't going to run themselves down."

7

OXLEA

The Black Hawk helicopter roared away. The berms, sand and nothingness of Anais Kiefer's black site prison sloughed off like the traces of a bad dream.

Wren's fingers flew over his laptop's keys while Rogers shouted into her phone by his side, arguing with CIA Director Humphreys. He was understandably furious at Wren. Only four months back, Wren had been Humphreys' prisoner. Now he was an Agent WithOut Protocol, taking liberties when he'd barely banked any trust at all.

Rogers was making his case; it didn't sound like she was having much success.

Wren didn't care. He was in the FBI vault right alongside Hellion and B4cksl4cker, hunting for the record of an Indian cult leader.

The FBI kept extensive details on all established religious organizations in the country; the small-time cults numbered easily in excess of ten thousand, encompassing those engaged in woo-woo mysticism cults, domestic terrorism, doomsday predictions, polygamy cults and many more.

At various times in his career as a CIA cult-breaker, Wren had cast his eyes across them all. It had been years since he'd actively scoured the database, though, and the membership changed constantly.

He knew someone who did, though, and dialed in the number for an old contact in the FBI. The line rang three times then connected.

"Go for Oxlea," said a bored-sounding voice.

This was Oxlea Karam Day, a very unique, highly specialized basement-dwelling FBI analyst Wren had spent many hours with, searching for records in the FBI's paper vault in Washington, D.C.

Oxlea was a true son of the sixties, born into a free-love commune in Nevada very different from the Pyramid; the members of his commune had genuinely cared only about flower power, LSD and mind-expansion. The commune had been so lax that the mothers had no idea which babies belonged to them, let alone who their fathers were. Children were raised by the collective and entrusted largely to educate themselves.

That indulgence had left Oxlea with a lifelong fascination for the esoterica of cult belief systems. He combined that with a purists approach to curating the FBI's absolute listing, collection and history of cults. Every single cult idea, cult leader and cult diatribe describing the rules of life and behavior had at some point been strained through his razor-keen mind.

He was also a deep believer and adherent to the policy of 'radical honesty', which meant telling only the whole of the truth, without any white lies, at any time. It had bought him his own set of detractors and devotees in the subfloors of the FBI, as well as something of a sect of his own in the wider world.

"Oxlea, it's Christopher Wren. I need your help."

A few moment passed. "Is this the same Christopher Wren I used to know? The one who was arrested for

34

murdering hundreds of child abusers on a boat in the Atlantic?"

Wren gritted his teeth. With Oxlea, radical honesty often meant he felt the urge to give a rundown of everything he considered relevant to the immediate topic.

"Yes, that Christopher Wren. Not the architect, who's dead. It's about a cult leader I'm hunting."

"Is it about your father? I'm afraid my records on the Pyramid ended the day the Apex died. I suspect the blame for this falls on you. It's been said you went around destroying all the records."

"It indirectly involves my father," Wren allowed, ignoring the accusation. "I'm looking for a man of Indian descent, most likely a cult leader in the United States, who crossed paths with my father at some point in the last four or five years. He may be associated with a location stinking of rotten eggs."

"Rotten eggs," Oxlea repeated. "Fascinating. Christopher, I'm going to have to ask you directly. Were you the one destroying those records?"

Wren sighed. Radical honesty often meant for slow conversations. "Sure. I did that."

"Why?"

"Does it really matter?"

"I'd like to know why."

That was the other thing about Oxlea. He was obsessive and compulsive when it came to protecting the Vault.

"Why did I destroy the records that linked me to my father, the mass murderer?" Wren repeated, praying for grace and patience. "I suppose I didn't want that connection. I didn't want to live in my father's shadow. Now can you help me?"

"Why not?"

"Why not help me?"

"Why didn't you want to live in his shadow? You have

35

since, in the past year, confessed to being your father's instrument of burning, haven't you? You confessed to being the one who set alight the Pyramid one thousand. Person after person, you burned them all."

Wren squeezed the phone tightly. "I was twelve."

"Then you burned the records from my Vault."

That was Oxlea's third characteristic that made him difficult to deal with. He considered the FBI's cult Vault his own personal property. "I shredded them. I didn't burn them."

"Ah. Did you happen to keep the shreds? You could potentially reconstruct them, given time and patience."

Wren was already running out of patience. "I can't imagine I kept them, and I wouldn't spend the months necessary to reconstruct them if I had. They're gone, Oxlea. Now, this is a pressing matter of national security. A cult leader of Indian descent, in a compound that stinks of rotten eggs. What have you got for me?"

"I'm going to ask something of you, Christopher, since I have you on the phone."

Wren squeezed his eyes tightly shut. "Is it about the Vault?"

"I'd like you to sit for an interview. To reconstruct the records. It would be very helpful."

"I can't really spare the time right now, Oxlea, but maybe-"

"One question now, then. I'll record this call."

Wren sighed. Rogers to his left seemed to be having no more luck as she dug into the Mall of the USA burning. "Fine. Shoot."

"How did it feel, when you were burning the thousandth person alive? They were your friends, your family, the members of your cult. People you knew and loved. How did you justify that to yourself?"

"I don't know. I can't remember. Probably I was just following my father's orders."

"Don't guess, Christopher," Oxlea said sharply. "Think back, this is a record for posterity. It happened to you, not to me."

"OK." Wren reached back. He thought back to the Apex's hand on his shoulder, and those sparkling blue eyes, and the stink of napalm in the air, and the feeling that now, after such a grand work, something truly incredible had been achieved. "It wasn't just orders," he said. "I believed, back then. All those people? Even the ones who were unwilling, even the children, my father had me convinced that they were going somewhere in aid of a war. A holy war, in which they would all be righteous warriors. I wanted to join them." He took a breath. The memory had brought a flush of sweat to his skin, remembering the intoxicating power of the Apex. "Good enough?"

"Not quite. I don't think belief is enough to do what you did. There's more to this story."

Wren's knuckles whitened. This was exactly why he'd shredded those records.

"Turn off the recorder."

"No. Tell the truth now."

Wren cursed, almost hung up, then restrained himself. He could go and dig through the Vault himself, but that could take days. "This is irrelevant, Oxlea."

"It's relevant to me."

Wren squeezed the bridge of his nose. "Fine. Maybe there is more to it. You want it on record? OK. The truth is, I loved my father, Oxlea, just as much as I feared him. I respected him. I wanted him to be proud of me, so I did what he asked. It's as simple as that."

Oxlea said nothing for a moment, then offered a prim "Thank you."

37

"So you'll find me some cults."

"Yes. First I'd like to book you for a longer interview, say July 13th, can you block the whole day?"

Wren had no intention of doing that. "Sure thing. Whatever. We'll delve right in. Now can you help me?"

"Of course. I've already collated three prime examples of cult leaders of Indian descent."

Wren wiped his brow and leaned in. "Let me have them."

"Two were major cult movements in their heyday, and continue now without their original leaders. The first is the Bikram yoga cult out of California, led by Calcutta-born Bikram Choudhury, who pioneered hot yoga in Speedos in massive warehouse-like tents in the 70s, while he verbally assaulted the members. At one point there were over a thousand Bikram yoga studios around the world. Choudhury allegedly used intimate sessions with his female 'students' to abuse them, however, and since fled law enforcement to India."

"Right, I've heard of that. I think we can rule it out, too famous, too much FBI surveillance from early on. Every cult my father's surfed so far has been largely below the radar."

"Agreed. The second is the Rajneesh movement, an anti-Christian sect founded by the mystic Bhagwan Shree Rajneesh in the 70s and 80s, whose followers always wore orange. They were the first US terror group to use a bio-weapon, interestingly, introducing salmonella into the salad in Oregon restaurants and shops with the goal of achieving political power in an election. Of course, Rajneesh himself died in 1990, though like with yogi Bikram, his followers continue the movement."

Wren nodded along. Many of those details were familiar. "OK. He's dead, but offshoot leaders might be possible, leading smaller cells. You've got the terrorist connection, too. Any link to rotten eggs?"

"None that I can think of. The Bikram yoga studios used to be carpeted and reportedly smelled very bad, but that's all different now, and anyway, I can't imagine it was sulfurous. Salmonella is unpleasant, but unless the Rajnesshis were still producing great vats of it, which I'm quite certain they're not, as we've been watching them closely as well since that first attack, I cannot imagine the smell would pervade very far."

Wren grunted.

"Now to the remaining cult."

8

CINCINNATI

"Christopher!"

Wren ignored the shout from Rogers by his side, gaze buried in his laptop screen, researching the last cult Oxlea had given him. There were scant images of the leader, a man named Jamal Jalim, but he found one from several years ago and sent it through to the black site, with express orders to show it to Kiefer and get a confirmation.

Now a thump came on his arm, and he looked up to find Rogers glaring at him, holding up her phone. She looked like she'd aged ten years in ten minutes; pale and drawn.

"Director Humphreys wants to talk to you."

Wren looked at the phone. Of course. He took the handset, pulled out the battery and SIM then handed the pieces back to Rogers. She stared at them.

"Are you kidding me?" she shouted over the Black Hawk's rotors.

Wren tapped his earpiece, transferring to throat-mic. Rogers glowered and tapped her earpiece too.

"What was that?"

"Humphreys is just going to screw things up. You know he is. Tell me one time he actually helped."

Rogers opened her mouth then closed it again. "It's difficult," she allowed. "But he's my boss. Technically yours, too."

Wren let that one pass. The exact boundaries of his working relationship with the CIA were fluid. As an AWOP Agent WithOut Portfolio, he'd been given wide latitude by the President herself.

"I have a lead for the Indian guy," he said.

Rogers brightened. "That's good. Who is it?"

"An ex-engineer called Jamal Jalim, he heads up some crazy pseudoscience outfit in Utah. I've got his photo out to Kiefer now, and the stink of rotten eggs? It could be the relic of the Great Salt Lake, where Jalim's got his compound in some old ruin. There's huge tracts of the dried-up lake that stink of sulfur, apparently. Something to do with it being an inland sea. But that's for me to deal with."

Rogers frowned. "What do you mean, that's for you to deal with?"

"I'll take a Foundation team. There's plenty of my trusted assets who live around there. As soon as Kiefer confirms, they're all boarding flights. As for you, I need you in Cincinnati."

Rogers cocked her head sideways. "At the Mall of America? Why?"

Wren checked his watch. It was coming up on forty-five minutes, now, since the woman had burned. "Because I've got a working theory about it, but it's pieces only. I need your eyes on the scene and interviewing her associates to figure out if I'm right."

"While you go strike a cult in Utah?"

"It only might be in Utah. Nothing's confirmed."

She sighed. "You kill me, Boss."

"Inadvertently. Now, you have been looking into the woman, right?"

Rogers glowered. "Yes."

"So brief me." He looked in her eyes, read the anger there and added one more word. "Please."

For a few seconds Rogers just stared, then she sighed again. "Damn it. OK. I guess you haven't even read her file yet?"

"Not yet. It's your case as far I'm concerned, that's what you're for."

"That's what I'm for, lovely. So." She brought up her phone, ostentatiously put the battery back in though not the SIM, and opened the notes app. "The woman's name was Rachel Day. 29 years old. Husband, part-time job at an accounting office. Two kids, boy and a girl, seven and five."

Wren flinched at that, but hid it well. Wren himself had two kids, a boy and a girl, the same ages. It seemed quite a coincidence, and if not a coincidence, then another message to him. Maybe a threat.

"Go on."

"She looks to be an exemplary citizen. Happily married as far as all evidence indicates. Yearbooks dating back to grade school show a well-adjusted, well-socialized girl. Father a pastor in the Baptist faith and local community leader, mother an activist for animal rights, but nothing extreme. Marching band, she played the trumpet, led taps at summer camp on Lake Erie eight years running, four as a camper, four as a counselor. No hint of involvement with any kind of terror activity, offline or on. Nothing unusual in her daily life, no cheating, no radicalization, no odd behavior. As all-American as you can get."

Pretty much what Wren had expected. All except the children. He nodded. It was all connected. "Then one day she burned herself alive. So tell me why you think she did that."

Rogers closed the flap on her phone wallet. "I think this whole thing's more bullshit."

"How so?"

Her head tilted slightly to the side, amused at his manner, like this was class and he was some professor using the Socratic method. "The timing. I was down in the black site with Kiefer right around when it happened. This was targeted at us."

She'd always been a quick study. "Agreed. For what purpose?"

"I have no idea." She took a moment. "Intimidation?"

"That's probably part of it," Wren allowed. "But think about what Kiefer told us. Above all, it was our first confirmation that the man on Keller's stage was the Apex, correct, as well as our first lead to hunting him down? They're both huge news."

"They're circumstantial," Rogers countered, "hearsay straight from the mouth of a mad killer. It's not proof."

"Maybe not, but the media would run with it, wouldn't they, if we released it? Start asking questions, start digging, maybe unravel the whole filthy conspiracy."

"I guess. What's your point?"

"What's on all the news sites right now? The only thing you can see, engulfing the media landscape?"

Rogers chewed on that for a moment. Wren glanced at his phone. Forty-seven minutes gone since Rachel Day burned.

"You're saying he burned Rachel Day alive, or, correction, got her to burn herself alive, as a *distraction*?"

"Exactly that."

She stared at him, perhaps trying to punch holes in the argument, perhaps failing. "That's crazy."

"Maybe. For the minute just accept the hypothesis that Keller works for the Apex, OK? Once you accept that, you'll see the distraction's necessary. Keller can't let anything come out linking him to the Apex; he'd never make it to the actual Presidency. So this is how he ekes it out; make sure any evidence we find never makes it into the mainstream."

Rogers looked like she was trying to swallow that. "It's wild, Boss, I'll give you that. A lot of moving parts."

"The Apex was always a master logistician. And just think; the media aren't going to listening to anything else now, are they? Rachel Day's burning has sucked all the oxygen from the room. Not even Hellion and B4cksl4cker could make Kiefer's data go viral over that. Even if we put out actual solid proof Keller was working for the Apex, nobody would hear it, nobody would see it, it'd be like it never happened."

Rogers sat silently for a second, then took Wren's phone, started scrolling through the major news websites: ABC, FOX, NBC, CNN, the BBC. Every page was headed by news of the burning. Everything else had been flushed off the front page.

"They stole the news cycle," she said.

"Exactly. Our intel's dead in the water. It isn't real if nobody hears about it, and this burning just flooded the zone."

"So…"

Wren felt the gears clank into position in her head. "OK. The timing is wild. Maybe they really did burn a woman alive just to muzzle us? But surely that'll only last for a single news cycle, maybe a few, but not past a few days. If we had a real scoop on the President, it'd break through soon enough." She thought a moment longer, then her face went dark. "But doesn't that mean..."

She trailed off.

"Say it," Wren said. "Check my working."

"Two things. Either Keller's got an attack planned in the next few days, which wouldn't make sense. Most attacks will only be possible once he's President in 53 days. But then one burning now won't keep us quiet for that long."

"Which means?" Wren prompted.

Rogers set her jaw. "It means more are coming. Many more. Every day, at least. Maybe more frequent than that. And they'll need to keep coming every day for 53 days."

Wren gave a sad smile. "When is it ever just one death with this guy?"

Rogers opened her mouth, closed it, then opened it and cursed loudly.

"I know. Picture a stream of burnings flooding the country, enough to drive the RQ up into the stratosphere and guarantee nothing we say will be heard for as long as the burnings continue. If it was me I'd schedule them every hour until the inauguration, after which we won't matter. Keller brushes us under the rug with a single executive order, and we'll be in a black site gulag right alongside Anais Kiefer, waiting out our execution for treason."

Rogers turned a sickly ashen gray. "One every hour? That's like," she did a quick calculation, "over a thousand burnings. You can't be serious."

"He burned that many people in just one day at the end of the Pyramid," Wren said. "He can do it again."

Rogers looked like she was going to vomit. Wren knew how she felt.

"Either way, we'll know soon enough. It's almost been an hour since Rachel Day. Let's find out."

He held up his phone, fixed to a breaking news feed. Messages slotted in rapidly as the seconds ticked by. Fifty-nine minutes gone. Wren's heart thumped hard. They both leaned in.

9

SIXTY MINUTES

A t sixty minutes there was nothing. More updates firing from the major news corporations, the latest information on Rachel Day, the names of her kids sourced by some amoral paparazzi.

Sixty-one.

Sixty-two.

Snippets rose up about the last moments of Rachel Day's death, linked to interviews with survivors from the food court: an old woman sobbing uncontrollably beside her car; children crying, slumped in the parking lot; a man trying to explain what it had been like, the sound, the smell, and getting overwhelmed.

Sirens wailed. Blue lights flashed. Ambulances were still rolling in and out. A teen boy flashed by on a gurney, unconscious. There was a a pale teen girl slumped against the mall's cream plaster wall, lodged in a panic attack, panting and weeping.

They looked like refugees after a bomb strike, with stunned faces and wide eyes, not comprehending what had just happened. Some had minor injuries sustained during the stampede. Fire engines encircled the building, but there was nothing for them to do.

"Good Lord," Rogers said under her breath, so softly Wren barely heard it. "More of these would break us."

Sixty-four minutes.

Sixty-five.

"I think-" Rogers began, and then it came.

It was a short message only, quickly buried off the Iota front page but enough to rock Wren and Rogers.

BURNING IN SPOKANE

There was nothing for maybe thirty seconds more, then the flood tide began. Jostled video. Maddened messages out on social media. Screams. Terror.

Not a mall, this time. A bowling alley. Another woman had walked out into the middle of the lanes and doused herself with gasoline, just the same as Rachel Day. There were hundreds of people watching, their games forgotten. In the live feed she was burning still, fallen on her side.

Rogers looked up at Wren with the horror bedding down in her eyes. One an hour, maybe. Every hour.

"Oh no," she said.

Wren met her eyes, then turned back to the coverage, waiting for confirmation of the details. Moment by moment the names and numbers trickled through, and it was just as he'd feared.

The victim was a young mother with two children, a boy and a girl aged seven and five. The mirror image of Rachel Day, and exactly the same as Wren's kids.

A message to him.

"Rogers..." he began, voice thick, but she was already cycling through her address book.

"I see it," she said. "The kids ages? Trust me."

"I don't even know where they live now," Wren said. "They're in Witness Protection, right? I-"

47

"I have them," Rogers said.

It helped. Still he put a hand over her phone. "I trust you, not the government. Please, tell me where they are."

She stared. A simple step to make. "You think witness protection's compromised?"

"I can't take that chance."

She stared back. They'd come a long way together since she'd put him in the black site.

"You can't move them," she said at last. "Overwatch I'll accept. Only make contact if it's absolutely necessary."

"Agreed," Wren said quickly, feeling like he was teetering on the edge of a very high drop. "I promise."

Rogers let out a breath. "Then here."

She held out her phone. Wren swept it up, found the address, the number, the new fake names and memorized them at once.

Rhode Island. East Coast still. His family. The sense of relief shuddered through him.

"Thank you."

He handed the phone back, heart feeling full and desperate at once, blood pumping like he was about to have a cardiac event. Holding his children in his hands. His fingers trembled as he logged into his darknet, put up a secure thread for Foundation CEO Teddy to see, along with Hellion and B4cksl4cker, slotted in the address, gave the order, then sat back.

"I'll spin up teams for both Rachel Day and the bowling alley," Rogers said. "We'll stop this."

Wren nodded numbly. It was hard to think with his family under threat.

He looked out of the Black Hawk's open bay into the rush of wind while Rogers shouted orders into throat-mic. They'd be at Tucson International soon. A road whipped by below interspersed with fiery red canyons carved out of primordial sandstone. Winding streams puddled into oak-strewn meadows. A boy flying a drone waved up at them, like a remnant from an earlier age. Wren half expected him to burst into flames.

Too many innocents. Maybe there was something he could do about that. He tapped his phone to open a line.

"Hellion, are you there?"

"Yes, Christopher," she answered. "We are working on bringing team together. What is it?"

"I need Director Humphreys."

A few seconds passed in a flurry of keys. "He is at the White House. One moment. Phone switched off. It will be difficult. Yes, I will force through. Bypass security. Activate ringer." A few seconds passed. "His phone is ringing," Hellion said.

The line picked up. Hellion made the impossible possible.

"Who the hell is this?" came a hissed response, and Wren imagined Humphreys ducking out of an Oval Office meeting, head down, hand curled around his mouth.

"It's Christopher Wren, Director. I have three words for you. Lock it down."

"Lock what down?" Humphreys answered. "Wren, you can't do that to my phone, it's-"

"You'll want to hear this right now," Wren interrupted. "First off, we believe these burnings are the beginning of a massive campaign by my father to flood the media zone and prevent an essential truth getting out; that the Apex is behind David Keller's meteoric rise to the presidency."

Humphreys was silent a second. "Have you got evidence for any of that, at all?"

Wren gritted his teeth. "Not yet, but we will. I'm en route to pick up the Apex's trail right now. Rogers is headed to Cincinnati to work on breaking the firestorm. Between us we'll get this thing under control, but there's one thing you can do right now to help."

"What?" Humphreys snapped, working up his own anger now. "Do tell me, because I'm only the CIA Director, in the middle of briefing the President when my damn phone starts wailing like a fire alarm, and-"

"Forget the phone," Wren said. "You need to start thinking about locking down the country. I know you won't do it now, maybe not in the hours to come, but by nightfall you'll be considering it, and the sooner the better. The whole country needs to shut down. Complete and total, everyone in their homes, nobody on the streets, in bars, sports events, schools, churches. Anywhere people gather, those are his targets. Rogers sent you Kiefer's RQ graph?"

Humphreys blustered something.

"We're in the first wave and heading up an exponential panic curve. The second burning cements it. We need to flatten that curve as soon as we can, you know this as well as I do, Director. President-elect David Keller wants all of this. We've had two burnings and more are coming, and with every one the people will just get more traumatized. Pretty soon the RQ's going to let Keller do whatever he wants. Shut things down now and you can slow the spread, buy us some time to get some evidence into the media mainstream."

A long few moments passed.

"Even if I believe everything you just said," Humphreys began, "and maybe I could, maybe I even do, what you're suggesting is near politically impossible. The President's a lame duck, Christopher. She's got less than two months left, and there's no way she has the political capital to shut the country down. You can't-"

"So do the impossible. This is a new order of attack, and they're going to fight dirty. It's going to get ugly. Buy me time and I'll get your President the capital to get re-elected next time around."

He hung up.

Rogers looked over at him. "Lockdown?"

"Lockdown," he repeated, then turned back to his phone. They were already calling it a 'firestorm' on CNN.

10

ANAXIMANDER

I n forty minutes the cityscape of Tucson appeared on the horizon through the Black Hawk's open bay, gunmetal gray against the ochre desert. At Tucson International Wren and Rogers stepped out onto baking blacktop, already most of an hour passed since the second woman had burned, leaving ten minutes until the next.

Two jets lay ahead of them on the apron. A ONE Aviation Eclipse 550 on the left, an Embraer Phenom 100 on the right.

"Yours is the Eclipse," Hellion said in Wren's ear.

He looked at Rogers. Getting her own directions from Hellion now. She nodded at him. "Find the bastard, Christopher."

He smiled as she strode away for Cincinnati.

"How's my team looking?" he asked Hellion.

"They will be waiting."

"Good."

Wren cycled through news channels on his phone as he headed to the Eclipse jet. They were in a frenzy. The President was still preparing her initial statement. David Keller was already out and channeling the country's anger from his Texas front porch, fiercely decrying the attacks and promising to strike back. He looked like Commander-in-Chief already.

Wren boarded. The jet taxied to the runway. Eight minutes until the next burning was due. In his seat as the Eclipse took off, Wren swiped through the FBI brief Oxlea had sent over.

The Anaximanderians.

Based in Utah, their story began in the mid-80s, when the Great Salt Lake expanded due to unprecedented rainfall. Properties on the eastern shore were damaged, and the State response was to construct a huge pumping station in the Bonneville salt flats to the west. It housed three industrial pumps capable of moving millions of gallons of water along a freshly dug canal, out of the Salt Lake and into the desert. The pumps ran for years, shifting trillions of gallons onto the open flats where it evaporated, leaving a thicker crust of salt behind, until finally the lake's water level fell. The pumping station was retired in 1989 and left to the elements.

In 1998 the Anaximanderian cult moved in.

Wren skimmed their ideology. Followers of the ancient Greek philosopher Anaximander, the first in history to have recorded his thoughts on paper. Apparently few of these recorded writings survived, however, until in 1984 when second-generation Indian-American engineer Jamal Jalim 'discovered' a trove of them lodged at the bottom of a salt bog in the Bonneville flats.

So the Anaximanderians were born.

Jalim had only been a second-string engineer on the pumping station, but he began recruiting followers in the local towns as a charismatic leader, hawking his unique brand of 'scientific religion', proposing a single universal element underlying all matter. He was a skinny young guy in the photos, with a nerdy look and awkward frizzy hair, but once he'd chosen this new path he somehow channeled a charisma others found entrancing. He invented an intricate system for Followers in his new mystic 'religion', where everyone started at the bottom of a system of 55 levels leading toward 'scientific one-ness' at the top, gaining badges as they climbed.

"Like the Boy Scouts," Wren murmured to himself.

"What?" Hellion answered.

"These Anaximanderians."

A moment passed.

"There has been third burning, Christopher," B4cksl4cker said.

Wren cursed. "Not again!"

"Every hour was correct. We are sorry."

Wren brought up the news; it was another woman, married again, two kids again, the same ages as before. In the foyer of a middle school as they were letting out. The bell had just rung, the kids were pouring out, and boom.

Wren didn't watch the video in depth. He knew already the effect it would have. Instead he buried himself again in the Anaximanderian file.

It seemed that, up until two years earlier, they'd been entirely inward-looking and completely peaceful. No complaints from nearby residents, no cult escapees offering tell-alls of abuse. the FBI let such cults go about their busiess wholy unmolested.

However, at the two-year point they shifted. This shift manifested itself in an extreme level of fortification. Then abruptly started buying up weaponry, began zealously training and reinforcing their pumping station. It was now a fortress, completely impregnable.

This placed it higher on the FBI's alert list. Ever since Waco they'd prioritized overwatch of heavily armed cults. If they weren't causing trouble, though, they were left alone, and until, now the Anaximanderians had never caused trouble.

"Impregnable," Wren said. "Send me everything you've got on the pumping station, their armaments, schematics, member count, the lot."

"Sending," B4cksl4cker answered.

Within seconds files began appearing in Wren's phone, straight from the FBI database amongst other government-branded sources. He surfed the data, beginning with specifications on the pumping station itself.

It didn't look good.

Far thicker walls than Waco. Much stronger armaments. Better training, more people, more warning time. B4cksl4cker wasn't kidding when he'd called it impregnable.

He dug deeper. It was a dam, essentially, a concrete construction with walls many feet thick, so there was no way to ram or blow his way in. There were six sentry stations, two above each pump, with military-level M61 rotary Vulcan autocannons capable of a hundred rounds a second. Add that to a deep stockpile of smaller arms: a range of British, US and Russian sniper rifles good from over a mile out; AR-15s with bump stocks for automatic fire; man-portable M1A1 bazooka rocket launchers, plus multiple barrels of ammonium nitrate/fuel oil ANFO explosives good for IEDs in the field. All wielded by a standing army of at least a hundred cult devotees who doubtless spent every waking hour drilling for an end-of-world attack.

Somewhere in the middle of all that lay Jamal Jalim. The man who might hold the key to the Apex, tucked away like a pearl in an oyster. It looked impossible.

"This is what I'm going to need," he said, and began listing out gear.

11

FOURTH

Minutes before the Eclipse put down in Utah, the fifth young mother burned herself alive.

This time it was in the middle of a water park. Top of the slide. Visible from all around, going up like an ancient Greek lighthouse. Apparently she'd hidden the gas in her kid's inflatable ring, torn it to douse herself then lit the spark. No time for anyone to lean in and tip her into the flowing water. Just instant conflagration.

The nearest children were injured, backed up into the crush of bodies leading down the steps. The guard on attendance had been hemmed in and dived down the chute, leaving the woman to fall on her side and just keep on burning.

By the time the footage came out the plastic material of the slide had started to catch, igniting with a green flame that unleashed vile black smoke. Terrified children were still flooding still down the steps, cheeks tear-stained, parents rushing amongst them crying out names.

Wren watched as the Eclipse descended. The crowds fled out and fire crews came in, but their jet hoses couldn't reach high enough. Soon the whole top of the ride was on fire, and the structure was judged unsound to ascend.

They wrote it off. Stepped back and waited for the blaze to end.

Anchors on news stations were left stunned. Trying to find some way around calling this a complete surrender.

"We must lock down our country at once!" a soundbite came through. Wren recognized the voice and gritted his teeth as the video came up. Standing on a makeshift stage and shouting at a growing gaggle of reporters and protesters was David Keller, arguing against his own secret interests.

Wren cursed. The plane touched down, taxied to a halt and he called Rogers.

"Rogers," she answered curtly.

"Are you seeing this?"

"Keller?"

"Exactly."

"These burnings are sick, Chris. When you said every hour, I didn't really think…" She trailed off.

"I know. Where are you up to?"

She took a breath. "I'm almost to Cincinnati. I've recruited an advance team from local cops and early arrival FBI. We're hunting those three people you pointed out in the CCTV."

Wren cast his mind back. It already felt like the first burning was days ago. "Shoe guy, greeter, helper boy?"

"That's it."

"Anything so far?"

"I've already ruled out their phones," Rogers said. "There are no messages or calls in or out. I remote-interviewed Rachel Day's husband, he says she's been completely normal. Her boss at the accounting firm said the same. No burner phone we can find, no unusual Internet usage. She's had no time to join a cult since they had their kids, apparently."

Wren chewed that over. "Maybe she's a sleeper agent."

"For eight years?"

It seemed unlikely. Eight years to wait to commit suicide. Have kids, raise a family. People had done worse, but only with extensive conditioning prior.

"Dig deeper," he said. "Go to her past. She crossed paths with the Apex at some point. My hackers are on it too."

"And your strike?"

"Wing and a prayer. I just landed at the staging ground in Utah. It's heavily fortified, we'll make contact soon."

"Keep me apprised."

"Likewise. Good luck."

He ended the call. It felt good to have Rogers out there picking up the slack, someone he could rely on.

The Eclipse taxied to a halt and Wren opened the fuselage door. Outside the jet, sunlight blared every bit as bright as the Sonoran Desert. He pulled a pair of wraparound Oakleys from his shirt pocket and slipped them on while the stair car rolled up.

Brigham City Airport was a single blacktop runway with a clutch of aluminum siding hangars, backed up against the ochre flanks of the Wasatch mountain range. Wren sucked in a breath. The scent of salt hung faintly in the air, like he was closing in on the ocean, underwritten with the tang of rotten egg. That would be sulfur compounds in the dense, mineral-rich Great Salt Lake substrate, off-gassing.

It was only going to get stronger as they approached the Bonneville Salt Flats, some fifty kilometers away; exactly what Anais Kiefer had described.

Details of the raid to come swirled in his head along with lessons from Waco; taking on the double threat of extremists poised between trying to kill you and trying to kill themselves. The trick came in bypassing both, but in the stark sunlight of a late fall day, on a white salt expanse with zero cover and dark many hours away, the options for stealth were near non-existent.

But not completely.

The stairs rolled up and Wren jogged down. The first members of his team were gathered nearby beside an Airbus H160 helicopter.

Mason stood slightly apart from Doona and Henry, leaning against a large wooden crate, 6' 2" and solid with muscle, as befitted a former Marine. Even from two hundred yards out Wren could pick out the brand marks that covered his face, each stamped there by the Order of the Saints. He'd survived three bullets, spent a year in Foundation rehab and emerged on the other side stronger.

Doona was 19, a Nigerian child soldier Wren had shipped out of a war zone four years back, a slender 5' 10" with tight cornrow braids hugging her skull. Wiry but strong, she knew a dozen ways to kill a man, and had probably used most of them during her days with the 'Peace Lords' militia. Wren was always wary of using her in combat, but she was mentally tougher than most seasoned operators, so…

Henry stood tallest and broadest of them all, an expert sniper at 6' 3" and thicker than Wren in the chest, with short-cropped sandy hair. He'd been instrumental in taking down the Order of the Saints. Battle-scarred after the loss of his Afghanistan brother Abdul in the service of the Foundation, he'd worked through counseling then gotten right back in the harness.

Wren rolled up to them with a smile, arms spread. "Thank you all for coming."

Doona smiled. Henry laughed. "When the savior of the Republic calls, we come." He pulled Wren into a tough hug.

Wren snorted, clapped Henry on the back. "You've been watching too much David Keller."

"Man's persuasive," Henry allowed. "I voted for him."

"He's impressive, I'll give him that. Didn't kneel when I asked him to, though."

Henry laughed.

"This is your father's work," Doona said, getting straight to business. "The burnings."

"It is," Wren said, sobering as he leaned in to clasp her arm, forearm to forearm, the way they'd done it in the Peace Lords. Her grip around his elbow was hot and firm. "He's running Keller as his front man. Something we're going to make him regret."

"The brief looks wild," Henry said.

Wren nodded. "Only way to take down a pumping station in the middle of a salt desert." He took the few steps extra to stand in front of Mason, held out his hand. "Good to see you again, Mason."

Mason shook his hand. The grip was crushing. As part of his coin-level rehab he'd taken up rock climbing, bouldering in Yosemite looking for new routes to break, often free-climbing without a rope.

"And you, Christopher."

Up close the brands smothering his face were ugly, but all Wren saw was the inner strength. A Marine who'd fought the Saints' brainwashing with everything he had, then come back to sanity before it was too late.

"We need to get you in to see Steven Gruber," he said, as the thought occurred. "You could help him a lot."

"It would be my pleasure."

"Thank you." He looked back to the others. "And Alejandro?"

"Thirty minutes out," Doona said.

"Gear?"

"All here," Mason said, patting the crate.

Wren checked his phone. Fifteen minutes until the next burning. Always on the clock.

"Let's unpack and run a trial," he said, looking from face to face. "What do you all know about diving?"

12

STRIKE

The sky was a raw and immense blue. The Bonneville salt flats were Arctic white, even and smooth as a fresh fall of snow stretching out to the horizon. The pumping station squatted in the midst, bisecting sky and land with brutalist gray concrete, spiky with gantries, gun lookouts and the barrels of Vulcan autocannons.

Wren barely saw any of that, immersed beneath five feet of water and cruising along the salt-crusted bottom of the pumping station's intake canal from the Great Salt Lake. He was positioned at the head of his strike team, clad all in camouflage-white scuba gear with white tanks, being pulled along by Seabob F5 scooter propellers at nine miles an hour. They were a convoy on stealth approach.

Wren focused on the tablet screen banded to the back of his Seabob, showing the topdown view from a high-flying spy drone above.

"Do they see our approach, Hellion?" he asked.

"It does not seem so," she answered. "I count six guards on top of station, but you are clear so far. Ten seconds to central pump, Christopher. Prepare to surface."

He watched the gargantuan pump's intake tube nearing like a lunar eclipse, shadowing the sky. His pulse thrummed.

"You are under cover of the pipe," Hellion barked in his ear. "Surface."

He inclined the scooter, covered the short gap to the surface in seconds then killed the engine as he broke through in the mouth of the intake valve. It was a huge tube ten feet across, looming like an archway half out of the water. The rest of his team surfaced around him in near silence.

Wren pulled off his scuba mask and shrugged off the air bottle, turning to take in the cramped tube mouth. It looked just like the same as their scout drone had shown, a tiny submersible Hellion had sent ahead an hour earlier. The intake pump itself, a rotary version he'd been hoping to slip directly through, had been completely backfilled with cement. No way through there. A pair of security cameras watched over from above, but Hellion had already hacked and looped the signal.

Wren let the Seabob sink to the bottom of the canal.

"Ready?" he asked.

"Ready," said Mason, followed by Doona and Henry.

"Tell me the middle gun emplacement is empty," Wren said to Hellion.

"Currently empty," Hellion confirmed.

As planned, they'd arrived in the midpoint of a garrison changeover. Wren reached to his back, where the huge Battelle TAIL grappling rifle was strapped. Bigger than a harpoon gun and powered by scuba tank air at 300psi, it was capable of firing a two pound titanium grappling hook one hundred feet straight up, towing a six-millimeter Kevlar line.

"Get ready to dive the drone," he said to Hellion.

"One minute descent time," she answered. "As ordered, it's packed with explosives."

"Then dive," said Wren, and pushed off the cement-filled

pump out into the open blue of the canal, looking up at the gun emplacement some seventy feet directly overhead. A Vulcan gun left vacant, an iron railing. He shouldered the Battelle at a near vertical, emerging four feet out of the water with the six-hooked claw hand of the grapnel flowering at the end.

Under the grappling rifle's thirty pounds he immediately began to sink into the water, but Doona and Mason swam down to form a human pyramid, supporting him even as Henry beaded his CheyTac M200 sniper rifle on the railing above.

Wren waited. At the west corner a guard group came into view. any second they'd see Wren and his team in the water down below.

"Hellion," Wren urged.

"Should be coming in range now."

Then they heard it, the high buzzing of the surveillance drone on a steep guided dive toward the pumping station. The guards atop the station turned their attention toward the sky. Wren couldn't see the drone yet but the sound of its rotors grew louder every second.

"Impact in ten, nine-" Hellion began.

"Good enough for me," Wren said, and pulled the Battelle's trigger.

It launched with a burst of compressed air through the diffuser, propelling the grapnel up in a silent arc toward the top railing of the pumping station. Miss now and they'd have to recharge the rifle's gas and re-spool the Kevlar cable, a near-impossible feat while floating in a canal, certainly impossible if they came under fire.

The grapnel soared, a slim black claw against the burning blue sky, overshot the railing then fell with a clank on the other side. Loud enough to grab the guards' attention, but just then Hellion's drone plummeted out of the sky, hit the dam on the far side and blew. The ensuing explosion was so vast even the water in the canal carried the vibration.

Wren jerked the grapnel back until it lodged on the railing then swiftly fed the cable into the winching mechanism of an APA-5 Atlas Powered Ascender. Twenty pounds in weight, a foot long with the profile of an old school film camera, it could haul up to six hundred pounds of dead weight straight out of the water.

"Clipped in?" Wren asked.

"All harnesses attached to you," Doona answered, bobbing up from underwater with a spare karabiner in her hand. "Good to go."

"Ascent," Wren said and hit the button. Within three seconds the APA-5 plucked them all out of the water like fish on a multi-hook line. They bounced up over the huge pump inlet then slapped against the sheer concrete side of the pumping station. Within ten seconds all four of them were ascending at a fast walk up the pumping station's sheer concrete side, already a quarter of the way to a top that was now shrouded in a thick cloud of concrete dust.

Within that cloud several of the Vulcan autocannons spun up. There was no target with the drone already destroyed, but that didn't stop them.

"A patrol's coming over to your side," Hellion warned abruptly, "estimate they will see you in three, two, one-"

A shout came first then a shot followed, bullet ricocheting off the wall and stinging Wren's right arm with stone chips.

Henry leaned out far to get the angle and fired back at two figures above. His second shot took one in the shoulder and spun him, the other returned fire, then Wren got his hands around the railing. He unclipped the karabiner smoothly, rolled over the edge and sank to one knee, steadying his SIG Sauer P320 .45 ACP and taking aim. "I have east," he said calmly then fired, taking the second guy once in the belly, once more in the side as he went down.

Behind him Mason dropped into position, followed by Henry and Doona, while Wren was already running low and fast along the top of the pumping station, through the whirling storm of powder dust.

"One dead ahead of you," Hellion warned. "They're trying to turn the autocannon. One incoming from the north side emplacement."

Wren could just about pick out the Vulcan emplacement through the white. He unclipped a flashbang grenade from the bandolier around his chest, pulled the pin and tossed it high. Three seconds on it landed, six seconds on it burst, and Wren ran into the thunderclap of light and sound.

Two figures lay beside the autocannon, unconscious and heaving, and beside them was a hatch leading down. Wren tried the metal handle but it didn't budge; they must have locked it at the first sign of trouble. Good job that wasn't the only route in.

"Ten yards north," Hellion called in his ear, and counted them out as he ran. At ten he stopped and looked down; beneath the metal grill lay a stretch of frosted gray glass. High-altitude surveillance had revealed that this part of the roof had been refitted by the Anaximanderians, presumably to allow natural light into the otherwise windowless concrete block.

Wren latched a speed rope to the railing, clipped it to his belt harness then vaulted over and onto the glass directly, landing with a crack that shot thin spider's web lines across the triple glazing. Not enough.

"Bolting," he called, and pulled the captive bolt gun from its holster.

"We're holding our own back here," came Henry's response. "But they're closing."

66

Wren heard the sound of their evac helo coming in. He racked the bolt gun, a .25 Cash Special packing 265 milligram blank cartridges that fired a retractable stainless steel bolt with enough percussive force to shatter a cow's thick skull. A mag of ten, he hoped to get the job done in four.

"I'm picking up some internal comms," Hellion blurted in his ear. "Sounds like they're beginning a mass suicide protocol. Hurry."

Wren pressed the bolt gun's muzzle flush to the glass, tracking one of the spiderweb cracks from his landing, and pulled the trigger. The whole pane of reinforced glass sank an inch as the bolt crunched in and jammed the crack wider. He picked another spot along the web and fired again, then again, and on the fourth shot the whole pane shattered and Wren dropped straight through.

13

JAMAL JALIM

The safety line caught Wren and left him swaying some twenty feet high in the cavernous gray canyon of the pumping station. The speed rope slack fell and thwacked against the concrete floor below.

"Dropping," he said over the earpiece comms, took his weight on the speed rope and unhooked the karabiner.

The rope raced through his gloved hands, working up a little heat as he fell into gloom. Raw gray concrete walls rushed by on either side then he was on the ground with his SIG .45 held up.

Nothing and nobody.

He was at the western edge of the station's central corridor, three foot wide and never intended for human habitation; merely an access route for engineers to service the pumps, nightmarishly tall and utterly functional. It made Wren feel insignificant.

"Hurry, Christopher!" Hellion said.

Both directions on the corridor looked alike. Blueprints said this corridor ran the length of the whole structure, with storage spaces and offices for the engineers alcoved to either side. Access hatches led below to the pumps in four places, but Wren figured those would have been sealed up just as fully as the pumps' outer access.

That left the control deck, a large hall offset from the corridor and directly above the pumps, accessible at the east end of the corridor by a narrow flight of stairs. Judging from the blueprints, it matched the space Anais Kiefer had described.

Wren set off running.

One of the alcoves opened to the left of him, revealing desks and chairs arrayed in rows before a low stage, atop which sat a huge rectangular glass box, easily fifteen feet across, ten tall, filled with what looked to be black earth. Above it hung a huge metal grill, like a guillotine blade ready to fall.

Through the next opening lay a dormitory hall stacked with bunk beds rising bed upon bed perhaps a dozen high, like shelving in a fulfillment center, reinforced with brutish iron ladders. Each bed was neatly made up with thin brown sheets.

Almost at the end, Wren ran past another two openings, each with more chairs and desks, a blackboard and surgical gurney at the head of one, a strange-looking altar with an oversized, upturned rough crystal cup at the head of the other, then he reached the stairs.

"Christopher!" Hellion cautioned. "They are seconds away from suicide completion."

He sprinted up two stories of tight square stairs then burst out into an open space.

Light flooded in from diagonals in the fifteen-foot high glass ceiling, dazzling him like floodlights on a stage; some kind of sun tunnels bored through the station's solid roof. He held up a hand to ward off the glare, picking out an open oval arena of tiered seating filled with people dressed in varying tones of khaki, sepia and brown. A perfect match for what

Kiefer had described. All the followers sat perfectly still, hands flat on their knees, staring at a figure in the center wearing white cotton robes with his arms spread wide.

Jamal Jalim.

Not the slender young man Wren had seen in the photographs. He was in his late fifties now, cheeks riven with deep lines, his frizz of nerdy hair all gone leaving a bald and imposing dome. His dark eyes stared directly at Wren.

"Stop whatever you're doing," Wren ordered, striding into the center of the arena.

"There is no stopping the forces of nature," Jamal Jalim said, and lifted his right hand to his mouth. His people responded like an honor guard on parade, raising their hands to their mouths also.

There were small red pills in every hand. Wren had seen it many times before; the endgame of all death cult leaders. Wren recognized the look in Jalim's eyes, too, the authority blurring into joy as he assumed absolute command over life and death; the same look on David Keller's face atop his acceptance stage.

"You can stop this, Jalim," Wren said, voice low and measured, gaming this out. He could just shoot the guy, or take five long bounds and clothesline him to the throat, but what about the followers?

He swept his gaze across them, seeing steeled eyes and braced bodies. Their discipline was impressive. He doubted he could save any of them if he tried to take Jalim by force; they'd follow his last order and end themselves first.

Wren didn't want another hundred dead on his conscience.

He lowered his gun and addressed the crowd, Jalim's true source of power. "I apologize for the way I've arrived. I apologize to all, but I have received visions from Anaximander himself, calling me to seek your counsel. My name is Christopher Wren." He focused on Jamal Jalim. "I think you knew my father."

Jalim's eyes widened, but the moment of shock was quickly buried in enforced calm. He was clearly trying to work some route through this moment for himself too. He'd spent a lifetime building this group up to service his needs, and surely he didn't want to kill them all if he didn't have to.

Wren placed his SIG .45 on the ground, trying to make it easier. "I come as an emissary. The world needs to hear the words of Anaximander, so I come here seeking your guidance."

There, he saw a twinkle of recognition in Jalim's eyes. Maybe amusement? He recognized what Wren was doing. Not all cult leaders were bound up in their dogma. Some were quite capable of extricating themselves from the nonsense when the moment came.

In some ways they were the worst kind.

Seconds passed. The light flooding in through the sun tunnels lit Jalim up like a holy beacon.

"I know who you are," he said at last. "I know why you're here. I have been expecting you. Now, your trials await."

14

TRIALS

W ren licked his lips.

"I only hope to talk," Wren said. "There need be no trials."

Jalim's eyes turned cold. The momentary amusement turning sour. "You shoot down my anointed sentries. Ram vehicles filled with explosives into this holy compound. You say you're seeking wisdom in Anaximander's name, that you are an emissary to save the world, then you say there is no need for trials?"

Wren blinked.

He'd walked into that. He felt this new reality rising up either side of him like the prison walls of the central corridor. In here, with his followers' lives on the line, Jalim held all the cards. Wren had already come halfway. So go a little further.

"Very well," he said. "Trials."

Jalim swelled with power. "Put down your equipment. The earpiece in your ear. The camera on your chest. There is no need for such things here."

Wren had been caught out. Now all his backup would be gone.

"Do not do what he says, Christopher," Hellion warned.

"He will wear your skin as suit. I have seen this in movie. Now I am scrambling Doona to join you, Henry will follow. Helicopter is nearby, ready to transport Mason. He is injured. Delay."

"Don't send them," Wren whispered firmly. "Hold the top and get Mason out, but otherwise no ones in or out."

"But Christopher, he will-"

"He won't kill me," Wren replied, loud enough for everyone to hear. Not taking his eyes off Jalim. "Not if I am who I say I am."

Jalim smiled.

Hellion protested further, but Wren just tapped and twisted the earpiece so it dropped to the sand, where it continued to protest tinnily. He unfastened his bodycam with all the gentle care of a suicide bomber disarming and set it on the ground reverently next to his SIG .45.

Jalim nodded. Two children ran in from either side to snatch up the gear.

"Christopher Wren," Jalim said, that strange note of amusement firing in his eyes again. "You should not have come here. I said precisely this to your father also, all those years ago. Apex of your Pyramid. We entertained him and his heathen acolytes some years ago, but he ultimately refused the trials and therefore was not welcome."

Wren's heart skipped a beat. That was a solid confirmation. "So you saw my father?"

Jalim raised one hand, and abruptly every person in the room stood.

"You have trespassed," he intoned, his voice changing now to something ceremonial, almost sing-song. "You have claimed Anaximander's blessing. Let the trials commence. Until death or ascension."

Wren's mouth opened, but there was nothing much to say.

He'd have to see this through. "Death or ascension," he repeated, "in Anaximander's name."

The people began filing silently off the bleachers toward the stairs, still clutching their pills. Wren met their eyes one by one.

"Go in Anaximander's name," he said as they passed by. They ignored him but he kept it up anyway. It was all going into their heads. Whatever BS Jalim had soaked them in, there was always a way to up the ante.

Jamal Jalim gazed at Wren. He was shorter, maybe 5'11", thin but wiry with muscle. Four tall, strong men in pale togas gathered at his sides. He waited until all the others were gone, then spoke.

"The truth is, the trials were actually your father's idea. I owe him everything, really. But I'm afraid I can never pay the price that he asked. If you're here to collect it, you will be sorely disappointed."

He strode to the stairs, and his men took Wren's arms and led him along behind.

15

ONENESS

I t was the room with the big glass box filled with dirt.

Wren's head raced as he entered the first of the rooms off the central corridor, trying to fathom Jalim's relationship with his father. Did he hate the Apex or adore him?

The men in togas led him up to the stage. The people were settling into their chairs like schoolchildren waiting for a lesson, though there were not nearly enough chairs, so the rest stood at the back and around the sides, circling the glass box.

Jamal Jalim took to the stage and spread his arms like a natural showman. Wren kept the judgment off his face. The guy wasn't much to look at, but he had conviction. All cult leaders were manipulators. Everything you thought was wrong. Everything they said was right. The trick to longevity was keeping the people so off-balance and so in love that they never realized how completely they'd been had.

"The trials," said Jalim, his voice carrying over the ranks of his followers. "Following the teachings of Anaximander, we seek to achieve oneness with all the elements of nature. Fire. Water. Earth. Air. In all their myriad combinations."

The crowd repeated the last few words, "In all their myriad combinations."

"Today we have a man who claims to come from Anaximander himself. A man who claims he is a messenger. So there must be a trial of all elements, beginning with Anaximander's prophet on this Earth. Myself."

The people gasped.

In one smooth movement Jalim stripped off his robes, and the gasps redoubled. He was naked underneath; pale brown skin, washboard abs, arms, shoulders and thighs thin but striated deeply with cords of muscle. Extremely low body fat, Wren figured. He'd be slippery as hell in a fight.

Standing naked before his people he seemed more in command than ever. Wren weighed the possibility of snatching the guy there and then. Elbow to his head, toss him over his shoulder and run. Maybe he'd make it out of the room. They'd probably all kill themselves, though.

He wasn't so keen on that.

"Trial 1 asks us for oneness with both Earth and Water," Jalim went on. "An ability to change our form to mimic our brethren elements, to flow like protons, neutrons and electrons."

Wren grunted low. Pseudoscience was a staple of many modern cults. He didn't bother to point out that while electrons might 'flow', protons and neutrons never really did. But whatever, as an engineer Jalim certainly knew that already.

A steel cable descended from above, with a steel hoop on the end of it. It lowered until it hung just overhead. Jalim looked over at Wren like he was tossing a gauntlet, then reached up with one hand and took hold of the hoop.

At once it lifted him. There were more gasps. The cable receded into a pulley mechanism in the high ceiling. Wren had seen a lot of grand exits, but never one quite like this.

Fifteen feet high it lifted him, well above the lip of the huge glass box, then it shifted gears and moved him backwards like the grapple arm in a funfair crane game, positioning Jalim immediately above the box's left side.

Wren didn't have a clue what was happening. Undeniably, Jalim looked good hanging there. Ripped. Completely at ease. All his weight hanging on one arm but clearly comfortable.

"Befitting the moment," Jalim said, speaking as clearly as before, though now his voice was loaned added depth by his height above the crowd, "failure at this test will mean death. Lower the division."

The huge grate that hung like a portcullis above the center of the box began to descend. Excellent production values, Wren thought. Ready to go on a whim. A team in a back room somewhere. He scanned the walls looking for the control booth. Watching through a spyhole, maybe, too small to see.

The lower bar of the portcullis reached the dirt and its descent paused. Jalim reached out to the top bar and twisted one of the poles, which released a long thin metal rod. With this rod in hand, Jalim attacked the portcullis in a frenzy, hitting every beam and crossbar in the grid. The sound of metal clashing rang out discordantly, filling the tall room with violent echoes even as it pulled Jalim's muscles into tight, startling relief.

Wren realized what was happening. Proof that the portcullis was solid. Not a trick piece of gear. Like a magician testing the blade he was about to stick through the woman in the box.

Thirty seconds of that passed, sound barraging out, then Jalim slid the metal rod back into the top of the grid and looked out at his audience as if to say 'see'.

The portcullis began sinking again, this time directly into the dirt. Not solid dirt, then, Wren realized, but liquid. Earth and water made mud, of course. It sloshed thickly as the portcullis slid in, slow waves rippling across the surface.

The people leaned closer. Wren felt breaths drawn and held. There was a grating sound as the portcullis worked its way down guiderails on the tank's inner walls, then a dull clunk as it hit the bottom.

Just what the hell was going on?

"As I was so granted oneness upon ascension as Anaximander's prophet on Earth," Jalim intoned, still hanging immobile, "so any emissary for Anaximander should exhibit oneness too."

Wren's eyes were wide now. Taking in every detail.

The steel cable holding Jalim began to descend. First his feet touched the surface of the mud and sank out of sight. His shins followed, his knees, his thighs. The mud level rose slightly against the glass as his body displaced it. Next his chest, his shoulders, his neck, his face, until he was completely submerged.

The steel cable reeled up and away, pulling the hoop dripping after it.

Wren just stared. In all his years of cult activity he'd never seen anything quite like this. This kind of staging. The Apex had buried people alive, his own children with Wren amongst them once, but those had been rough-hewn efforts dug out in the desert wastes, barely stage-managed at all, with no helpers in back rooms bringing such class to the proceedings.

The show wasn't done though. With Jalim swallowed in the mud, a second huge grate began to descend from above. A roof for the cage, ten feet on a side, the perfect fit to enclose the left side. It came down in seconds and slotted into grooves smooth as a Porsche changing gears, chased by clanking sounds as locks sealed it in.

Wren's mouth went dry.

Seconds ticked by.

78

As far as he could see, Jamal Jalim had just put himself in a solid steel cage inside a box full of mud. Thirty seconds already and counting. Was it a feat of holding his breath? He looked around at the people. Men, women and children stared fixedly at the glass box of mud, utterly rapt and leaning in.

It was crazy. Wren almost laughed but it wasn't funny. The silence got hot and thick.

A minute, now?

The portcullis divider rattled and people nearby jerked. Nothing was visible through the mud walls. A minute thirty. Wren started to think about calling for the divider to be raised, the roof to be lifted, thought about grabbing a desk and putting it through the glass himself. Jalim was no good to him dead.

The divider rattled again. People gasped. Mud shifted against the glass, then began to spiral.

Wren's jaw dropped.

A slow counterclockwise whirlpool in the left part of the tank. Clockwise in the right. A magic trick like nothing he'd seen before. Topping two minutes now. More rattles. More spinning. It was incredible.

Then it all stopped.

The mud slowed. More seconds ticked by. Wren envisaged Jamal Jalim suspended in the mud of his cage like an unborn baby sucking in fetal liquid, convulsing as his lungs tried to filter oxygen from wet dirt, failing to exhibit the 'oneness' he'd so trumpeted. A trick gone wrong, the magician stabbing his assistant right through the chest.

Then the steel cable descended once more, this time directly into the right half of the tank. The steel hoop struck and sank. The line went taut. A second passed, then it began to reel in.

The mud parted. Jamal Jalim's fist emerged, followed by his arm then his head. Coated in thick brown muck. His neck followed, his shoulders, his torso, his hips, legs, feet, ascending until he was completely clear of the vat. He casually wiped his face, rising calm and clear the rest of the way, breathing normally, eyes white searchlights against the dark mask of black.

Wren stared in silence, as awed as the rest.

The cable shifted forward then descended, setting Jamal Jalim down on the stage a scant few feet from where he'd been plucked up. Wren racked his mind trying to figure out the trick. The whirlpools were easy enough; a couple of wave makers in the bottom of the vats would do it. This was a pumping station after all, so that wouldn't be hard.

But the transition from left to right through the portcullis?

Clearly he hadn't 'become one' with the mud, flowed his protons and neutrons through the portcullis, then 'rematerialized', so was there a trapdoor leading to a tunnel down through the stage and up to the other side? Wren dismissed that as too complex; the mud level would bob and sink if a hatch was opening underneath. Maybe the portcullis had a built-in trick hinge, which could simply be opened under the mud?

Jamal Jalim gave nothing away. Not even breathing hard. He looked out at his people calm and triumphant.

They burst into a wave of cheering, and Wren couldn't argue. It was one hell of a trick. He considered again just taking the guy out there and then, but it was the worst possible timing. Just when he'd proven himself to be Anaximander's prophet, some kind of living god?

No. They'd definitely pull the pin on all those pills in their hands.

There was only one thing for it. He had to pick up the trail on his father, and this was the only way.

He began with his gloves, followed up with the bandolier around his chest, his rubberized boots, his rope harness, then peeled off his all-white wetsuit until he was standing on the stage naked as the day he was born.

The people saw him. Saw his confidence, even if it was a front. Jalim saw it too and there was that look of amusement again, the recognition by one conman of another.

Wren had no idea how to pull off the trick, but fake it 'til you make it. He could hold his breath pretty long. That gave him a couple of minutes to figure it out. Failing that, maybe he could punch through the glass itself and drain the box that way.

Maybe.

16

EARTH & WATER

F irst came the grate roof, lifting up from the left side of the box trailing mud. Next followed the portcullis divider, sucking out of the thick liquid and rising to hang just over the center, mud-slathered but intact. Wren scanned it rapidly, looking for hidden seams, joins, hinges, but nothing stood out. A good craftsman could conceal them easily, though. He began to wonder how good an idea this was.

Showing none of that doubt on his face, he took up position at the left side of the box. Being naked didn't bother him. As he looked out at Jalim's people he replayed everything he'd seen, trying to figure it out. The real magic in a trick like this was usually baked into the physical structure. You thought that was a woman being cut in half? Nope, two women were already there in two separate boxes, contorted into tiny spaces. The magician slides in the guillotine blade, one sticks out her head, the other sticks out her legs, abracadabra.

Either that or it was a simple misdirection, pulled off before the show even began. Think a card trick's amazing, so complex and randomized? But go back and watch it a dozen times and you'll see the magician palm the card right at the start while you're enjoying the patter and waiting for the trick to begin.

So how did that apply here?

The steel hoop came down. Wren imagined himself suspended in the mud like a dinosaur fossil, unable to figure it out, sucking in mud then just hanging still, perfectly embalmed and unable to help anyone. No use to his Foundation. No way to stop the Apex or David Keller. Firestorm rolling on.

That outcome could be very real. Standing closer to the glass now, he realized how thick it was, and didn't like his chances trying to break through with just his fists and feet.

He would be quite dead.

Still, this was his lead, and he had to pursue it all the way, just like Jamal Jalim had said: death or ascension. He raised his right hand, took hold of the hoop and at once it lifted him up.

Just like Jalim. He thought back on the Apex and all his tricks, homing in on the one time he'd shown little Christopher Wren, then known as Pequeño 3, the secret tunnel running out from the first 'buried alive' pit he'd had his people dig into the Arizona desert. None of the people who'd died in that pit had known about the tunnel, concealed behind a few flat stones in the wall. Instead, they'd dutifully died. But the Apex had shown his Pequeño 3.

Soon after that, Wren had been buried with all his brothers and sisters in another pit. Galicia. Chrysogonus. Zachariah. Gabriel. Grace. Only Wren had believed there was another tunnel in the pit's smooth-walled sides, and only Wren had kept searching until he'd almost suffocated, and in the end only Wren had survived.

The steel cable swung him out over the mud, and there he

hung, spooling his mental footage of Jalim's trick backward and forward.

His money was on some kind of trick switch hidden in the portcullis. But it wouldn't be easy to find. It looked like this mud vat underwent constant use, Jalim's means of keeping his people busy as they sought to 'flow with the mud' and achieve 'oneness'. Likely they spent all day, every day dropping in and out and trying to push their way through the portcullis. If there was an easy switch that opened a trick door in the portcullis, one of them would have hit on it already by accident.

The portcullis was descending again already.

Wren's mind raced on.

It couldn't be anything a random movement could trigger. That left some kind of key. But Jalim had gone in naked. Hadn't had time to prepare, to secrete the key somewhere about his body, unless he carried it with him at all times like a drug mule making an endless border crossing, and why would he do that in the safety of his own cult?

No.

The room full of faces was staring up at him, a few with faith, most with derision. A pretender who deserved to die for his arrogance. Now the portcullis was grinding down into place, met with clanks as it struck bottom. He could still pull out of this. Jump off the loop, scale the box before the lid came down, but he knew where that led.

His mental footage looped. His arm began to ache. Where was the key? He thought back on card tricks where the 'magic' happened before anything had really happened, and highlighted the points Jalim had touched as he went into the tank. The steel hoop itself? Wren looked up, then swapped hands. Right hand to left. Feeling for anything on the hoop. A magnet, maybe. A place a key could be attached. But nothing. It was perfectly smooth with no indentations.

His steel cable began to descend. Now or never.

"Wait!" he called. Remembering one last thing.

The cable kept descending.

"Wait!" he called again, this time booming. "Don't I have the same rights as the prophet in this trial to the death? Shouldn't I be afforded the chance to test the divider?"

The line descended a moment longer, until his feet touched the mud. It was uncomfortably cold. He sank deeper, into his calves, then the cable halted.

"Very well," came Jalim's voice.

The cable reversed direction. Wren was lifted out. He swapped arms again. He couldn't hold his own weight for much longer, being so much heavier with muscle than Jalim. Already his shoulder blade was throbbing. His grip could give out any moment. It didn't help that Jalim had left the hoop slick with mud.

The portcullis rose beside him, and Wren reached over to the place Jalim had touched earlier. He found the rod, thin and flexible, inserted into the top bar of the grate. Once in the mud, it would be rendered inaccessible by the roof grating.

He pulled a half-inch of it out, and felt rather than saw the indentation worked in the end. Small. Insignificant. Round. Deep enough to contain a specialized key? He pulled the rod all the way out, three feet and slender, and made a show of inspecting it. There was no indentation in the other end. No reason for there to be one. He brought it up before him and used the angle to sneak a look into Jalim's eyes.

There he saw the same recognition and momentary fear. It takes a con to spot a con.

This was it. A key embedded into the end of the rod, which Jalim slipped out every time he had to perform, then replaced it afterward. So where was it now?

He attacked the grate with the rod, playing the part and sending concussive clashes ringing around the room, while also looking for a tiny keyhole. Mud rattled off and slapped down as he beat it hard, looking for tell-tale bubbles, the mud shifting strangely, until-

Yes.

Bottom right. A tiny dimple. If the grate were dry he'd never have seen it, but the mud glistened and picked out contours. Light and shadow. Achieve oneness.

Now he just needed the key. The worried look on Jalim's face had told him everything he needed to know. It was a hell of a gamble, but there was only one place it could be now, unless Jalim had swallowed it or stowed it another orifice, but Wren didn't think so. That wouldn't be practical.

No.

That meant the key was still in the tank.

Wren hit the portcullis with such vigor that the rod slipped out of his hand and fell into the tank below him. He looked up, acting like this was nothing.

"I'm ready," he said.

The portcullis descended into the mud, clanking firmly into position as locks engaged. Seconds later, so did Wren.

The mud engulfed him like a barrel of cold fish. It was more watery than he'd expected, but buoyant enough that he sank slowly. Silty and stinking of the Great Salt Lake's sulfur. His knees, his thighs, his hips submerged. He took deep rapid breaths, not nearly as cool as Jalim, hyperventilating his lungs.

He'd always had strong lung capacity, had even taught himself as a child to enter 'aortal flutter', an unconscious state that feigned death and required very little oxygen to maintain. His max had been seven minutes. Out of training, now he could probably push that to three or four, if he undertook no vigorous activity.

The mud rose up his chest, his shoulders, his neck, then

he took one last breath, closed his eyes and ducked below the surface.

Instant dark. Instant cold and disorientation. He swiped a few strokes, pulling himself down to the bottom. Within seconds his fingers closed on the rod that he'd dropped on purpose. There was no key inside it, but that didn't matter. He swiped further down until he lay chest-flat like a catfish on the bottom of the tank, reaching out to take hold of the portcullis grate. It was as solid and impassable as granite.

If the key was anywhere, it would be on the other side of the portcullis. No way Jalim would leave it on the left side, where Wren might stumble on it and realize what it was.

Holding to the portcullis, he slipped the rod through the grating, then followed with his arm up to the shoulder against the metal. Call it protons and neutrons becoming one with the mud. Still lying flat, he pressed the rod to the floor of the box's right side then gently swept it flush to the front glass, then back across to the left in a half-arc like a windscreen wiper.

He felt nothing. Maybe he wouldn't. If the key was light, if the mud was too thick, maybe this would never work. Thirty seconds. Along with his arm, that made for a six foot radius. Enough to cover just over half the right side of the tank. He had to hope the key was on that side.

He dragged the rod back toward him until it lay flush along the portcullis base, then worked his left hand along the grate, feeling for the key. His fingers fumbled through mud, working swiftly between the bars, but there was nothing. No tiny sliver of metal.

A minute already. Time enough for several more swipes.

This time he picked a different spot, pushing his right arm through the portcullis at the middle, strained against the metal and ran the rod all the way to the left side of the box, dragged

87

it gently back to the grate, then repeated his scavenge through the mud.

Again, nothing.

Two minutes?

Once more, left to right this time. The biggest sweep he could make, with his lungs already starting to rebel. Demanding air. As slow as he could bear to drag, then gathering it in. Moving along the grate, scavenging his catch with both hands, fingers probing until they caught on something.

Metal!

A tiny chunk, barely larger than a screw. Wren clasped it and pulled himself sideways, positioning himself blind at the bottom right corner of the portcullis, where he probed for the hole. It took him three stabs with the tiny key to find it, insert it and twist. There was the tiniest click and the portcullis moved.

His heart surged. He pushed and the grate split smoothly, opening outward on an invisible hinge into the right hand side. Three kicks sent him through, surging straight to the surface where-

His head struck metal, hard.

For a second he was stunned and saw stars, almost shocked by the impact into sucking in a breath, though he regained his wits swiftly and felt around at this new ceiling.

They'd lowered a second roof grate!

This considerably upped the challenge, forcing him to the prove his 'oneness' with the mud twice if he wanted to be released back into the air; a feat he knew even Jamal Jalim had never managed, because it wasn't possible.

Panic bloomed and he tamped it down.

He'd always known this was a possibility. Ten foot square cage, a roof lattice made of thin bars, held by locks at the edges. Not too strong, he guessed, but at ten foot tall there was nothing he could brace his feet against to squat the roof up and off.

But with the portcullis swung open? He saw the way instantly.

Around two minutes thirty, with his pulse banging in his head and his lungs gulping at his throat, he swung the hidden portcullis out to the middle of the cage, set his feet on rungs two thirds of the way up, pressed his shoulders against the roof and pushed.

His whole 6' 4", two hundred twenty pound frame bent against the grid like he was squatting five hundred with the devil on his back.

The cage roof strained. Flexed. Wren almost gulped mud, relaxed for a second, strained again. Something popped as the metal flexed in its locks. Three minutes, and Wren dug deep as a red glow bloomed across his eyelids. No way he was going to die in a bucket of mud. Not after surviving everything the Apex could throw at him, not after letting down his family, Rogers, all the Foundation. He had things still to do.

He pushed again, throwing everything he had into the curve of his back, then felt something shear, like a vertebra slipping. He would have roared if he was above ground. He pressed again even harder, Atlas squatting the whole world, and another latch slipped, then another, then the whole grating popped up and out like the triggered arm of a mousetrap, admitting Wren roaring and filthy into the light.

He surged up, mud spraying from his mouth and nose, rubbing at his eyes and ears, standing tall on the portcullis door and staring out at the people through the half-cocked roof grate. The whole audience were splattered with mud that he'd catapulted across them. That felt pretty good.

There was a stunned silence.

But Wren wasn't done yet. He seized the edge of the

glass, pulled himself over the edge like a turd escaping the toilet bowl and slipped down to land on his feet with a splat beside a shock-faced Jamal Jalim.

Wren wasted no time.

He punched Jalim square in the face.

The prophet flew. A hundred-forty pounds soaking wet, Jalim didn't stand a chance against the wrecking ball of Wren's fist. Two hundred pounds per square inch of force, and that was hardly even trying. The thin, wiry bastard took wing off the stage, hit the deck and rolled.

Wren didn't follow up, just stood in front of the people. Cult devotees. Staring at him now with something like wonder. The first person since their prophet to cross from one side of their stupid mud tank to the other. The first person ever to 'achieve oneness' through the damn roof.

Wren felt their minds flexing before him. Windows of possibility opening up in their eyes. for a second he thought it might be enough, that this victory would prove Jalim was a false prophet, and they'd unclench their fists and drop their suicide pills to the ground.

But they didn't.

If anything, they clutched them tighter. Wren saw white knuckles everywhere he looked. Very well.

"Trial two," he announced, booming the words so loud the people nearest flinched. "And pick him up," he ordered, pointing at Jalim, who was now struggling to get to his feet.

Wren strode right past him, through the gawping ranks of the members and out of the tall open doorway. No idea where he was going, but it didn't matter. He was in charge of this nonsense now.

17

FIRE & WATER

Wren turned left onto the spine corridor, panting a little as he recaptured his breath. His feet burned where the narrow portcullis gratings had dug in. Probably he was leaving bloody footprints behind, but he didn't stop to check. It wouldn't kill him.

He went past the dormitory room with its stacked beds reaching a dozen high, thinking how ridiculous it all was.

To the right lay another room, another stage, more chairs, and Wren stamped in and onto the stage. In the center was a plain wooden altar topped with a huge smoked-glass bell jar, like a giant's shot glass, rim down. Wren laid his hands on it as people came in, lifting it carefully. It was heavier than it looked. Inside was a crystal goblet filled with water, atop a metal plate flush to the wood.

Curious.

Wren set the outsized shot glass back over the top and just stood, naked and covered in mud, staring down each person as they came in.

Jamal Jalim entered last. Blood streamed down his chin, neck and chest from what was doubtless a shattered nose, along with maybe a few broken teeth, mangled lips and possibly cracked jaw.

Wren didn't care. The guy had just tried to kill him with mud. Wren stood with his arms behind his back like a Marine awaiting inspection.

Jalim's eyes didn't have that cocky, knowing amusement anymore. There was anger there now, and there was fear too; of Wren, of the trials, of potentially losing his cult.

Good.

"Trial two," prompted Wren.

"Trial two," repeated Jalim, trying for gravitas and missing. He didn't sound right. Wet with the blood and nasal with his crumpled nose, but off balance. "As with all such matters of Nature, Anaximander states-"

"Get on with it," Wren snarled.

Jalim's eyes sparked as anger burned through the fear. Who was Wren, after all, to challenge his authority in his own compound?

"Trial two," he intoned, slowing his speech to reclaim status. In a stately manner he took up position beside the altar, mirroring Wren and not flinching away. "Fire and water. The true Anaximanderian can absorb both within his body, unharmed."

He nodded a signal, and a sound like rushing wind came from the altar. Wren studied it. Coming from the giant shot glass. Maybe a minute passed, then something unexpected happened. The water in the crystal goblet within began to boil. Bubbles formed at the bottom of the glass and shot their way to the top.

Fire and water.

The rushing sound stopped. Jalim strode to the center behind the altar, showing no fear of Wren, laid both hands reverently on the giant shot glass and lifted, revealing the goblet underneath. A few bubbles were still working their way from the base to the top.

He turned to Wren and said a single word. "Drink."

Wren stared back at him. He stared at the goblet. He couldn't figure out what the trick was here. He knew well enough that sometimes that 'magic' was actually just phenomenal training and preparation. Magicians who put a nail through their hands weren't doing magic, they'd just pierced a hole through their hand in advance.

But drinking boiling water? There was no way to train your body to accommodate that.

He leaned over and touched the goblet. The glass itself was blazing hot. He held it for a second only, shielded partly by the layer of mud on his hand, but didn't even try to raise it to his lips. If he tried to pick it up his palm would be irreparably burned. Third degree, most likely, permanent damage deeper than the skin down to the ligaments beneath.

To drink it would kill him. Boiling water would blanch his mouth, gums, esophagus, stomach. There was no treatment for internal burns. He'd just die in unimaginable agony.

"You first," he countered.

Jalim nodded gravely. Getting some of his mojo back.

"You have polluted the cup. It must be boiled again."

He set the crystal dome back over the goblet. Wren couldn't help but admire the ritual nature of it all. Clearly all thought out, all planned, all worked through. The metal plate had a heating filament. Impressive to wire that into the altar and show no signs of the wiring, but not that hard.

The rushing sound came again. Again bubbles appeared in the goblet, racing to the top. Again Jalim let it boil for nearly a minute. Wren's confidence began to ebb a little. The extra time wouldn't make the water any hotter, but the goblet itself? Glass could climb to a temperature in excess of a thousand degrees before it melted. It wouldn't even turn red hot until it hit eight hundred. Just touch that and you'd lose your hand in an instant.

The rushing sound ceased. Jalim lifted the oversized shot glass and set it down to the side as the last few bubbles raced up in the goblet. He took a moment, breathing deeply, eyes closed, centering himself, then took hold of the glass.

He didn't scream. His flesh didn't sizzle. It was almost as if he truly had mastered fire and water, achieving Anaximanderian oneness. For a second Wren only stared disbelieving as Jalim raised the goblet to his lips, showing no sign of the pain.

Wren seized the glass off him before he could swallow. Jalim didn't expect that and his grip gave out easily. Barely a drop of water was spilled. This time Wren lifted the goblet to his lips and threw it back in two big gulps.

He didn't scream. He didn't start to spit up blood from a fiercely scalded windpipe. If anything, the water went down as a pleasant balm.

Jalim was left staring. Panic in his eyes now. The people saw it. Wren saw it.

"I am one with Nature," Wren said, and slammed the goblet down on the heating plate. Smiled at Jalim.

Science.

Wren was no engineer, unlike his namesake, but he was no slouch either. There was only one possible way Jamal Jalim could lift a blazing hot glass and drink boiling hot water, and that was if the water wasn't boiling hot. From there the suppositions had come fast and found proof in Jalim lifting the goblet. It was actually a simple middle school lab trick, child's play for an engineer of Jalim's caliber to pull off, based on one simple law of thermodynamics.

Water didn't have to be hot to boil.

Carry a kettle to the top of Mt. Everest, the water would

boil at 160 rather than 212. That wasn't because of some difference in temperature up there, but because of the low air pressure. How to replicate that in the lab?

Make a vacuum.

From that hypothesis onward everything fit perfectly. The heavy giant shot glass was airtight when flush against the wood. The rushing sound of 'heat' transferring was actually the sound of air being sucked out of the shot glass; difficult to disguise so Jalim hadn't even tried, letting it become part of the ritual. A simple air pump disguised in the wood or the heating plate would convert the crystal shot glass to a depressurized bell jar with ease.

From there it was easy. Suck the air out, reduce the interior to a vacuum, and water would boil at room temperature. Jalim had first heated the glass up for Wren, then switched the plate off and let the vacuum pump run for a good minute, boiling the heat right out of the water and by conduction from the glass itself, leaving it barely lukewarm to the touch.

Wren felt angrier than ever. How many people had Jalim permanently damaged, forcing them to handle burning glasses and drink boiling hot water? It was sick. He turned on the man, sorely tempted to hammer him in the face again, or better yet, make him drink the boiling water.

But there was no time for any of that.

Still, Jalim clearly read all that on his face. He looked terrified.

"Trial three." Wren growled.

18

AIR & WATER

The third room. It had the same bare cement walls, the same encircling chairs, the same people standing around the outside, though the atmosphere was very different now.

The people were abuzz. Whispering to each other. Staring at Wren with a new kind of wonder, maybe disbelief. He approached the stage at the center and felt their eyes on him.

They were all deluded.

He was probably the first person they'd seen pass a single trial other than Jalim. His successes alone were already bending the Anaximanderian cult to breaking point. The stakes for them were enormous. Like any death cult leader worth his salt, Jamal Jalim would have them worked up about talk of a coming doomsday, the forces of good and evil, eternal life and death, with himself as the only source of truth and light. Barely thirty minutes ago they were all ready to swallow pills and die at Jalim's word.

But now?

Now their minds were being forced open. If a stranger could pass the trials, and strike their prophet, and still survive, what did that mean for the rest of it?

Wren looked into their faces as he passed. A young pregnant woman holding her belly stared up at him. Two children with dark eyes gawped. A heavyset older man with hands pressed close together, eyes closed, whispered some scientific prayer. These were the same kinds of people Wren had seen on the streets of Salt Lake, New York, Chicago, just dropped into a prison of faith. Minds bent. Guzzling down Jalim's bullshit magic tricks.

The stage was ready for him. A reinforced metal surgical table sat centrally on a thick metal pole, inclined downward at the head, with four leather restraining cuffs for wrists and ankles. A water spigot hung from the ceiling above, and Wren knew at once what it was all for.

Air and water.

Waterboarding.

Head at this end. Arms and legs strapped here and here. A cloth over the face to aerosolize water from the spigot and force it to be inhaled into the lungs, where air and water met and blurred into agony.

It only fired Wren's anger hotter. Delve into any of these mind control cults and the core was sickeningly rotten. He was ready to just rip the whole thing apart, but that required a little more patience, a few more moments only.

Jamal Jalim strode through his people with his head held high. The blood down his chest and chin had hardened into the dried cakes of mud. He'd gotten over the punch, it seemed, gotten over his loss on trial two, and was probably plotting some path through to still keep his cult. Maybe give Wren what he wanted, crown him as Anaximander's emissary and hope he would leave. Roll with the punches and write Wren into his mythos somehow, anything to keep himself on top.

Wren couldn't allow that.

This had to end now. Those pills in the people's hands

were all bullets on one-way trajectories. If Wren left them with Jalim, one day those bullets would find their targets. He preferred to stop the barrage without a single shot fired.

Jalim gave him a look as he took to the stage. Not the amused look now, but maybe supplication. An offer. You scratch my back here, I'll scratch yours. You want to know about your father? Keep what I've built here intact.

Not a chance.

Wren fixed him with a hard glare, then dropped off the stage and picked up one of the chairs. Wooden, solid, thick. He hefted it, stepped back onto the stage and raised it over his shoulder. The nearest members flinched back. Jalim's eyes widened.

"What are you d-"

He didn't get to finish the question. Wren brought the chair down hard on the tilted end of the surgical table. There was a deep metallic bong matched by an enormous crack, as the table jerked slightly lower on its axis. One of the chair legs broke away and gasps filled the air. Wren raised the chair and brought it down again.

Another massive bong, the table tilted further and now the chair smashed into fragments.

Wren turned. People were on their feet now. Outrage was morphing into terror on Jalim's face.

"What are you doing?" he demanded. "That's the sacred-"

Wren tuned him out, went to the next chair and hefted it. Like a lumberjack selecting his tool, the demolition work was just beginning. He spun and rang the chair hard off the table again, smashing this chair into kindling in one massive strike, steepening the table's angle a few more degrees.

In the shocked silence that followed, Wren heard a faint hissing.

He smiled.

Two more chairs broken over the table left it see-sawed to

a near vertical, with the hissing sound climbing to a gushing flow. Exactly as Wren had expected. There was some kind of retractable air pipe built into the frame. Perfectly aligned so that when the cloth was placed over Jalim's head, and the water was poured over the top of it, an air tube circled around and into his mouth.

That was how he'd endured waterboarding.

Now the mechanism was broken along with the table. There would be no air tube. No trick. No concealment.

Wren's chest was heaving. He turned. The people were on their feet. Jalim was staring at his ruptured table with pale-faced horror. Broken chair pieces festooned the stage. Wren owned it.

"Here," he said, voice booming so loud they all shrank back, and pointed to the front of the stage. "As good as anywhere. Right, Jamal Jalim?"

The people's eyes turned to their leader. Pissing himself, most likely. Thin-looking. Reedy and pale now. He was looking at them and trying to muster his customary command in the face of an impossible demand, looking at Wren with an expression that wavered between rageful defiance and obsequious pleading. Wren read it all in his eyes.

There was no way he could endure the test now. Nobody could endure waterboarding. Everybody had to breathe. Maybe you could hold your breath for a few minutes, but at some point your lungs would give out. You'd suck in a breath of aerosolized water through the cloth and at once your throat would tighten, your lungs would palsy, the burning pain and the choking terror would be overwhelming.

Wren knew. He'd been waterboarded before.

He watched the decision happening in Jamal Jalim's eyes as the last of his 'trials' came crashing down, maybe before Jalim himself even knew it.

His hand was halfway to his mouth, red pill in his hand,

when Wren hit him. A long snap kick in the gut, enough to double him over, followed up with one hand grasped around Jalim's wrist to shake the pill loose. Wren let it fall and crushed it under his bare foot.

"Please," Jalim gasped, in one last effort to avoid losing everything in front of his chosen people. "You can't-"

"Trial three," was all Wren said, and lifted the man bodily. He laid him kicking and wriggling at the center of the stage. Fury propelled him. How many of this man's followers had been forced through this torture without the aid of an air pipe to carry the day? How many times had he encouraged them to waterboard themselves, all the while damned in their own minds for their inability to achieve 'oneness' with the water and the air?

It was unfathomably cruel. Day after day, hour after hour, with nothing to look forward to but more pain and more failure in their efforts to 'ascend' his nonsensical 55 layers.

Wren straddled the smaller man's chest, easily pinning down his arms. No way Jalim could move, though now he was trying. Struggling for all he was worth. Crying out. Whimpering. Leaking crocodile tears. Wren just looked to the side.

"Cloth," he said, and held out a hand. The people were struck dumb. Eyes wide. Uncertain how this fit into their Anaximanderian ideology, but straining their minds wide to swallow the reality.

A piece of cloth appeared in Wren's hand, embroidered with what looked to be atomic bonds. More pseudoscience BS. There was no pleasure in any of this. Only justice.

"Please!" Jalim whimpered. "I'll tell you everything. About your father. I swear it."

"Not enough," Wren said, and laid the cloth over his face. Electrons, protons and neutrons covering up those terrified eyes. Held out his hand again. "Water."

Jalim's jaw worked frantically beneath the fabric. "Then what?" he cried, voice muffled but high. "What do you want? Tell me, I'll do anything you ask, I promise!"

A bottle of water appeared in Wren's hand. Delivered by a child. It was horrific. It was nothing these people hadn't seen a thousand times before, though never to Jalim himself. If anything, the successful torture of their leader might finally break the spell.

"Anything?" Wren asked, leaning in.

"Anything!" Jalim howled, like he was in pain already. "Anything at all!"

"Achieve oneness," Wren said, and poured the first splash of water onto the cloth. It sucked the fabric tight to Jalim's gasping mouth, immediately blocking his airways and aerating liquid directly into his lungs.

19

ANYTHING

The people were cleared out. Into their bunks. On the way they stared at the mud tank with its broken roof grate, at the crystal goblet on its metal hotplate, at the upended and hissing waterboard gurney. Whatever.

Wren didn't care.

What mattered now was Jamal Jalim. Sitting in a chair in the center of his upstairs 'arena', bathed in a flood of sun tunnel Utah light. His body coated in a dried mask of mud and blood. His face smeared where the cloth had clung, mud washed away by water, vomit, more water.

Panting now. Humiliated before his cult. Much reduced. Wren almost felt pity for him.

Almost.

"Tell me."

Jalim looked up. The rage was gone. The begging was gone. Massive loss could be transformative. Now he just looked broken.

"I never did it like that," he said, his voice hollow.

"But you did it," Wren said.

"Not like that."

Wren resisted smacking him across the face. The man should have been jailed twenty years ago. If not for the terrible example of Waco, he would have been.

"But you did it. You drowned them in mud. You made them drink boiling hot water. You waterboarded them. You don't think you've earned this?"

"They never actually drank boiling water," Jalim mewled, looking up. Spit and blood clung to the corners of his mouth. Too shocked to rub them away. "It was just a trick!"

"I don't believe you," Wren said. "Like I don't believe you weren't also abusing them in every way imaginable. Jalim, I've seen this routine a thousand times before. Don't forget who you're talking to. I grew up in the Pyramid. The Apex is my father. So let's cut the pity party and get down to it. You had a cult. Now you don't. But it can still get worse for you."

At that Jalim mustered a disbelieving snort. "How?"

"Push me and find out. Now let's talk about my father. He came here several years ago. You already confirmed it. So spill."

A haunted look stole across Jalim's expression like a shadow. "I can't."

"Why not?

The fear deepened in Jalim's eyes, and that fascinated Wren. This man had already tried to swallow his suicide pill. He'd just experienced the ignominy of losing his cult. Wren's threats didn't bother him, but mentioning the Apex?

"He'll destroy me."

This fear went deeper. It was primal.

"I've already destroyed you. The Anaximanderians are in ruins. I'll have my people in here next and de-indoctrination will begin. What's left to be destroyed?"

Now Jalim managed a faint chuckle. "You don't even know who your father is, do you? You don't know what he's really capable of."

Wren's tone turned hard. "I saw the Pyramid burn, Jamal. I was there at the end."

Jalim laughed a little more. Like something was loosening inside. Wren had seen it before, shock and awe leading to a kind of mania, leading in turn to stroke-like events. Extreme moments of emotion could cause lasting damage, shift personalities permanently. People came out of such episodes changed, maybe unable to think coherently, unable even to speak.

"You think the Pyramid was bad?" Jalim wheezed. "You don't even realize that you and your desert groupies were his favorites. You had it *good*!"

Growing louder now.

"The hell are you talking about, we had it good?" Wren asked. "He burned every one of those 'groupies' alive, Jalim. Before that he buried all my brothers and sisters alive in a pit as a test of their faith. I was there, just nine years old, and I'm the only one who survived. What's good about that?"

More gulping laughter. "You really don't know a thing, do you?"

"So tell me!" Wren hissed. "Tell me or I'll send you to him. The Apex. Put up a flag on the Internet, spike your position, out you as a CIA collaborator."

That woke Jalim up.

His next mad bark of laughter came out like a shout. More followed swiftly, escaping his lips like autocannon bullets, out of control and manic. Raw panic filled his eyes and he wrapped his hands across his lips to hold the sound in, but he couldn't halt the convulsive gulps.

"You'll give me to him?" he managed to gasp. "You do all this to me, take everything, and then you'll hand me over?"

Wren dropped to one knee. The playing field was shifting now in a disturbing direction. Worse than a panic attack.

Jamal Jalim was on the edge of hyperventilating himself into an aneurysm.

"Tell me," he urged. "If you give me the Apex, I'll protect you. I'll fight for you like I fought for your people. You know my record. I help people like you, Jalim. The victims of the Apex. Take off the blinders and see what he's done to you. Give me what I need and we'll turn all this around."

The laughter only intensified. "Turn it around? It's over, you idiot! When he hears you came here I will be destroyed. There is no protection against what he'll do."

"What will he do?"

Jalim began shuddering violently, the impact of extreme duress mounting on his nervous system. "The human zoo," Jalim spat, and abruptly blood bubbled up from the back of his throat then worked a ropey trail down his muddy brown chin. "You never saw the zoo, did you? The real extent of his human experimentation."

Wren leaned in. "What zoo?"

Jalim laughed. "The human zoo! Once you've seen his research, the true depths he's willing to reach, no place is safe from him." The mad laughter overcame him. Wren squeezed his shoulders, trying to help him ride it out as his eyes rolled and his pulse raced. "What do you even think I've been doing here, Christopher Wren?" Jalim said. "All these weapons, all this training, all these pills, you think I was afraid of your government or your idiot FBI? I was protecting myself against him!"

Wren blinked. "Against the Apex? Why?"

"Because he wanted me for his collection!" Jalim hissed. "Like all the other groups you already broke! Don't think I haven't watched it happen. The Saints? Richard Acker was here! the Reparations? Yumiko Harkness was here! I was supposed to be one more in his stable, a deal with the devil after he helped me set all this up in the beginning."

Wren blinked. "In the beginning? Wait, you mentioned that already. You said the trials were his idea. But you've had this cult for over twenty years. You can't mean-"

"Of course I mean it!" Jalim hissed, spraying blood in Wren's face. "It was his idea to take it this far. The pumping station, the trials, he promised me glory, fame and riches, but it would come at a cost."

"What cost?"

"To help him in his campaign, when the time came." Jalim went slack, like he'd given up. "So I followed along. I went to his meetings. I invited him here. I followed his rules. I saw his zoos. But I couldn't do what he wanted me to do."

Wren felt like he was hovering on the edge of something huge. "What did he want you to do?"

"Attacks on religion! Not like our little groups. Real religions, like Christianity, Islam, Hinduism. He had it all planned it. My people, my peace-loving Anaximanderians, he wanted us to crucify Christians inside churches, and burn Muslims on a pyre, because of some belief that the prophet Mohammed died of a fever." Jalim squeezed more tears. "But I couldn't do it. I couldn't!"

Wren felt disgusted and pitying in equal measure. It was an odd pleasure to see a cult leader like Jalim draw the line somewhere, even as he'd undoubtedly killed his own members in the course of his trials.

"You were meant to be another stage in pumpijng up the ERQ," wren muttered.

"The what? RQ?"

"Never mind. You refused, and he threatened you?"

Jalim shuddered and gulped. "He said he'd make me a permanent feature of the zoos."

Wren nodded. "The zoos. Human zoos. Just what's so terrifying about them? What are they?"

Jalim's face worked between extremes, lips pulled back

like a death's head, mouth flaring wide with white tension lines, eyes flashing side to side like a fox with its leg in the trap and the hunter closing in. "I saw them twice," he managed through gritted teeth, cheeks puffing. "In cities. In skyscrapers. He takes a whole floor and blocks it out then moves in his zoo."

"Skyscrapers?"

"Atlanta was the first," Jalim croaked, sucking wind hard now. "Louisville was the second. I'm never going back!"

"You mean like an office floor? Like a CIA black site?"

Jalim's laughter grew out of control. "Worse. The worst thing I ever saw, and he promised to send me to the biggest one yet, in New York! Now, I think-"

Abruptly his eyes rolled up into the back of his head, all his muscles went limp and he sagged in the chair.

Wren checked his pulse.

A high, threadbare beat. Worked himself up half to death. Wren leaned in and carefully, almost tenderly, shifted the thin man's weight onto his shoulder.

20

SURFACE

J amal Jalim's Anaximanderians were all in the bunkbed room. Two or three to a bed, stacked tall to the ceiling like battery chickens in a wall full of hutches. The smell of them rose like the stench off a refugee camp.

The children had voided their bowels. Maybe some of the adults. Some were weeping. Some just stared at him with a thousand-yard glare. He'd broken their world. Was now carrying their Lord and Master away.

It broke Wren's heart. Now they were free, but real freedom would take years, if it ever came. The illogic of what Jalim had drummed into them for decades would butt up against the reality Wren had just unveiled and clash, maybe breaking some of them permanently.

Left alone like this they'd stay in the pumping station, maybe elect a new leader, but none of them would have Jalim's tricks. Leadership would rotate as pretenders rose and fell, until someone figured out a new set of tricks or mastered the old ones. The cult would roll on, though vastly diminished, because at this point there was nowhere left to go.

"I'm coming back," Wren said, casting his eyes over them stuffed into their bunkbed cells like animals in a zoo. "My people will come first. They're going to help you. Things have to change here. I passed your trials, so you know you can believe me. No one's taking any pills. This is a changing of the guard. I'll see you very soon."

They only stared, bereft. No words. The pills were in their pockets still. Bullets on trajectories he hoped he'd stopped, but you could never be sure.

He moved on. The speed rope hung where he'd left it. He looked up, thirty feet high into a white rush of sunlight. It felt like he'd been down here in this human cave for a whole day, when it had probably barely been an hour.

No faces peered over the top. That was fine. He moved on, tracking the schematics as he remembered them. In one of the smaller pump access rooms there was a wall-mounted ladder leading up. He climbed with some difficulty, though Jalim wasn't all that heavy, just an awkward load. At the top was a platform and a doorway leading out to the roof.

Heavily reinforced with braces and bolts. Wren unclasped them one by one then swung the door open, stepping out into the light. Fresh air hit him in a wave, tinged with the stink of the Great Salt Lake's sulfur and salt, along with the slight astringent aftertaste of whatever explosive Hellion had packed into her drone. The light was brighter and all-consuming after the gloom of the pumping station, forcing him to blink against the glare.

In seconds they were upon him, Doona and Henry.

The smoke had cleared from the blast. His team looked well.

"Boss," said Doona, "you're naked."

"And covered in mud?" Henry asked.

Wren gave a sheepish smile and shrugged the shoulder

upon which Jalim lay. "The cult leader insisted. When in Rome. Tell me Mason's alive?"

"He's alive," Henry said smartly. "Already landed at Brigham City. Initial triage in the helo suggests he broke some ribs after a fall off the station, shattered his wrist, maybe dislodged a vertebra, but he's alive. They've got him queued for a CT scan to check his skull."

That was all news to Wren. "How did he fall?"

"Saving me," Doona said. "I was fighting two at once. Mason took one and they fell off the side together."

Wren nodded, and laid a hand on Doona's shoulder. She'd carry that debt now. If he knew her well, she'd find a way to repay it.

"He's stable?"

"Within reason. He fell a long way."

Wren grunted. That was the best news he'd heard all day. Mason had already died on him once in the Jib-jab headquarters, and he couldn't handle it again.

"Good." He kneeled and carefully set Jalim down on the raw concrete. When he came back up Doona offered him her jacket, which he wrapped around his waist like a skirt. "Thank you."

"It's nothing. Boss, what happened in there?"

Wren paused. Looked both Doona and Henry over. Didn't know where to begin. "Stupidity. I don't even want to say it. There's probably bodies buried all around here, people who drowned on mud. It's…" he paused, reaching for words that escaped him. "Just stupid. Mud vats. Oneness with natural elements. Fear of the Apex. The people below will tell you all about it. We'll hear no end of it, I'm thinking." He paused for a second, cataloguing all that he'd seen, then filing it away and moving on. "Right now, I need to get up to speed. Do you have a spare earpiece? I left mine with my clothes."

"Here," Henry said, already holding out his extra. "But you may want to, um, give yourself a rinse first."

Wren stared at him a second, saw Doona was holding out a water bottle, then grunted. He tipped his head, poured water into his ear until most of the residual mud was out, then inserted the earpiece and took the cell unit that paired with it. While the fuzz of reception crackled in his ear canal, he looked at Henry's wholesome, strong-chinned face and Doona's brushed, perfect complexion, thinking thoughts he'd already tried to banish.

About the cost he'd asked of them. Mason had almost died. But even with the benefit of hindsight, he couldn't see a better way through. The cult had to be cracked, and he pulled himself out of the brief reverie. Doona was looking at him oddly, had just spoken.

"Are you all right?" Wren figured, or something like it.

"Just distracted," Wren answered. "And thankful you were both here." He cleared his throat. "Now, they need you down below. Babysit them please. Tell them you come from Anaximander's emissary."

"Emissary?" Doona asked.

Wren shrugged. "Ask them, if you like. It's a sweet story."

Doona cracked a smile. "We will. Well done, Christopher."

He smiled, then strode a few paces away along the metal gantry. The white salt flats spread lone and level in every direction, slit only by the white line of the pumping canal. He put one hand to his new earpiece to activate the comms line.

"Hellion?" he called. "B4cksl4cker?"

"Christopher," came B4cksl4cker's cheery Armenian baritone. "I have banished Hellion from the room, as you are far too naked for my liking. This is, what is the word, immodest? Hellion has been calling out insults since you emerged."

Wren held in a sigh. Of course, they'd be watching. He turned his gaze to the sky to pick out their overwatch drone.

"To your left," B4cksl4cker corrected. "Too high to see."

Wren grunted.

"Hellion is shouting to me now, Christopher. Yes. OK. This is a question. She says you look like as if you have been making sexy time with a sewage tank. Is this the word, sexy time?"

"She's nailed it," he said, too tired to fight back. "That's exactly what happened. Me and the sewage tank made a baby, and it came out as a fifty-year-old man. His name's Jamal Jalim. I need Teddy to take custody and see what else he blurts out."

B4cksl4cker chuckled. "Yes? Good. Meanwhile Hellion says you look like, hmm, she says 'stinking pond scum rolled in steaming fresh turd'. Is this the expression?"

Wren just about cracked a smile. B4cksl4cker knew well that that wasn't any kind of expression. They were just bringing him back with their trademark black humor.

"Bullseye," he allowed. "Tell Hellion her English is really coming along. Now, I need a helo inbound, a direct line to Rogers, an update on the firestorm, and I need you to start researching New York skyscraper ownership records."

"New York skyscraper?" B4cksl4cker repeated. "That is exciting, Christopher. Did your sewage child already blurt something?"

"A little. He's terrified. Claims the Apex had some kind of traveling human 'zoo' which he kept in whole floors of skyscrapers. First up was Atlanta, second was Louisville, and most recently it was New York. If we can find that, maybe we can find him."

"Whole floors? And what is human zoo?"

Wren gritted his teeth and strode toward the northeast

corner, where the helo would set down. "I think it is what it sounds like. Bad."

"Of course, this is bad. Yes. Atlanta, Louisville, New York, we will find it. Hellion is already working. Your helicopter is twenty minutes out. As for Rogers and the firestorm, I will let her tell you yourself. Connecting you now."

Wren leaned against the railing and listened to the phone line ring.

21

CINCINNATI

Rogers picked up, and Wren heard first the sounds of many people bustling in the background, phones ringing, raised voices.

"Christopher," she said, sounding harried and worn down, but then who wouldn't be, facing off with the firestorm head on?

"It's me," he answered, leaning against the pumping station's railing and looking down into the canal they'd come by. "I just extricated myself from a two-bit mud cult in Utah, now it looks like we have a couple more data points to narrow down the Apex's trail."

That took Rogers a second. "Mud cult?"

Wren spat grit. "Don't ask. It was some of the dumbest nonsense I've seen. Upshot is, the Apex keeps something called a 'zoo' for humans, sounds like a roaming dungeon with past appearances in Atlanta and Louisville, now based in New York. He uses it as a precautionary tale to control other cult leaders, from what I can gather. My hackers are currently searching real estate ownership records, hopefully they'll be able to narrow it down some."

He let a few seconds go by, giving her time to absorb all

that. Imagined her lips pursing, dark brows drawing tight, like they did any time he presented her with an unfinished jigsaw puzzle.

"I suppose that fits," she landed on. "If your father's behind the firestorm and all the past attacks too, it's a fair bet he had some way to corral his sub-cult leaders. Incentives and punishment."

"He's a master manipulator," Wren agreed. "I'm going to head to New York. Do you have anything from Cincinnati on how he's getting these women to kill themselves?"

Rogers sighed. "Frankly, no. All I'm hitting here are dead ends."

Wren cleared a space in his head. "Tell me."

"There's nothing to tell." Her frustration came through clean. "First off, we can't find those three guys. Shoe salesman, greeter, helper kid? They were plants, it looks like, not employed by the Mall of Cincinnati at all."

Wren cursed. "Nothing to track back?"

"We're looking, but not yet. Actors they shipped in, it seems."

That complicated things. "And Rachel Day's family?"

"We're all over them, taking Day's house apart, her Internet footprint, her phone, her family, but there's nothing. No manifesto, no secret hard drives, nothing on her social feeds other than cupcakes and grinning pictures with the kids."

Wren rubbed his forehead. Working on an oxygen deprivation headache. Crusted mud scratched free and fell the long drop to the water below.

"Work computer?"

"Every damn computer," Rogers answered. "Her mail. Her colleagues. Her husband's a sobbing mess, I could barely get him to drink a Dr. Pepper to steady him. We swept the house, ripped up the walls and floorboards, but there's no bugs, no stash, no sign of the Apex anywhere in her life."

Complicated. Of course, Wren hadn't expected this to be easy. "You have her routes tracked via phone GPS?"

"The Freedom of Information request's before a judge right now, but we've already assembled most of her movements from other sources. Takeaway is that there's literally no time for her to go anywhere or meet anyone, let alone get indoctrinated. Her daily routine is crammed. She went to work, went to pick the kids up, took them to their activities and that's really it. Maybe a brief minute here or there unaccounted for, but that's traffic, red lights, the short walk from her car to her office, maybe a neighbor stops to chat once she's home. Her life is a piece of clockwork, Wren, and this dates back years. They had a holiday to San Marino last summer, five days all told, but as best as her husband can remember, he was with her all the time. Not a minute apart." She sighed. "Right now, it seems every thread I pull is a short straw."

Wren considered. "How many minutes?" he asked.

"What?"

"You said there were minutes unaccounted for. Commutes, traffic stops. We need to tally those." He paused for a moment, thinking. "We're dealing with a long-term psychological operation here, Rogers. Either she's a sleeper cell since whenever she was last properly free, maybe college, which I doubt, or her brainwashing was conducted at a glacial pace, in tiny increments, over time. Radicalization always takes repeated exposure, but not necessarily a lot of face time."

"Face time? What are you talking about?"

Wren took another breath. More mud grit in his mouth, and he swished a few pieces out with his tongue. "We're used to thinking of cult indoctrination as this intense experience, right? Like Gruber with the Ghost, like you while Jessica Grimes burned by your side. You lock someone up in a box, degrade them, deprive them and torture them into accepting a new reality. For Gruber it took three days. It didn't work with you, but I've no doubt it would have done, if it had lasted long enough. No offense meant, that kind of treatment gets everyone in the end."

Rogers was quiet.

"Even me," Wren went on. "Especially me, even. I was born into the Apex's mind control, remember? I grew up with him wiring my brain, and I'm still not right in the head."

Rogers let out a half laugh. "You can say that again."

"Happily. But the fact is, the rewiring doesn't always have to be so all-consuming. It doesn't need to be an incredibly intense experience that just lasts and lasts. Think about something like a violent mugging. How long does that last?"

Rogers took a second. "Minutes. Seconds, maybe."

"And the effect?"

A beat passed. "I see what you're getting at. One event that happens in seconds can shape a person for the rest of their life."

"Exactly. Even more so if they dwell on it, if the emotions remain strong."

"OK. So, what's your point here?"

"I'm not sure yet," Wren said, chewing on his lip. "But those actors, the plants? Maybe he did it like that. Random people crossing her path, but again and again. Make those intense experiences, play them out repeatedly like depth charges blowing up her personality, and ultimately she could be shoved in any which direction he wanted."

A long silence passed. Wren watched as a helicopter emerged from the heat haze over the salt flats, black and clamoring closer. He hadn't thought through this before, but when the evidence pushed you in a given direction, there was no use resisting.

"You're saying he spoon-fed her radicalization," Rogers said. "Baby steps over months, maybe years. Kept it on the back burner, so she led her life throughout, like everything was normal?"

"Deep cover," Wren said, making sense of it as he said it. "People can partition their minds incredibly well. A young woman gets mauled by an abuser in a changing room, you'd think she'd come out crying and calling the cops, but that's not what often happens. Most times she bursts out then goes back to chatting with her friends like nothing happened. We don't know how to react in the face of such trauma, so we just don't. Afraid anything we do will just make it worse. Maybe that we were complicit somehow, brought it on ourselves. Sometimes it seems the only way to play it." He paused to game it out. "But that few seconds of abuse, the humiliation, it sets a fuse burning. We can pretend, but it still happened, and it's going to have its day in the light. It's going to hurt that woman, and everyone around her, when the bomb finally goes off."

No sound from Rogers' end. He imagined her chewing her lip, reflecting on her own experience; how what the Ghost, Anais Kiefer, had done to her was going to play out down the line.

"Right," she said. "So find those three plants, and if I can't them find others, hidden in the empty spaces. The missing minutes."

"The missing minutes," Wren repeated. "And stay in touch. I'll let you know when I have a target."

"Good," she said, but didn't ring off. "And Wren."

"Yes?"

"Good job with the mud cult. Hellion says you almost died."

He hadn't expected that. It took him aback slightly. That Hellion was saying nice things about him behind his back.

"Uh, thanks."

"Just wanted to say," she said, then ended the call.

Wren was left looking at the cell phone as the helicopter dropped down to the salt flats below.

22

CITATION X

Christopher Wren jerked awake with a start, rubbed his eyes and sat upright. Low lights picked out the contours of the jet's eight-seater cabin. After the Black Hawk ride to Salt Lake City International Airport, he'd boarded a private jet to New York. The route was two thousand miles-plus, clocking in at around three hours flight time in a Cessna Citation X.

He hadn't meant to sleep, but sleep had found him, and along with it came the nightmares.

He could still vividly remember how it had felt, flat on his back in the desert as a child, the Apex's favored 'Pequeño 3', after another beating by his elder brother, Chrysogonus-with-Bared-Arm. He'd just watched Chrysogonus murder their brother, Tomothy-Where-the-Giants-Roam.

He could still hear Tomothy's twitching last breaths, and feel the weight of Chrysogonus crushing his chest, and taste the rust of his own blood filling his mouth.

Wren looked out the window and saw a dark floor of clouds below. At fifty thousand feet there wasn't much else to see. He rubbed his dry lips and gritty eyes, then pulled his phone from his pocket. 3 a.m.. Thirteen hours since this whole thing began at the Sonora Desert black site, and four hours since he'd left the pumping station behind.

He flicked the overhead button for light and a private beam switched on. He noticed his hands were shaking. There were dark half-moons under his fingernails; leftover mud from Jalim's vat. He pulled his fingers tight into fists but the shaking continued.

Thoughts of Chrysogonus haunted him. He squeezed harder. Not something he'd thought about for many years; how his big brother had held him there, bringing the knife down to his throat. One hand unconsciously went to his shoulder, where Chrysogonus had opushed the blade in, still wet with Tomothy's blood. His fingers worked beneath the taut black fabric of the strike suit and found the scar.

Jamal Jalim had brought this on, he figured, with his talk of a skyscraper dungeon in New York.

The thought sent shivers down Wren's spine. He'd lived in New York since the birth of his first child. Even now he remembered the moment Loralei had handed tiny baby Quinn into his arms, wrapped up in white, so beautiful. Now even that golden moment was poisoned by the Apex's touch; maybe he'd been there the whole time, watching down from his zoo.

Wren stabbed a button on the armrest, opening a channel to the cockpit.

"How long until we arrive?"

"Good morning, Sir," came the clipped, professional voice of the pilot. "We are forty-five minutes out from LaGuardia. Would you like a breakfast service?"

Wren grimaced. He'd never liked being served. As if on cue, though, a grumble came from his stomach. "Yes, thank you. Two of whatever you've got, the greasier the better."

"Coming right up."

The line crackled away, replaced by a shuffling sound

from the front. Private pilot, private air host. A man in white shirt and black tie began opening small metal closets in the narrow galley, pulling out trays and assembling Wren's meal.

"Do you have coffee?" Wren called.

"Yes sir," the man said attentively. "How would you like it?"

"Black, hot, and lots of it."

"On its way."

Wren pushed off the seat arms and stood. His legs trembled slightly. In the cup holder next to him he found a bottle of water and knocked it back in three long gulps, washing away the gritty mud taste. Clearing the way for the coffee.

He placed the call to Hellion and B4cksl4cker. B4cksl4cker answered.

"Christopher?" he rumbled. "You are awake, and I see almost to New York. Do you wish for current update?"

"Yes, please."

"You shall have it." Keystrokes thudded in the background. "Humphreys has not yet instituted a national lockdown, though there have now been twelve burnings. The first five you know. The most recent two, all women, all with children similarly aged to yours, one died in front of a preschool and the other ran out onto the field of an NFL game, New England Patriots vs. the Miami Dolphins."

Wren winced. The scale was getting bigger. "How many saw it?"

"Game was carried live to some three million viewers. They cut line after she caught fire, but many people filmed on their phones." A second passed. "It is disturbing viewing. Many have seen it. This was forty minutes ago. Next burning is due soon."

Wren didn't know what to say. He felt anger and disgust.

Anger at the Apex, disgust at Humphreys for failing to institute a lockdown.

"What about the RQ?"

"By any measure, it seems RQ is rising. Television pundits are shouting in each other's faces. People are running for their homes. It appears lockdown will be self-imposed before your current President enforces it. Nobody wishes to have this happen near them. To have their children witness it."

"It's horrific."

"It is. Now, more disturbing than this is David Keller. Of course, he is speaking at every chance he can. He is channeling both fear and rage very adeptly, Christopher. He is not President yet, but it seems your military are listening to him. They are not taking to streets, but we are seeing mobilizations in bases, logistics being prepared to shutter USA. Worse still, he is attempting to pin all this on you."

They always did. That was nothing new.

"What's he saying?"

"He is claiming you lied to him and to American people. The 'largest con in American history', he is calling it. He got down on knees and apologized for calling you his hero. Now he says you and your Foundation must be behind firestorm."

Wren's fists tightened. Of course Keller would get on his knees again. The people would love that.

"And my family?"

"Secure. Teddy arranged their rapid exit from safehouse one hour ago. I know we were not supposed to move them, but Teddy approached and they agreed. We have training facility three hundred miles north, and we are flooding forces there. They will be safe."

Wren's heart skipped a beat. Even thinking about Loralei and the kids mixed up in this terrified him. The possibility that maybe he could talk to them, attempt to reassure them, only made his heart flutter harder, though he knew that wasn't going to happen. He'd promised Rogers, and wasn't about to break faith with her again so soon.

"And the ownership records in New York?"

"Records, Christopher, are full of information. We believe your father's zoo is located within area of new super-tall buildings in central Manhattan. We will narrow this further and send you the map before landing."

Wren grunted. That was something. "Thanks, I'll call when I'm on descent."

The air host stood by politely, holding a tray heavy with steaming plates. It was plane food, but it still smelled divine; looked like bavette steak with mushroom sauce over steak frites on one plate, sweet and sour chicken over rice on the other, alongside a veritablr tankard of black coffee.

Exactly what the doctor ordered.

23

NEW YORK

In thirty minutes the Cessna Citation dropped through dark clouds into an abyss of night over New York. Soaring buildings glittered yellow like the eighth circle of hell, millions of sinners and saints stacked atop Manhattan's volcanic bedrock, spewed up millennia past.

Wren's fists squeezed the seat rests hard as he gazed through the window, seeing only loss written across the glass, steel and concrete of the city. Last time he'd come here it was in the hope of reuniting with his family. He'd approached his old family apartment in Great Kills, Staten Island on foot with his pulse booming in his ears, dreaming of seeing his children, Jake and Quinn, of holding his wife Loralei in his arms, of maybe being forgiven.

But they hadn't been there, and there was no forgiveness. When Rogers sprang her trap and brought the black bag down over his head, part of him had been relieved. It was finally over.

Now he was back.

The Citation swept over the mouth of Hudson Bay, circling the Freedom Tower like a spoke around the world's hub. Looking out at the countless skyscrapers grasping for the sky, it seemed obvious that his father would have a presence in Manhattan. Sutured to the mainland by twenty-one bridges and fifteen tunnels, the island was a Frankinstein-like creation, home to the greatest, sickest examples of humankind.

Capital of the world. A fitting place for the Apex to keep his human zoo.

"We'll be landing in five minutes," the pilot said over the PA system.

Wren brought up his phone and clicked through to his darknet, where a map of Manhattan awaited him, highlighted with yellow squares. In the last half hour Hellion and B4cksl4cker had narrowed the zoo's target zone significantly to 'Billionaire's Row'; a patchwork crop of luxury skyscrapers recently erected along 57th Street in Midtown, just south of Central Park.

As the Cessna descended over Brooklyn for the La Guardia approach, Wren called his hacker collective.

"Christopher," came B4cksl4cker's deep voice. "Hellion is sleeping. It is late for us here."

"Got it. I appreciate this, B4cksl4cker. Now, the map; how certain you are that the zoo is contained within one of these target locations?"

"Absolute certainty, Christopher, if such a place exists," B4cksl4cker replied. "We have found no records for your Apex, as you know, but all of these structures are ideal for him. He could have been to any of these multiple times and we would not know for sure, but construction and purchase records align with his ghost imprint in the world. They all have private access, the means to ship his 'exhibits' in unseen, secret mezzanine and mechanical floors where a dungeon could be kept."

Wren shuddered at the terms 'dungeon' and 'exhibits', swiping through a few of the buildings in the list. They were all relatively new build residential skyscrapers, pencil-slender and ultra-luxurious, with penthouses in the upper floors going for hundreds of millions. Central Park Place. 57E57. 231 Madison Avenue. Home to hedge fund managers, Saudi oil magnates, tech moguls and Russian oligarchs seeking a money laundering sink.

"This is millions of square feet," he said. "Hundreds of floors. Thousands of apartments."

"Yes," said B4cksl4cker.

"You can't narrow it any further?"

"Nyet, Christopher. Our search algorithm has run many analyses, and short of knocking on doors directly, this is best we can do with digital record."

Wren grunted and went back to swiping through buildings. Two45. 200 West 57th Street. The Millennium Center. So many.

"Then I'm on my own."

"I am in your ear. But, yes. All the data that can be hacked and processed, we have hacked and processed it. Beyond this, we leave it to you."

Wren gritted his teeth, scrolled back to the map of Manhattan highlighted with yellow. It was far too many locations, and no way he could investigate all of them. Each tower was comprised of hundreds of private residences, rising fifty-plus stories in the air, encircled with security and accessible only via card-locked elevators. He might get Humphreys' support for an anti-terror raid on a handful, but without hard proof on breach he'd never be able to raid them all. If he atempted other means, whether subterfuge, phishing or stealth tactics, he'd do well to see even a handful before David Keller was sworn in on the White House lawn.

His knuckles whitened tighter on the seat rests. No way to brute force it. He could be standing on 5th Avenue no more than a thousand yards from his father's zoo with no way in hell to pick it out.

He needed a way to narrow it down more.

"Thanks, B4cksl4cker. Get some sleep."

"I will be here, Christopher. What will you do?"

Now the Cessna was sinking fast over Queens. Out the window Wren caught a glimpse of Calvary Cemetery, a dark oblong in the midst of a grid of street lights, rushing up toward him.

"Resurrect the dead," he said, and tapped the line shut.

24

THE DEAD

Wren was no fan of Manhattan.

He'd always disliked the overwhelming mass of people. There were just too many. Too much money. Too much noise and grime and achievement built atop human blood, sweat and bones. He was a child of the desert, raised in the wilderness, and though he'd adapted to cities over the years, he'd never gotten used to the concrete crush of Manhattan.

Riding in a taxi from LaGuardia along Northern Boulevard toward the Queensboro Bridge, he felt that old sense of unease swelling on all sides.

Manhattan wasn't like other cities, as if the weight of humanity crushed on top of each other in cage-like apartments and offices thickened reality like a pestilence, hanging in the air and sucking everything around it in for fuel.

Money. Souls. Decency.

It was a prison for ambition. Skyscrapers rose like fortress walls. Failed dreams were baked into the foundations. If you couldn't make it there, you couldn't make it anywhere, so why would you ever want to leave?

Either side of the cab the low battlements of Queens bled away as Astoria Park spread her dark arms and the support columns of the Queensboro Bridge rose up in verdigris-green. Dark sky, no stars, only the salt-fogged lights of Manhattan's eastern wall of buildings forming scattershot constellations against the night sky.

Wren had dark memories of an undercover sting on a human trafficking group shipping Vietnamese children in through the Red Hook Docks in Brooklyn, thirteen years back. He'd thought he'd seen bad things back then, having come from the Pyramid.

He'd been wrong.

Either side of the cab the low battlements of Queens bled away as Astoria Park spread her dark arms and the support columns of the Queensboro Bridge rose up in verdigris-green. Dark sky, no stars, only the salt-fogged lights of Manhattan's eastern wall of buildings forming scattershot constellations.

Wren brought up his phone.

McKenzie Slade. He hadn't spoken to her for thirteen years. Not since the Vietnam trafficking operation had collapsed in on itself, as Wren systematically blew out its supporting columns. Not since they'd both stood at the entrance to an off-dock Brooklyn storage yard stacked ten high with thousands of twenty-foot shipping containers, knowing full well dozens of children were trapped in one of them, and not knowing which.

He'd been hasty back then, burning through middlemen in his rush to reach the kids in time. Back then he'd thought the top dogs had to know the locations of all their cargo. There'd be records. A track back.

Unfortunately, he'd killed all the middle men who knew where the kids were being kept. After that, there'd been no track.

The East River flew by. Wren made the call. It rang exactly seven times before she answered.

"Slade," she said.

She sounded the same. 3:40 a.m., and maybe she'd been sleeping, maybe not. Strict as a slide rule, hard as graphite slate, she'd never been impressed with Wren's past or his pedigree in the CIA or as a DELTA Marine. A redhead, even at 5' 3" she was all lanky angles, performing the Escherian trick of seeming taller than anyone around her simply by the commanding sneer of her sharp green eyes.

In those early years he'd loved that attitude. She immediately punctured whatever mystique had formed around him in the long wake of the dead Pyramid. Consultant to the NYPD, FBI, CIA, she made Wren's pattern analysis skills pale into insignificance. A savant, they called her, when they weren't calling her a cold-hearted bitch for usurping their authority, solving cold cases right under their noses and sneering as they thanked her.

"It's Christopher Wren," he said.

Her response came like a bullet. "What?"

"Christopher Wren. We worked together-"

"I know who you are," she interrupted with frosty precision. "I understand your name. What do you want, Christopher Wren, at 3:41 a.m., when I told you very clearly thirteen years ago to never speak to me again?"

She had him there. With her help they'd found the children. Working both deductive and inductive logic loops, they'd pinned down an immigrant stevedore already halfway to Argentina who confessed to witnessing an off-book movement of container boxes in the hours before dawn. Slade had walked the terrified man through the maneuver ten times, having memorized the exact contours of the container stacks, then churned the blocks in her head like a pre-teen genius speed-solving a Rubik's cube, coughing out the answer seconds later.

As he'd lifted the first of the children out of the container, her hand had come cold and firm in the crook of his elbow, her eyes burning into his. "This was your fault. You're sloppy. You coast on luck and charm. It is a wonder either of us survived. I won't do it again. Consider me dead to you."

Of course, she'd been right. He'd learned a lot from that indictment.

"You did say that," Wren allowed, trying to sound as sincere and forthright as her, and not rely on any hint of the 'charm' she so despised. "I'm sorry to infringe on our agreement. McKenzie, I need your help."

"I'm not interested in helping you."

He felt her finger moving to kill the call. "It's like the children again," he went on swiftly. "Something I should have seen. I screwed up then, McKenzie. I may be screwing up now, and there are far more lives at stake than before. You know New York like nobody else. I don't think I can do this without you, so please don't punish innocents for my mistakes."

Silence. No click came, though. The line remained open and he pushed on.

"You've seen the hourly fires. I'm sure it's my father's work. He's linked to David Keller. They're using the firestorm to swarm the media, not allowing any proof to get through on what they've been planning. I've got a team working to break that stranglehold, but I still haven't got solid proof on their connection."

Still nothing. Maybe she was listening. Maybe she'd dropped the phone in a fish tank.

"He keeps a 'human zoo', McKenzie. A dungeon high in a Manhattan skyscraper. Innocent victims. I'm crossing Roosevelt Island now. I'll be outside your apartment in fifteen minutes. I've got the location narrowed to a few blocks in Midtown along Billionaire's Row, but I've got nothing else. I need your pattern analysis skills to pin it down."

Another long silence. He would wait for as long as it took. There were other analysts he could call, but none who had both the skills to rotate potentials like a quantum difference engine, and who already lived in Manhattan and knew the city and its people like the back of her hand.

"Los Angeles," she said at last. Each word a rap from the schoolmarm's cane. "Explain yourself. I've seen your works these past few years, Mr. Wren. If anything you have become sloppier still. Foolishly enamored with your own infamy. Luxuriating in a legend you do not deserve. Explain why I should help a man with so little professional regard?"

Wren rubbed his eyes. He'd forgotten how McKenzie talked, like every word was an arrow perfectly flighted to the task. If anyone could hit bullseye then split that arrow down the middle with a second, it was McKenzie Slade.

"Desperation," he said, part telling her what she wanted to hear and part just speaking the truth. "Limited resources and ability. Rough guesswork combined with a reliance on charm. It was sloppy, you're right, but it's all I had at the time, and it worked."

Another silence. He craned to hear some sound of her breathing but there wasn't even the faintest whisper.

"You call *this* worked? Calling me in the middle of the night. A firestorm of fourteen dead women across the nation. A confidence man who claim is two months out from the Presidency. Your father resurgent, a dungeon in a skyscraper, and people burning your effigy across the nation where once they lofted you as a hero? How has your arrogance fared since then, Mr. Wren?"

He winced. Mr. Wren. "Poorly. I'll cut you a deal,

McKenzie. Help me in this, you can tongue lash me all you want. I-"

"But I don't want," she interrupted. "There is nothing I'd rather do less. When I said to consider me dead, I meant it. I have no interest in dissecting your twisted family or your countless mistakes. Thirteen years ago you were profligate, reckless, highly emotional and came close to getting not only both of us killed, but all those children too. I cannot see how any of those attributes have changed. It is for that reason that-"

"So take it over," Wren said sharply. Charm wasn't going to help now, that was clear. Time for a little of that reckless, profligate emotion. "If you can do what I do better than me, I'll gladly hand the whole thing to you. You take responsibility for my father, for the firestorm, for bringing Keller down and I'll hand in my notice. It's yours if you want it. It'll all be-"

"Mr. Wren," she said, sharp as an elbow in his gut.

"It's yours. That's all."

"You are not listening to me," she went on coldly. "I want none of that. I am done cleaning up your messes. Do not call this number again, do not-"

He was losing her. Charm hadn't worked, neither anger nor appealing to her better angels had worked, and that left only one path left.

"You have a daughter," he said.

It knocked her silent. He'd done his research.

"Adelaine. She's nine years old, yes? I've since had children too, my girl's eight, my boy's six, and I just had them moved out of witness protection because my twisted father's targeting them. You may not know this, but every woman that burned is my wife's age. Each one had a boy and a girl that are the same ages as my kids. It's no coincidence, McKenzie. He'll kill everyone in his path to get what he wants. You've seen the burnings. You live near 5th Avenue. Can you imagine what impact it'll have for your daughter to see something like that? I've seen it and look what it did to me. Use me as your cautionary tale. He wants that for your daughter. For everyone's daughters."

He fell silent. Heard her breathing. Tight, furious, controlled.

"This is repellent," she said. Her voice was utterly devoid of emotion now, cold as the Marianas Trench. "To mention my daughter. Even for you."

"I'm sorry, McKenzie. You never asked to be a soldier, but when he wages war on civilians, we're all in the trenches. We all have to fight or we'll lose what we have. He must be stopped."

Long seconds passed. Wren feared he'd pushed her too far.

"Thirty minutes," she said. Sounded strangled, forcing up the words. "I will see you outside Central Park Place on 57th Street. Do not come tom my apartment. Do not be late."

The call ended.

Wren stared at the phone. He hadn't expected that, and felt part-elated, part-sickened; that she was going to help, and that he'd brought up her daughter as leverage.

He gazed numbly out of the windscreen. There was sparse traffic. Distant offices shone like a wall of stars, as they raced ever-closer to the dungeon mouth of Manhattan. Moments later the cab shot off the bridge and was swallowed whole into the city's maze-like intestinal tract. The sky pulled back. The horizon disappeared. The city had him, now.

25

CENTRAL PARK PLACE

C entral Park Place was one of the skyscrapers highlighted in yellow on the map. Wren clicked through the building's profile in fascination. Under development still, it had topped out only a few months earlier, with condos in the lower fifty floors finished and sold, though none were yet inhabited. Standing at 1,450 feet across 131 floors, it was already the tallest residential building in the world, with 174 apartments starting at $8 million for a two-bedroom on the lower levels.

The cab stopped and started at intersections along West 57th Street, or Billionaires' Row, five narrow lanes flanked by gleaming luxury goods stores, designer office blocks and upscale restaurants, and Wren caught glimpses of other buildings highlighted on his map. The silver wave front of 231 W 53rd to his left, all 742 feet of it rippling in the moonlight. 231 Madison Avenue lay beyond that, a beast of white and glass blinking 1,425 feet into the sky. The razor taper of 447 East 58th Street loomed on the right, an unlit spine occluding stars a thousand feet high, still buttressed with a great-boned construction crane.

As they advanced Central Park Place emerged ahead, a

slim square column of glass rising into darkness, though it was soon cut off by the angle of the cab's roof. In moments they were outside. Central Park Place looked unassuming from the ground, builders' scaffolds shielding the lobby like wrapping paper on a Christmas gift.

"You're shopping for a condo?" the cabbie asked as Wren got out.

"Something like that."

New York was cold at 4 a.m., and smelled of concrete dust and raw iron, like the rusty tang of fresh blood. Wren stood on the south side of West 57th Street and drank it all in, acclimating to the city. Buildings hung over him. Vehicles buzzed by, mostly cabs and trucks on early morning deliveries. A few pedestrians passed, drunks on the walk of shame home, a handful of workers in suits heading early to the office, a young woman in pastel sweats out walking two huge labradoodles. They cast him glances then looked swiftly away, and he realized he was still wearing his strike suit: tactical black pants and jacket, harness belt, SIG .45 at his hip.

Nothing he could do about that now.

Central Park Place stretched impossibly up into the night. Lights fizzled near the upper floors. Wren imagined construction workers far above, plastering in contoured walling, wiring in dimmer bulbs and voice-activated AI. Room after room, finish one floor and move onto the next. Perhaps on one, a zoo.

McKenzie Slade had chosen this place without a moment's hesitation. What did she know that he didn't?

"Stop staring like the rube hick you are," came a voice nearby. Wren dropped his gaze and saw Slade standing barely three feet away. Holding a coffee close to her chest, appraising him with those cold green eyes. She wore all black, but where his outfit was utilitarian, segmented by pockets, zippers and straps, hers was a flowing single piece folded upon itself multiple times, like a cloak with different layers.

Her face had aged but not by much, in her late forties now, the nose thinning, her cheeks taking on the raw shape of the bones underneath, lending her gravitas despite her diminutive height.

"It's good to see you, McKenzie," he said.

Her green eyes didn't shift in the slightest. "Yesterday was the worst day of my life, dealing with fallout from your firestorm. Now you're here." She looked him up and down. "Inappropriately dressed for the city, Christopher Wren. Did you just overthrow a South American dictatorship?"

He chanced a smile. "A mud cult in a Utah pumping station, actually. But you don't care about that. You selected this building. Why?"

Her head tilted slightly to the side. He remembered this, just about the only sign of faint amusement she ever showed. "No attempt to romance me. No flurry of compliments melding into excuses."

"I'm not the same man I once was. Just as reckless, perhaps, but you've made your position very clear. You're dead to me. I won't waste time bantering with a ghost. Every hour another woman dies and Keller moves closer to the Presidency. Let's stop that together."

Her head tilted back to dead-level. "The very minimum, then. All I had hoped for. Come with me."

She strode out into traffic without looking. Wren almost reached out to stop her, but halted himself at the last moment. If anyone knew the physics of moving bodies, it was McKenzie Slade. Never once in his estimation had she failed to exhibit absolute command of her surroundings. Doubtless she hadn't started now.

He looked both ways and crossed after her, weaving a

path where she walked a straight line between honking vehicles. Not one had to slow or swerve as she passed smoothly through, though the same could not be said for Wren.

He arrived at the scaffold fence moments after her, as she received a key from a man in a high visibility waistcoat.

"I know the foreman," McKenzie said, then strode through a wire security gate just as it opened. Wren followed into a polyvinyl tunnel through the gaping mouth of the lobby. He caught some sense of the glorious, light-filled space it would soon become, in the triple-height ceiling, hanging stub for chandelier and twin escalators rising away.

"How do you know him?" Wren asked as she stalked ahead, a black messenger bag bouncing gently across her narrow shoulders.

"I solved an architectural problem for him," she said, then turned for a single beat. "With the mob."

He almost laughed but held it in.

"And you have some reason to target this building? You think the zoo is here?"

She didn't answer. They arrived at the elevator bank. Two industrial cars stood open in the central chute, metal cages dressed in chipped orange paint, and McKenzie strode in without pausing. Wren hated cages, but followed after her. She worked the control lever like she rode industrial elevators every day, and their ascent began.

"McKenzie," he started, and she turned to him. "If the zoo is here, I'll need more gear. A strike team."

She just tilted her head again in silent amusement. "I'm not a miracle worker, Mr. Wren. We're just getting started."

After that he was silent as the elevator winched them upward. Past open doorways into dark corridors leading away, lit only by the glare of the elevator's heat lamps. Ten floors passed, twenty, thirty, until soon the furnished corridors gave way to raw cement studded with spikes, ready for wooden boards to be slotted in.

Fifty floors. Sixty. When they hit the first of the penthouses, massive open expanses that gave a view straight through the building's exterior ribs to the city beyond, Wren was impressed.

"I took my daughter here," McKenzie said. "It is indeed a sight to see."

The elevator came to a halt on the 131st floor.

"After you," McKenzie said. Wren stepped out. The penthouse was a shell. A few support struts here and there, but very little to obstruct the incredible view. No maze walls either side. No clouds blocking the sky, nothing to obscure an uninterrupted view in all directions.

He stepped up to one of the floor-to-ceiling windows and gazed across New York; Manhattan, the Bronx, Queens, Brooklyn, Staten Island. His old home lay barely a mile away in Great Kills, their home where his kids had grown up until his dark past had ruined everything.

"I heard about your family," McKenzie said. Standing at his side. He didn't turn to her, expecting something cruel. "They're better off without you. You're a disaster. Now." She swung around her messenger bag and extracted an object, blocky and dark in the minimal light cast from the elevator. It took him only a moment to realize what it was.

"Binoculars?"

"You want to know which building your father's zoo is in? We look. There is no better vantage point on Billionaire's Row than the place you're standing right now."

26

VANTAGE POINT

Wren stared at the binoculars for a moment, unsure if she was making some kind of joke.

"You're serious?"

Her expression didn't shift. She extended the binoculars a bare inch closer.

"Of course you're serious," Wren said, starting to regret even calling her. Maybe she wasn't as sharp as she'd once been. "McKenzie, there's no way we'll see the zoo from here. Even if he has his prisoners pressed up to the skin of the building, the windows will be screened. There'll be nothing to see. It's pointless."

Still she didn't move, though it looked like her green eyes were judging him.

"What?" he asked. "What am I missing here?"

Again that head tilt. "What did you expect when you called me, Christopher?"

He didn't need to think. "The brilliance you showed me before. You found those children."

"So trust me now. Take the binoculars and look."

He took them. A model he recognized. He was surprised

she had them so readily to hand: ATN BINOX 4T 640, optical zoom to 25x with infrared built in. Hunters' binoculars, five thousand dollars plus, good for picking out the heat signature of deer maybe a field away. He held them up to his eyes and targeted the nearest skyscraper, 151 West 57th Street. It was a gray-scale set of lines running up-down. he dialed the zoom all the way in.

It did a little. 25x at this range moved his vantage point into the air maybe three hundred yards away from the tower. He ran the binoculars up and down, looking for tell-tale signs of human habitation. The lighter notes denoting heat spill through the structure's outer skin were scraps only. Not enough to identify anything, let alone exhibits in a zoo.

"This is-"

"Proof of concept," McKenzie finished.

He took the binoculars away from his eyes to find her looking at him intently. "What concept?"

"Primary research," she said. "Eyes in the field gathering primary data that we can trust. There is no other way."

Wren held up the BINOX 4Ts. He was halfway there already. "But binoculars from nearby skyscrapers aren't going to cut it."

"Of course not," Slade said.

Wren's mind hummed, the squares of his own Rubik's cube rotating toward completion. "We'd need blanket coverage of every tower in Manhattan. High-resolution thermal scans, ideally conducted before daybreak."

Slade brought up her wristwatch. The display glowed purple in the darkness, then she tapped it. "Send them," she said.

"Send what?" Wren asked.

Slade pointed out of the glass. Wren looked.

"What am I looking for?"

Then they appeared. Wren's jaw dropped slightly as an

array of lights flashed brightly, right outside the window. For a few seconds he was entranced, lost in the glamor of an unexpected magic trick.

"Still a child," Slade said, watching his expression cynically, though there was a hint of a warmth in her tone.

"Drones?" Wren said, picking out the black skeletons of the hovering light array. He counted a dozen of them, operating in tandem.

"Another favor," Slade said. "My architect friend, they use these all the time to survey their work; they're refitted UAS Air Rangers, ten of them. They can scan the exterior skin of a building in minutes, picking out structural faults, analyzing progress and highlighting areas for repair. This latest batch, to your great good luck, also come equipped with infrared. That's green energy in operation; these can identify areas of heat loss and inefficient energy distribution. They can also be reprogrammed to search for anything you like; bodies in shackles, floors masquerading as mezzanines that are actually dungeons, floors that don't exist on the submitted blueprints, anything you want."

She fell silent. The lights outside went dark and the drones disappeared against the dark sky.

"Twenty-seven-minute batteries, Wren," Slade said. "So pick your jaw up off the floor. I can supply the wireless access codes; can you think of anyone capable of designing a search matrix on short notice, taking into account the need to recharge frequently?"

Wren pulled his eyes from the window and focused on Slade. "This is incredible."

"You mentioned my daughter, so I acted. Now stop wasting time."

Wren nodded. "OK. I know who to call. Send me the codes."

She tapped her watch several times. His phone pinged. He brought it up to confirm then placed the call.

"Yes, Christopher," B4cksl4cker said.

"Wake Hellion up. I've got a job you're both going to love."

27

TESTIMONY

The night deepened.

Wren paced around the penthouse as Hellion spoke in his ear, walking him through the search grid they'd designed. She'd split the ten UAS Air Rangers into a square formation that swept up all sides of a building at once, plotting a three dimensional heat map. They began with Central Park Place: at five seconds per floor across 131 floors it took around eleven minutes to scan the whole structure.

"Is that fast enough?" Wren asked as he watched the drone array rise past the window, barely visible insectile black chunks flying in uncanny synchrony. "There's dozens of target skyscrapers. Do we really need all ten at once to check a building?"

"In order to achieve a minimal resolution, yes," Hellion answered easily. "Any fewer, there will be gaps. Our display will look like, how shall I say, an eight-bit video game?"

"Donkey Kong," B4cksl4cker supplied helpfully.

"More like Asteroid," Hellion said. "A wonderful game, but as a three-dimensional render searching for anomalies-"

Wren stopped listening. Looked at his phone, already half past five, just over three hours until the dawn.

"I take it this building's clear," he said, cutting through their chatter.

"Boringly so," Hellion confirmed. "Workmen working, you and McKenzie Slade. This is all. I am moving next to 111 West 57th Street."

"Where are we at on a strike team?"

Keys flew. "B4cksl4cker is working with McKenzie Slade to vet local SWAT police. There are no operational Foundation members in New York, Christopher; we already sent our best to Rhode Island to protect your family."

Wren gritted his teeth. "SWAT?"

"Apparently McKenzie Slade knows many. Some are, how shall I say, sympathetic to our cause."

Wren didn't want to ask what that meant. "I need to see them. I'm not going in half-baked and-"

"There is a call inbound, Christopher," Hellion interrupted. "It is Agent Sally Rogers. She sounds most excited."

"Rogers? Put her through."

The line clicked. "Sally."

"Christopher! You are going to love this. It's all going crazy out here, but the upshot is, Rachel Day had a secret phone!"

It took Wren a second to switch gears. "What?"

"Well, not exactly a phone," she went on. "At least not a normal one. And we don't have it yet, but we've heard all about it from witness testimony."

Wren blinked, dredging her progress from memory. "So you found the, uh, shoe guy? The greeter?"

She snorted. "No chance of that, it looks. No, we've been canvassing Rachel Day's life, waking people up, bringing them out, running re-enactments of what they might have seen on any given day, and-"

"What?" Wren interrupted. "Re-enactments? What are you talking about?"

"Like we did for the Blue Fairy," Rogers enthused, clearly in the throes of an adrenaline high. Her energy made Wren feel exhausted. "You remember how we ran the live e-fit performance in Chicago, had everyone stand where they'd been when the Pinocchios killed that guy? You chased down a ham and a crab shell, I got us a baseball bat and we watched some actors knock the crap out of it until-"

"I remember," Wren said. He remembered trying to fob a lecture off on Rogers about how people would perform better on a math test staged in a blue room if they'd studied math in a blue room previously. Sense memory was directly linked to recall. He'd drawn the parallel that anyone witnessing a trauma would remember it best when exposed to a re-enactment of the original trauma. Rogers had been skeptical, quickly becoming furious that he was just re-traumatizing the witnesses.

Maybe she'd shifted her values base since then.

"So you've been, what, running live e-fits on potential witnesses?"

"Exactly! You talked about those lost minutes? I'm digging in. The people in her workplace, we put them all back in position. The people along her drive to work, the walk from the parking lot, shops overlooking her commute, parents at the pickups where she collected her son from gymnastics class. Everything, and we asked them for anything strange. Any tiny thing out of the ordinary. And it shook something loose."

"You've got her sighted on a secret phone."

"Exactly. It started with a barber on Juniper Street; she walks a three-minute stretch of it from her company's parking lot to the office. He wasn't happy we woke him up, this was three hours back, but he came in. Of course he knew all about it on the news. We put him at his chair, full floodlights in the street so it looked like day, got him a customer in, scissors in his hand, and asked him if he'd ever noticed Rachel Day acting strange when she walked by. His chair looks right out over the street, so he must have seen her every day."

"And he did?"

"He did. Nothing momentous at first, day after day he sees her, so we pressed, and he came up with one time around three months back, when she stood outside his shop for maybe a minute, looking at her phone."

"OK."

"Nothing strange in that, until she did something a little odd. Out of character, anyway. She lifts her phone up and points it at the window. He has mirrored glass, reflective in the daylight, so he figured she was taking a picture of herself. Of course we set up a person matching Day outside with a phone in the same pose, and that jogged a little more loose."

Wren leaned against the skyscraper's cold glass wall. "Jogged what loose?"

"It was some kind of video on her screen, right after she took the photo. Just rippling red, like a video of flames. Not a photo of his barbershop, that's for sure. But he wasn't sure, he only saw it for a flash."

Wren considered. "OK, that is strange. But it could be-"

"It's not," Rogers said firmly. "Not a gif, not a video, nothing she would have had to access the Internet to download. There's no record of her using her phone in any way like that on any of her commutes. Of course the phone itself was slagged when she burned, but her cloud account has full updates. She streamed no video of fire, received no messages with fire flash files embedded, nothing. She hardly even uses her phone at all. So," she took a breath, warming to the story, "we get a fire gif rolling on our actor outside, and the barber remembers one more thing. Sense memory, right?

He says Day's expression changes as she looks at the screen. Her eyes widen, her jaw drops, like she's seeing something shocking. Maybe terrified, the barber says. It's what he remembered most."

"Terrified," Wren repeated. Picturing Rachel Day from the food court video, watching a fire on her phone. "OK. Three months back, you said?"

"Three months, right."

The gears cranked into motion in Wren's head. "Three months. So if we believe your barber, Rachel Day had a second, secret phone at least that far back. One that streamed video of flames when she took a photo." He thought hard, trying to piece it together. "I don't get it, but this has to be connected to how the Apex radicalized her. If so, there should be a record of that phone's cell carrier somewhere. Have you looked at carrier records in the vicinity?"

Rogers took a breath. "That's where it gets sticky. There are none. No phone line activating anywhere near her at those times."

Wren puzzled over that. "So maybe it's not a phone on a standard contract. Maybe it's piggybacking off someone's nearby Wi-Fi."

"I thought the same thing. We checked it, and there's nothing detectable or on the record. No data up or downloaded in that period of time, in that space."

"At least not through Wi-Fi," Wren murmured. "There are other ways to transmit data. Direct beam through the radio spectrum. It's not hard."

"If the phone is synced for it, absolutely."

"But there are no easy records to check for radio uptake," Wren went on, thinking aloud. "No simple way to track it, certainly not if we don't know the frequency." He thought some more. "And that's exactly the Apex's MO. Un-trackable. If he did this for Rachel Day, you can bet he did it for every other woman in the firestorm too. Deliver them some kind of ghost phone and beam his BS directly into their heads."

"I've already reached out to all the firestorm task forces," Rogers said. "They're re-canvassing their witnesses about phones displaying flames, cross-referencing to carrier records and looking for instances that don't sync up."

"We need to do more than that," Wren said, the gears grinding faster now. "We need to get some kind of detection net in place. Maybe we can narrow beam it if we catch the frequency. We need infrastructure in the field that can detect uptake of unexpected signals. If we can find it, we can cut it off. Stop the flow."

"On it," said Rogers. "Hellion's got some ideas of civilian infrastructure we can co-opt. But there's more still."

"What more?"

"We already started re-canvassing our own witnesses," she said, "bringing up this ghost phone with a red screen and Day's terror reaction. You're not going to believe the testimony that shook out. Seems he thought it was just a nightmare at the time, said he barely even remembered it, but the similarity's telling."

Wren felt a chill sink around his heart. Had a feeling he knew what was coming next. "Whose testimony?"

"John Day," Rogers answered. "Rachel Day's husband."

28

JOHN DAY

R ogers sent the video file of her John Day interview, and Wren brought it up. Eleven minutes and twenty seconds, the thumbnail showed a gray-faced man, mid-forties, hairline receding in a shallow widow's peak, eyes red from crying or lack of sleep or both, clearly in a heightened state. He was sitting on a rumpled double bed, ivy-green wallpaper in back, subdued lighting. Wren guessed it was the master bed in his house; Rogers again using the sensory environment to stir up memories.

He pushed play, and the video began with Rogers' voice off camera.

"Tell us what you saw," she said, not following the rulebook at all. No formal, 'This is Agent Sally Rogers at the interrogation of John Day in booth 3 at the Cincinnati PD'. Instead she'd bypassed it all, which alarmed him even as it warmed a strange kind of pride in his chest.

"Tell you what?" John Day asked. He sounded reedy, looking lost even in his own home. "You want me to do what?"

"Re-enact it," came Rogers' voice. "You told me you

woke up and saw your wife using a phone in the night. I want you to-"

"I said it was a nightmare," John Day protested haplessly. "I don't, really, I don't see what the point of all this is. I've been over and over-"

He froze. Mouth open, staring at something off camera, dead ahead. "What the hell is this?"

The camera panned across the dim ivy wallpaper, a tall bureau, curtain, an open window. Standing in front of the glass was a female figure, her back to the camera, blond hair tousled down her back, wearing a cream silk dressing gown and looking down at a phone in her hand.

"I told you this would be a re-enactment," came Rogers' voice. She was pushing her witness, a sudden widower still in shock from his wife's horrific death, so far it made even Wren uncomfortable.

"She looks like my wife!" Day gasped, then gulped like a swimmer just come up for air. The camera swung around to see shock and fear written on his face. "That's her night gown."

"It is," Rogers said, not offering him any way out. "Tell me again what happened."

"I don't want to do this," Day said, though he didn't stand. "This can't even be legal. You can't just take my wife's clothes!"

"We're not taking them," Rogers said firmly, "we're wearing them. But yes, you're right it might not be legal, and I may be fired when my boss hears about this. Until then, I believe it's our best chance to catch the man who radicalized your wife. Who brainwashed her, John. I'm sorry, but I need you to be brave and tell me anything you can remember."

Wren's mouth opened in a slight gasp of wonder. The reframing was crass and obvious, but he couldn't have said it much better himself. Rewrite John Day's involvement as an act of heroism. Get him onboard and believing that delving into this deep lake of pain could actually produce results.

The camera showed these emotions playing out on his face, fear and uncertainty breaking toward borrowed resolve.

There it is, Wren thought, and was surprised when a second later Rogers echoed his exact thought.

"There you are," she said. "Now, get back in the moment, two months ago, you said? I want you to re-live exactly what happened. You were sleeping. It was dark. We'll hit the lights."

The lights clicked out. The screen fuzzed and struggled to capture anything in the dark, settling on indistinct bands of gray except for the window, where the figure of Rachel Day was haloed by street lights from outside.

John Day's voice came through high and breathless. "Yes, that's exactly where she was standing. I woke up and she was right there, looking at her phone and facing me."

The actress playing the role of Rachel Day turned.

"Oh God," Day said.

"Keep going," Rogers pressed.

"I, well, she was just standing there. Maybe there was a reflection in the window?"

"Of her phone screen?" Rogers asked.

"I, maybe?" His voice shook as he tumbled back into the moment. Sensory states were powerful things, encoding memory locked to a physical sensation, a sound, a mood, a color. "I thought it could be a light outside, maybe a plane blinking, a neighbor's security alarm flashing, I-"

"Let's say it was her phone's screen. What did you see?"

"I-"

The figure of Rachel Day took a step closer to the bed, and there was the sudden sound of Mr. Day jerking in shock. "Argh! I, OK, I got it. It was red! Red, orange and flickering,"

"Like flames?"

"I, yes. Maybe."

The camera turned to the actress. She worked the phone; Wren guessed she was bringing up a gif of flames. A second later he was proved correct. The red spill light illuminated her face demonically, reflecting back off the window like a tiny window into hell.

"Oh no," said John Day.

"What's next?" Rogers pushed.

"I, uh…" his voice came through thinner now. This was a stress reaction, adrenaline pouring into his system and starting fight or flight, but there was nowhere to go. This was his own wife standing at the base of their bed, staring into flames on her phone in the middle of the night. Sweat poured down Day's face.

"What next?" Rogers insisted sharply.

"She held the phone up!" John Day gasped. "Pointed it at me."

A second passed, then the Rachel Day clone did just that.

"Why?" Rogers asked.

"The light came on. The flash? She was filming me, or taking a photograph."

That got Wren's attention. Clearly it got Rogers' too. It didn't distract the actress, who must have hit record in the phone's camera app, sending out a wash of white light from the flash.

"That's it," John Day said tightly. "Really, I think we should stop now. I don't remember anything else."

"Be brave a little longer."

The camera focused on John Day. He was clearly visible in the white flashlight now, curled up against the headboard, clutching a pillow close like a terrified child.

"She began crying," Day said. The words sounded like teeth being pulled. "I thought, I don't know, she was sobbing? Like one of the children had died. I think I said something, like, 'Honey, what's wrong?', but I don't really remember."

"You were still half-asleep."

"I was. I thought, I mean, maybe she said something back?"

"What?"

"I don't know. She wasn't saying it to me. Something like lines of poetry, like she was muttering to herself even while she was sobbing."

"What did she say, John?"

"Something about fear. Fear is a portal? It didn't make any sense."

Wren's heart chilled. He remembered that. One of the deepest tenets of the Pyramid.

"Anything about pain?" Rogers asked, sparking another chill. She'd studied up on the Pyramid, then.

"Yes," said Day, his voice rising to a squeak. "How did you know that?"

"Was it pain is a doorway?"

John Day's eyes opened so wide they caught the white light and glistened like knife blades.

"Walk in the fire," he whispered.

There it was. Conclusive proof of the Apex's involvement, at least for Wren; the final line in the Pyramid's credo.

Fear is a portal. Pain is a doorway. Walk in the fire.

"And then?"

Now Day was sobbing. "She told me to go back to sleep. 'Go to sleep, John,' she said. I'll never forget it now. I'll never forget it."

He raised his shuddering hands to cover his eyes.

Wren let out a breath. Now was the time for Rogers to finish the reframing, to ensure this moment didn't haunt John Day worse than the actual moment itself. He urged Rogers on, then she was there. Stepping in front of the camera, sitting on the bed beside John Day, putting one hand on his shoulder.

"She said that because she loved you," she said. "That was Rachel, John. And whatever happened to her, whatever was done, it wasn't by her choice. Don't ever forget that. She didn't burn herself, she was burned, and the things you've told us tonight give us a real chance of catching the man who twisted her up. We're going to save other people because of this. Hold on to that, and thank you for your courage."

He mumbled something. Rogers rooted in the covers to hold his hand. A long moment passed, then she nodded, someone hit the lights and the spell was broken.

29

WHAT IT MEANS

Wren pulled away from the screen, feeling overwhelmed.

"They'll fire you for that."

"I don't care," she answered. "What do you think?"

Wren tried to martial his thoughts. There were so many now, swirling across each other like cross-currents. "You took outrageous risks. The damage you could have done-"

"You would have done it, if you were here. Maybe you would have gone further."

There was nothing he could say to that. "Maybe."

"There's no maybe. You wanted me as a student? I've been learning the whole time. So stop playing games and tell me what you think."

He let out a breath. She had his number, no point denying it. "OK. Well, firstly, after the barber mentioned flames, I'm certain that all that did happen to John Day, just like he said. I don't think it was a dream." He paused, wondering how far he was going to take it, then plunged on. "Whatever Rachel Day was looking at, whatever she was filming him for, it ties directly to her radicalization. That phone is the key. We need to tie it to a person. How did she get it? Who told her what to do with it? How did they use it to radicalize her so completely? What role do the flames play? If we can build a pattern that matches the other cases, maybe we can narrow down the data stream it's receiving, predict the next one to blow and prevent it."

"We have those requests out to every victim team in the country," Rogers said swiftly. "There's seventeen now, Wren. Seventeen women."

He didn't need her to tell him that. Each one felt carved into his chest. His father, his responsibility. "Have you enlisted the Foundation?"

"Affirmative. B4cksl4cker says he's running algorithm searches back on every woman who burned, looking for evidence of incoming data, whether that's via Wi-Fi, cellular data or radio frequency."

"Good work," he said. "Keep the pressure on."

"Will you have proof against the Apex ready if this works and I manage to extinguish the storm?"

Wren gritted his teeth. "We're closing in on a location for the Apex right now. Some kind of human zoo in New York. Hopefully we'll have it before daybreak. We should get answers there."

"Answers," Rogers replied, then went silent for a moment. "Humphreys gave me access to deep Pyramid data, Christopher. Background on the Apex that was never released. Those mantras John Day mentioned, fear is a portal, pain is a doorway? They're not mentioned anywhere else. I need to know what they mean."

Wren didn't say anything. Whatever deep data Humphreys thought he had, it wasn't one tenth of what Wren had destroyed about the Pyramid in the years since. Oxlea had had a fair point about Wren's file destruction.

He blew out a breath. This was not something he'd wanted to think about again, but he should be brave, like John

Day. "It's his ideology. How he got a thousand people to burn themselves alive when the Pyramid fell." He squeezed the bridge of his nose, hard. In for a penny, in for a pound. "Those words, the portal, the door, they mean none of this is real, Rogers. The world. People. Governments. The air you breathe. The ground you walk upon. It's all fake. The real truth is - the truth 'the Apex' revealed through prolonged pain and fear - was that we're all suffering." He paused for a second, dredging up the past. "Story goes, we're all in hell already, Rogers. Everything we see around us is the lie, while in reality we're screaming our hearts out for mercy."

There was silence for a moment.

"Unpack that for me," Rogers said.

Wren almost laughed. There was a lot to unpack, something he'd avoided doing for anyone else, pretty much ever. "It's a shell game," he said, steeling himself. "The pits, the cages, the vats, it was all torture, right? As we know, the first step to indoctrinating cult members is to break the old frames of reference, and torture is a good tool to achieve that. Look at Steven Gruber. But for the Apex, torture was not just a tool, it was the whole shebang." He took a breath, realized he was being obtuse. It was hard to look at the Apex's works head-on. Rogers waited silently on the other end of the line, giving him the time he needed.

"At a basic level, he's saying pain is truth," Wren tried again. "When you're in pain or experiencing fear, your eyes are open, because you're already in hell. Not metaphorically, not metaphysically, but for real. You're actually stepping through a door into hell. You're experiencing one tenth of what your soul feels every hour of every day, glimpsed through the doorway and the portal." He took a deep breath. He'd thought for so long that he'd left the Apex's sickness behind. "He preached that through a thousand different lessons. Baked it into everything. This world isn't real. This world is a dream. The real you is suffering in hell all the time." He sighed. "Over time, that revelation crept up on people. It broke people down. They couldn't sleep for nightmares about what their soul was actually suffering, about what their children's souls were suffering, about all their family. He got people asking for more pain, more torture in the vats, the cages, whatever, because they were 'seeking the truth'. He told them to try and open their eyes in hell; something you could only do in the most extreme states of pain."

He said nothing for a moment. Rogers cursed.

"Yeah," Wren agreed. "So people pushed for more pain, so they could see. When they start to beg for it, he's got them. They believe. Then he drops the final 'truth', the one he's been prepping you for all this time: the only way to save your actual soul is to die in the most painful way possible. The more painful, the more chance you have of waking up 'in' your soul. It ends the spell. You come to as your soul in hell, but now you can act." Wren leaned hard against the glass, legs beginning to shake.

"Once you're in hell," he went on, "you gather with the other members of the Pyramid, an army of enlightened angels, waiting for you to come. You join their army and start working to free everyone else. All of humanity." Wren rubbed his eyes and was surprised to find them damp. It took genuine bravery and made it vile. "You become an angel sent to redeem others. It's your holy duty. So, that's what all those people, the ones I burned alive in the fake town, truly believed. They thought they were sacrificing themselves to go save all of humanity."

His voice trembled at the end.

"Sick," Rogers said. "That is, I mean..." She whistled low. "That is one head trip, Boss."

Wren laughed. "We all believed it, one way or another.

My brothers and sisters. My family. Me." He took another rough breath. "When he wouldn't let me burn at the end, I remember feeling like a traitor. I wanted to go be an angel with my family, but he said no. He needed me here as a messenger of what we'd done, to spread the word."

There was silence for a moment.

"I didn't know," Rogers said eventually. "You never said."

"Well, now you know. What he's doing to these women, I'm guessing it's the same thing. We're seeing flames on the phones, maybe that's a vision of hell, a way to outsource his brainwashing through technology. It took time back then, weeks sometimes, months, years, so it looks like he's refined the method. Maybe he can do it remotely, now. He can flip them through a ghost phone, make them believe that they're angels pressing forward to rescue the lost." He took a steadying breath. Time to turn this around. "When it comes to intervention, if you do manage to disrupt one of these women, remember that there'll be no reasoning with them. Right now they're bought and sold. In their eyes we're the blind ones; maybe we're even working to keep everyone enslaved. All you can do is shut them down physically, then worry about deprogramming their minds later on."

Rogers' breathing came heavier. Who knew what she was thinking.

"I'm sorry," she said.

That wasn't what he'd been expecting, and not something he was equipped to deal with. "We're going to bring him down, Rogers. Believe that."

"I believe it."

"Good. Now find these phones. Nail the frequency. I've got a zoo to crush."

"Thank you," she said. "For trusting me."

He smiled. A leap of faith. Sometimes faith was all you had.

30

SWAT

7 :15 a.m., and the blue glow of dawn spread up from the east like the glare of a flare light. In the back of a SWAT van peeling east along Billionaire's Row, Wren strapped a quad-load bandolier of 12 gauge 303 grain 'trocar' shotgun shells across his armor-plate Twaron vest, then looped a second harness of 410 Triple Defense 7-shell magazines across it. In one hand he held a Benelli M4 tactical shotgun, while a SIG Sauer P320 .45 ACP was holstered on his left hip.

"It's 231 Madison Avenue," Hellion had said three minutes earlier. Activating Wren, sitting with his new team of SWAT officers on loan from the city in their riot van, decked out to look like a florist's truck from outside. Every member wore a jawbone conduction mic, earpiece and bodycam synced direct to Hellion riding overwatch, and all wore base-jumping parachute packs, in the event of a catastrophe.

"How sure are you?" Wren had asked, surveying the specs for 231 Madison Avenue. Finished in 2016, 1,426 feet tall with 101 floors, 119 residences, it had been the tallest residential building in the world until Central Park Place surpassed it. Its construction design featured six independent building compartments stacked atop each other, divided by mechanical floors filled with reinforced concrete outrigger trusses binding the core to the perimeter framework; these increased stiffness and reduced the 'drift' felt by its billionaire residents as wind buffeted the exterior.

"We're seeing seven stacks," Hellion had replied. "Not six as all the schematics say. Slade was right. There's an extra mechanical floor hidden like a mezzanine in the upper reaches, floors 73 to 74. No elevator stops there, it's heavily shielded so we can't see any heat signature, but it's there, the only anomaly out of all the structures. If there's a zoo anywhere, it's here. Sending you the 3D model."

He gave the order and the florist van took off east. Barely a ten minute ride, five if they flashed blue lights, but the whole goal was to approach incognito. The zoo had to be caught before it could self-immolate.

Images flashed up on his phone and Wren scrolled through them; three-dimensional heat maps of Madison Avenue's upper floors laid atop a best-guess render of the physical layout.

"If there's no elevator stop, how do we access it?" he asked.

"Access must be through the floor above or the floor below. 73 and 74 are both penthouses, full width."

"I always liked my dungeons going down," B4cksl4cker said. "I think you hit 74."

"But you keep the madwoman in the attic," Hellion countered. "Hit 73."

Wren clicked the line open, admitting the seven SWAT members packed into the van with him. "We'll hit both 73 and 74 simultaneously. I'll take lead on 74, Jimenez you're lead on 73."

Corporal Jimenez nodded. Wren had never met him

before and knew none of the strike team, but their records were clean and Slade had vouched for them all.

"They can't be bought," she'd said, while Wren was putting the request through Humphreys' off-book channel. "If the mob can't buy them, I don't think your father can either."

That was good enough for him.

"Yes, sir," Jimenez said.

Wren studied his own sub-team. They were three-strong and adept at exactly this kind of strike according to their jackets: break-and-enter with no-knock warrants on cartel targets across the five boroughs. All were hardened, all with a history of good shootings, forged in the fire. Wren doubted they'd operated at 73 stories high in the sky before, but there was always a first time.

"The things we might see in there," he said to them. "I'm expecting hell. Think of the worst urban myth you've ever seen and 10x it. Human trafficking dens, coked-up flophouses, people on bath salts carving each other for snacks, that's what I want you ready for. There's no time to be horrorstruck; we'll have to act decisively."

His sub team stared back at him. Kato was lean and silent, thirty-four, ex special forces. McNeil chewed a cud of tobacco, thick-necked like a bull at just twenty-seven. Miller was a slender blonde, expert in demolitions. She was his only proof against a networked bomb big enough to bring the whole tower down.

"Drones are pulling back to avoid detection," Hellion said in his ear. "I'll close in for real-time tracking when you're there. Overwatch shows no signs they know we're onto them. Infrared looks like three people on 74, two on 73.

"Security?"

"We are in the main building's system," Hellion said. "Multiple cameras on every floor, several with capture angles overlapping the exterior, though of course not inside the zoo.

Seismic sensors throughout, fine-tuned enough to hear a single footfall. Remote elevator disabling with palm-locked floor selection, steel bar security doors, private escape rooms in every apartment, plus a security team ten-strong."

Wren dismissed the security team. If they put up a fight, they'd be downed with ease. The elevator controls and overrides were an easy hack. The exterior, lobby and elevator cameras were a simple matter for his hackers to copy and play on a loop. Steel-barred doors they could evade by blasting straight through concrete with compound ANFO shaped charges tucked into diamond-bit drilled holes.

"What about their own cameras? If the zoo's there, I guarantee the Apex has multiple feeds not synced to the building's system."

"At some point they will see you," Hellion answered swiftly. "We plan to kill building's power selectively upon breach, keeping elevators online. If zoo has backup generators, perhaps there is short window to kick in. Thirty seconds, maybe. This is your opportunity. You have to move fast."

Wren laughed. "Copy that."

"You are currently four minutes out, Christopher. Do you have any further questions?"

Countless questions. Only one for Hellion.

"Tell me there's a medical team on standby. If the interior of this zoo is anything like I expect, there'll be a lot of people in need of assistance."

"We have four ambulances on standby. New York Presbyterian Hospital has a trauma team ready. How's that?"

She'd thought of everything. While he'd been occupied with vetting and assembling his team she'd been prepping the rest. "You're an angel, Hellion."

"And me?" B4cksl4cker asked in his truculent bass. "Am I also angel?"

"Maybe a winged cherub," Wren allowed, "one of those pudgy babies with a bow and arrow."

"Very good," said B4cksl4cker. "I am youthful."

Wren strapped his Kevlar riot helmet tight and ducked down to look out the windscreen. The edge of Madison Avenue's segmented white front had just come into view.

31

STRIKE

T he lobby was dark as Wren sped through the glass doors of 231 Madison Avenue, his pulse pounding loud in his ears. The space was double height but understated in the ghostly wash of streetlight cast through the huge square windows. Silver marble veined with black lay underfoot, large laser-cut copper sheets clung to the walls and a floating desk in squared-off granite stood at the head, staffed with a receptionist who looked terrified in the sweep of their flashlights.

Wren ignored him and made for the second elevator. His team lined up behind him, the other team led by Jimenez alongside. The doors were already open and they swept inside.

"Hellion?" Wren said, as the door closed.

"I kept them warm for you," Hellion said. "Hold onto a railing. You will hit two-g."

Wren grabbed the railing and his team followed suit as the elevator accelerated upward. Wren felt gravity tugging down the skin of his face. He eased the SIG .45 from its holster.

"Almost there," said Hellion. "The zoo appears to be

reacting. They are dark, no power, but there is movement on 74. figures are coming toward the elevator."

Wren gritted his teeth. Of course. He watched the floor lights flashing on the readout above the door, ripping through the fifties now. He spoke on an open channel to both teams. "We go in hot, looks like they're waiting for us."

He received nods in the elevator and the OK from Jimenez. His squad readied their weaponry. Within ten seconds the elevator decelerated hard, sending his stomach lurching up, then halted and the doors sprang open. Wren briefly glimpsed the penthouse beyond, plush carpeting stretching away to the glass wall where the sun was just surfacing over the horizon, then he tossed twin 'vertigo' flashbang grenades and dived to the side.

His left shoulder struck a wall, he bounced off a side table then dropped to the lush-carpeted floor with the SIG .45 extended dead ahead, belly to the ground and eyes clamped shut, just as the flashbangs erupted in light, smoke and sound.

Wren fired and someone fired back, automatic bullets spraying the elevator's interior. Wren tucked his head low and crawled into the smoke.

"Left, Christopher," came Hellion's calm voice, watching via the infrared Air Rangers. "Five feet further and you will be clear of their field of fire."

In five seconds he cleared the distance, came up on his feet behind a sofa and put a bullet into the skull of a sniper proned out across it. The smoke cleared a little and Wren circled to level the Benelli M4 shotgun at the remaining two men, hunkered behind an upended mahogany table.

"Morning," he said, and fired.

The first 12 gauge 303 grain 'trocar' shotgun shell burst out and hit one of them in the face, the trocar-angled multi spikes of the exploding round splaying on impact and churning separate paths through his skull, shredding it to red jelly. The Benelli auto regulating gas pistons pumped a second shell into the breech and Wren pulled a fraction left, hitting the second guy in the chest and coring his heart like an apple.

"There are more coming from below!" Hellion shouted.

Wren plucked at his chest for a reload, slotted them into the Benelli then threw himself forward over the bodies of the two men as bullets raked the wood where he'd been.

In a brief avenue of visibility through the smoke, Wren fired, caught someone in the leg and took it clean off. The man screamed and fell. Wren surged into the moment, taking one other figure out with a trocar round to the face and the third with three bullets from his Sig dead through the heart.

The penthouse fell silent.

"Your team are down," Hellion said rapidly. "It looks like Kato's still alive, but no life signs for others. I've replayed drone footage and I see where they came from, up through a passage to your four o'clock, fifty yards, but you must hurry!"

Wren ran.

"There is heat building on mechanical level below, this looks like fire, perhaps destruction of evidence."

"Evacuate the building," Wren said.

"Already doing it," Hellion answered as he sped past a glossy grand piano pockmarked with bullet rounds and into a library. Books lay on the floor drifted by black smoke. There was a rug tipped over at one corner and cement stairs leading down. He reloaded his Benelli then dropped down into the zoo.

32

ZOO

Wren descended into the flickering gloom of the hidden mechanical floor. He was in a cave-like access shaft that ran east-west along the building's southern face, barely six-feet high, with red emergency lights blinking in the rough gray ceiling. There were no windows, and line of sight was blocked by interjecting bulkheads; likely the structural trusses binding the perimeter wall to the building's central core.

A scream rang out. Wren ducked his head and ran toward it. Concrete-sprayed beams jutted at all angles across his path, along with thick pipes and heavy swatches of electrical cables, partially blocking the tight passage like jungle overgrowth. His bodycam flashlight activated in the darkness, illuminating black finger streaks smeared on the walls.

More screams followed.

"I cannot pinpoint them," came Hellion's voice in his ear.

The tunnel tightened; Wren ducked beneath a thick diagonal truss, squeezed between two vertical waste downpipes and pushed through a beard of heavy cables until the shaft turned north and opened into a huge hall.

The space was some twenty yards wide and fifty long,

likely running half the footprint of the building's west side, though the ceiling was barely seven feet tall, which made it feel oddly claustrophobic. It was only lit by the epileptic flash of red emergency lights, revealing its horrors by pulsing degrees.

The right wall was studded with tarnished metal doors next to silvery one-way glass panes; possibly cells. To his left ran floor-to-ceiling iron bars, close-set and casting stroboscopic shadows as the red lights flashed, an undeniable cage. Beyond the bars low, shivering shapes clustered at the corners like flies on a horse's eye. Wren caught glimpses of skin lashed red, long strands of filthy hair, fire-blackened faces, the nubs where limbs should be.

The air hung with fetid smells. Wren approached and the bodies behind the bars shrank back and cried out as his bodycam light played over them.

"Christopher," came Hellion's warning voice, but he barely heard it.

At the cage door he yanked on the bolt but it was padlocked. He pointed the Benelli, thinking his trocars might chew threw the padlock, but at once the pitiful creatures on the other side surged like a tide, pressing their scarred bodies against the bars and reaching through.

Wren was startled backward, staring into what was left of their faces. Some were missing eyes, others noses, others ears or patches of skin. In a grotesque flash, Wren realized what they wanted; not to steal the gun or fight him, but for him to pull the trigger on them.

He backed away.

"Christopher, help these people later," came Hellion's shout in his ear, sounding very far off. "Find the Apex first."

Wren wavered, then nodded like she was there to see. "I'm coming back," he said to the figures inside the cage, though his voice sounded weak and reedy. "I promise."

"Move, Christopher! We are seeing heat levels spike in multiple places; there is high chance building is on fire. "

The bodies began to wail. Wren turned and ran. Pale arms plunged toward him through the cages, until at the end the hall narrowed and he lurched right to avoid them. He hit a cell door in the wall on the right and burst through into a wholly green space.

He dropped to his knees, the Sig discharged as his hand slapped onto the ground, then he was up and spinning. Everything was green: the walls, the floor, the ceiling, bizarrely bright under the roving beam of his flashlight. Twin green-framed beds stood side by side filling the middle, with green sheets, pillows and blankets, besmirched with a rich layer of greasy black.

Not black. He leaned in. Dried blood.

The air stank of ignited napalm, the tang of gasoline lingering along with the smoke of scorched flesh. The green walls were sprayed with more dried blood. His heart stampeded.

"Christopher, the Apex!"

Hellion's voice broke through and Wren stood still for a moment, the room spinning, realizing that her voice had been there all the time.

"I-" he began, but had no words to follow up with.

"It is all right, Christopher, you will give yourself heart attack," she said, and he heard the relief in her voice. "I have played many horror video games, so I have seen all this before. You must not panic. The door is to your left. Do not think about what happened here. We will; end this. Now there is definite fire in this building. You must move swiftly."

The words stamped logic back atop the terror. He'd said the same thing to his team, don't be horrorstruck, but that was one thing to say and another to live through. He'd seen plenty of horrors in his day, but nothing to match this.

He took a calming breath.

"Thanks, Hellion."

He exited back into the moaning hall of pale bodies pressed to the cage walls.

"It is only video game, Christopher," Hellion said in his ear. "Finish this level."

He ran on to the east, plunging back into another tight access passageway between the outer and inner skins of the building. He stumbled over pipes and scraped against the rough walls, weaved around a tree-trunk-thick rebar column and ducked through another cavern of looping cables until there was a glass door ahead that slid smoothly open at his touch.

Here lay a bright, clinical corridor. The ceiling was tall enough for him to stand upright again, the raw cement was gone, and now the red emergency lamps flashed off lustrous black tile flooring and cream-painted walls hung with-

Wren's eyes widened as he recognized one of the framed, sepia-tone photographs. It showed a place he recognized immediately, done artfully and enlarged, but without any of the drooping facades or burned-out structures of latter years.

The fake town.

His heart crashed violently in his chest, his mouth dried out and his vision tunneled tight to the image before him, capturing in stark technicolor a past that had only ever existed in the mists of his childhood memory. It showed the front façade of the old Bank building, just a stage set for a cowboy Western that was never made, since burned down by Wren himself.

No other photographs of this place existed; there was no evidence that it had ever been there other than a plain concrete foundation pad laid out in the Sonoran desert.

Except here it was wholly alive. Hundreds of people stood in front arrayed on tiers like children on school bleachers. Wren's gaze ran left to right, taking in the men in the back row, the women in the middle, the children at the front.

He knew them all. All were beaming like this was a happy day out at summer camp, with the orange desert in back and the blue sky above, and…

In the center, arms wide, blue eyes sparkling in his bodycam light's glare, stood the Apex.

It was undoubtedly him. Looming large out of nightmare. The same man as on David Keller's stage.

Wren couldn't breathe.

The Apex looked so young, straight out of his memory; with rich dark hair, a broad grin, wearing denim jeans and a check shirt like he was just another regular human. Looking happy. Maybe late twenties. A photograph Wren had never seen. He had no recollection of it being taken, and his eyes raked the rows hungrily, seeking something else that he'd never seen before. There'd been no mirrors in the Pyramid. The only glimpses of himself he'd ever caught as a child had been in darkened store fronts and car windows as he'd danced for new followers, as their drivers pulled away.

He'd been a phantom child only, dark from the sun, moon-white teeth, hale and healthy, performing for the masses as they passed.

Then he saw them, there at the bottom right corner; seven dark-skinned children. His heart skipped a beat. Not the same as a mismatched line of grinning kids beside them, not dressed in jeans and T-shirts like those part-timers who looked like they'd just had a wonderful day of activities, archery and s'mores and a singsong around the camp fire.

No. These children wore the hessian tunics of the Pyramid. These could only be the Pequeños, children of the Apex himself, and Wren's breath caught as he picked them out one by one and saw the Apex in each, his lost brothers and sisters lined up eldest to youngest.

Galicia-In-Her-Mother's-Heart. Chrysogonus-With-Bared-Arm. Zachariah-Of-The-Marsh. Tomothy-Whereof-The-Giants-Roam. Gabriel-In-Extremis, and there at Gabriel's left arm stood Pequeño 3.

Christopher Wren.

He gasped. He was so small. Barely six years old. There were two younger Pequeños to his left, one held in the arms of a nursing maid.

His breathing grew chaotic. This was him, trapped in the Pyramid just like the creatures he'd left in their cages. Happy in appearance. Healthy to the onlooker. Tortured only by night, on the Apex's whims.

"We were his favorites."

"We've all grown up," came a voice to his left.

Wren's head snapped sideways.

At the end of the corridor stood a woman. She was tall and olive-skinned, wore a cropped black halter top and a long aquiline dress. Even standing perfectly still she exuded grace, with high cheekbones over dark purple lips. Her thick hair was pulled skull-achingly tight into a complex confection of sweeps and curls at the back of her head. Strong arms were crossed over her chest. She gazed at him with something like recognition.

Wren felt like he was drowning.

"Though some of us are still living in the past, aren't we, Pequeño 3?"

The words washed over him. He stared into her eyes. They were gray with flecks of sparkling blue, similar to the Apex. It was impossible but the resemblance was undeniable. Last time he'd seen her she'd been dead, suffocated at the bottom of a pit when he was nine years old. All his brothers and sisters had died there and then, casualties of the Apex's war on faith.

Except.

The word trickled up through his throat, a name he hadn't spoken in nearly thirty years.

"Galicia?"

33

GALICIA

S he took a step closer and Wren almost dropped where he stood. His heart slammed madly. This was truly the dead resurrected.

"You're not looking well, little brother," Galicia said.

There was the confirmation. She was really here in the flesh, though all he could see was the solemn-faced teenager from the photograph imposed atop her. She'd been sixteen then, barely a shade of the proud and beautiful woman she'd now become, and he blinked hard, trying to dispel this twisted double vision.

"You-" he began, but nothing came out. Hellion shouted but he didn't hear a word for the blood rushing in his ears.

"I've waited so long for this moment," Galicia said, taking a languid step forward. Now Wren saw the knife in her hand. Long bladed, stiletto thin. "Ever since the pit, I've wondered which of us would cross your path first."

His throat jammed but he forced words out. "You're dead."

She took another step, one hand tracing the wall and caressing more framed photographs as she glided closer, a smile flickering at the edges of her lips. "Perhaps. You remember the mantra, I think? Pain is a doorway."

The old words buzzed back to the forefront of his mind. "Fear is a portal."

"Walk in the fire," Galicia intoned solemnly. "How we've watched you, little brother. Your trials and tribulations. All your suffering. Now you've come home."

His mind felt gridlocked. "This isn't my home."

"No," she allowed sadly. "But one day."

He fought for control, to stop reacting and start acting, but his thoughts were a storm and Hellion was just a noise in the back of his head. He'd come here for a purpose, but now that purpose had been swamped by the past. "How are you alive? I saw you dead in that pit. All of you."

"You saw a performance," Galicia said, sounding faintly bored. "Just another recruitment drive."

Those words made no sense. "You died. How was that a recruitment?"

Her smile spread, her tone turned chiding. "Little brother. How have you travelled the world and not yet learned this? Had the Apex not sacrificed his own children on the altar of faith, would the good people of the Pyramid ever have walked in the fire? We both know the answer to that one."

She gave him a wink. It floored him. Just like the old Galicia, and completely out of place in this dungeon.

"I…"

"Do you remember how we used to watch the babies crying together, little brother?" She took another step closer. "How the night desert's warmth enveloped us, just you and I in the dark, out of our beds and knowing our father would be angry if he found us, buzzing with fairy lights and standing hand-in-hand to watch them for hours, mewling themselves to sleep?" Her delicate fingers ran along the lip of another framed photograph, this one showing just the Pequeños standing side-by-side in the desert. "Do you remember when I taught you how to take notes at your first drowning? I can picture the man today still, just beginning to glimpse the world lying beyond the door. How he grew hungry and begged for more. How our father slowed him down, ensuring the portal was fully open."

Wren listened transfixed; this was the same sing-song tone she'd used to whisper lullabies to him as a small, scared child. "Do you remember huddling down in the blankets with me, hiding from our brother Chrysogonus? He was always so furious with you." She smiled at the memory. "Untying all his barometers of progress. Monkeying with his knots." The smile grew wistful, and Wren felt like he was floating on some kind of drugged cloud. "I remember your little hot body pressed close to my thighs, your thin arms around my back, your face in my belly, your tiny high pulse racing like a baby bird, and I remember thinking, if I break his poor neck now to spare him this fear, will he still walk in the fire?"

Her heels clacked closer on the marble tiles.

"I love you still, little brother. I always have. I always will. I only ever want what's best for you."

She was close now, maybe ten yards, and he could almost feel the forgotten heat of her body against his, trembling beneath the sheets while Chrysogonus stalked the night, ready to douse him in candle wax or lash the soles of his feet with an ocotillo arm as punishment for even the slightest offense. He remembered her heavy pulse as the soothing staple of his earliest memories, always there at his side, stroking his back, smoothing out his wild hair as the nightmares bled away.

"I remember," he said, and everything else around him was forgotten.

"I'm glad," she said. "We've been too long apart. Sharing whispers on the rooftop, watching the new people flow in. Like a river they came, little brother, never ending. I can see them even now, from all the corners of the world to see the great wonder our father was building. Every inch of their pain mounted up like blocks in a great testament of stone, rising toward the ultimate feat of a pyramid framed from human grace. Do you remember all the ways we used to imagine shaping them, you and I as they tumbled in, lives stacked atop lives atop lives. You were always the architect. I was never surprised at the name you took for yourself, in the days after we parted. Christopher Wren. How could you choose any less of a man? How else could you hope to follow in our father's footsteps?"

He was adrift. Didn't know what to say. "Galicia…"

"They were such fools, don't you think, those converts?" she pressed on. "In their jeans and their flannel tops, with their air-conditioned vehicles and handheld technology, thinking they could one day truly belong to the monument we were constructing. They were mere mortar to hold the blocks together, when all along we knew that we were the true pillars of the pyramid. You. Your brothers. Me. Five disciples and one prodigal son. Our father's true legacy. The pathway to a brighter world for all humanity. Because fear is a portal, little brother. Pain is a doorway. Will you walk in the fire with me?"

She lunged.

The stiletto blade came sweeping in, cracking the fog around him like a skin of winter ice. Two yards out now and Wren moved too slow, but the blade caught on one of his armor plates, slicing off to dig into his shoulder.

He lurched into the wall and the stiletto blade whipped clear. His right arm suddenly hung numb, the Sig clattering to the tiled floor.

Galicia didn't wait, and sent the blade out again in a frontal thrust backed with her whole body weight, straight toward the hollow of Wren's throat. He threw his left hand up to bat the blade away but took it instead directly through his open palm.

The pain was instant, and tore an animal cry from his lips. He pulled his hand off the spike, streaming blood.

"Little brother," Galicia said sadly, "if only you saw what I see."

The blade swept in again from above, and this time his left elbow rocketed up, and he caught her forearm on his own. He sent a straight punch out, but there was nothing to catch as she spun away, pirouetting to bring the blade around toward his right ear.

He barely got his hand up in time, and watched in horror as the blade stabbed through the meat of his right palm. This time he was more ready, and shoved her away. The blade pulled free and he followed on, both hands dripping blood to the black tiles.

"Pain is a doorway, little brother," she said, eyes flashing blue. "Don't fight me."

He took another step closer, sick of feeling sick and confused, tired of being caught off balance, and raised his ruined fists before him.

"You call this pain?"

Her lips split in a proud smile. "For the Apex so loved the world that he gave his most favored son." She came in hard then, the blade clattering off Wren's forearm plates before she leaped easily away from his answering grab.

"I've waited so long to guide you through this door," Galicia said, eyes glittering. "My sweet little brother, finally taking his place in the tombs of the Pyramid."

She sprang in again with the lightness of a ballet dancer, this time putting the spike into his left shoulder. Fresh pain ignited down his left side.

"Don't be afraid, little bird," she said, and came in low toward his belly. His armor saved him, but she stepped into another pirouette that sent the blade slamming toward his ribs.

Wren was ready. He caught her wrist, twisted hard enough to send the blade skittering over the tiles, then dragged her into crushing headbutt square in the face.

She pulled free, but the feel of her nose crumpling against his forehead remained hot on his skin, the sound ringing in his ears. Now blood streaked her glamorous lips and down her elegant throat.

"There you are," she said, eyes afire as she pulled another blade from a sheath at her waist and leaped back into the fray.

Wren ignored the blade, put his shoulder down and charged. Maybe the stiletto peppered off the armor panels, maybe it sliced through the Twaron fabric, but he didn't care. He was too injured to dance any longer. Weight was his advantage here, and he lifted and slammed her with ease.

Her back thudded to the floor and she gasped as something crunched in her chest. The blade spun out of her grip and ricocheted off the wall, but somehow she snuck an elbow into his face, throwing his head back.

He rolled back on his feet like an old boxer fighting the count, weaving and punch-drunk, her stiletto blade now in his hand. He flung it, even as she-

Stood, leveling the Sig at his face.

"Walk in the fire, little brother," she said, and fired.

34

ALL YOUR GLORIES

The gun clicked empty.

The blade struck Galicia's chest and near punched her off her feet.

Wren laughed. It took a second to comprehend. There were no bullets left in the Sig; he'd been saved by the Apex's grace.

"Don't kill her, Christopher!" came the shout in his ear.

For a moment he forgot who was speaking. He felt torn and disoriented, looking at the elder sister he'd thought dead so long ago. Now she was on her knees.

"Are they talking to you now?" she asked, blood spraying from her lips with each word, "the false prophets in your ear?"

"We came here for the Apex!" the voice came again, and Wren pressed one hand to his ear and touched cold plastic, remembering the earpiece. "For proof."

Hellion. She felt like a figment from another life.

"We need her alive, Christopher," Hellion called. "She is everything we need, but you need to move! Jimenez is on the mechanical floor with you, and he says there's enough C4 strapped to the support trusses to blow out the core. Christopher!"

It barely registered. He didn't care. He advanced on his sister through a roiling red mist.

"I can help you, Galicia," he said. "I help lots of people. You could still be free of him."

She laughed low and tugged on the blade sticking out of her chest, but her hands were slick with blood and slipped on the grip. "Are they telling you about the bomb, little brother? How today we will all walk in the fire?"

She was two steps away. All he had to do was lay hands on her, hoist her, carry her away, but now the corridor was zooming and refocusing like a concertina and his feet didn't land where he wanted.

"Two minutes, Christopher!" Hellion called. "Jimenez cannot break the circuit. You must go now!"

"I escaped," he slurred, and held one bloody hand out as he sank to one knee before Galicia. "I escaped our father's shadow. You can too."

Galicia pulled on the blade again, and this time managed to draw the weapon out. Fresh blood welled from the wound and her face blanched pale. "Escaped his shadow?" she asked, so close now, like they'd always been as children. "Little brother, you have never once been out of his shadow. All your choices belong to him. All your glories are his. There is no world beyond the reach of his touch."

"Galicia," he said, reaching for the blade. "Sister. We can-"

"I love you, little brother," she said, and raised the blade high. "I will wait for you on the other side."

She brought the blade down. Wren couldn't move fast enough. The tip sank into the hollow of her throat and down into her chest cavity. The fire went out of her eyes, her knees buckled and she dropped to the floor with a thud.

His elder sister, the one who'd always protected him from his elder brother, finally dead.

35

OFF LINE

W ren swayed.

Blood leaked from his palms and his shoulders and the corridor spun around him. Black tiles. Cream walls. Photographs of the Pyramid hung to either side while his dead sister sprawled on the floor.

He took a step and almost fell, recognizing that this was the blood loss emptying out his head.

"Listen to me, Christopher," said Hellion, "forget proof, you need to get out right now!"

He blinked, inundated with memories of his big sister.

"Ninety seconds," came the voice.

His legs moved. The corridor tumbled. He hit another wall, slid until he came hard against the same photograph from before, now flecked with blood. Little Pequeño 3 so small in the corner. The Apex at the center. All those dead people. A memory of a forgotten world.

He put his elbow through the glass, scratched out the shards, snatched the picture and stuffed it into his jacket; about all the proof he could manage.

"Seventy seconds!"

He ran, slapped off another wall, slipped on the tiles and

rounded a corner. He passed a large office space decked with large speakers and screens, where people stared back at him from chairs like regular office workers, while C4 packages strapped against the central core blinked down their timers.

Nobody moved.

"Sixty seconds," Hellion shouted.

Wren rounded the southeast corner and careened into another jungle of beams and struts as Hellion counted him down from fifty. At forty he hammered his head into a low metal beam, and he crawled through thirty, then was up again and lurching forward.

"Twenty seconds, Christopher, get the hell out!"

On the count of ten he reached the concrete stairs, cornered hard and was charging up when the blast struck. It punched him the rest of the way up into the library, feeling the explosion more than he heard it as the building's steel trusses instantly buckled.

Books tumbled from shelves around him. Plaster dust and stinking chemical smoke fumed up from noxious green fires in the tunnel below.

"Go, Christopher!" Hellion shouted. "The top of the building is swaying, it looks like it's going to-"

Wren rose to his feet then the world shifted beneath him, like the moment you hit the top of a rollercoaster and begin to tip, the arrogance of height giving way to the cold truth of gravity.

"You should see the hole in the building's side, Christopher!" Hellion called, sounding struck by awe. "It is coming down now, get out!"

Numb calculations ran through his dimming head. He started to run just as the floor tilted hard right, sinking to an incline of maybe ten degrees toward the south. He was at the south side now. One thing he'd learned from his days in the forests of Maine: never run in the shadow of a falling tree.

He had to get offline.

Smoke surged past him in a foul green river, heading for a smashed window pane off to the east. He let the tide sweep him along as the floor swayed more steeply, stinging his eyes and bringing the Benelli up for one final task.

As he ran he cracked the breech and fumbled a single shell from his bandolier into the tube. Thirty degrees now? Hellion was a siren in his ear, and Wren leaned one hand against the south side's glass as the whole penthouse rolled and furniture slid toward him like he was on a sinking ship. The conference table jammed into his path and he pulled himself along the side. The building jolted again, closing fast on forty-five degrees with the floor to ceiling windows glowering out over the incredible drop. Wren glimpsed tiny vehicles racing across intersections below, people like dots, and knew that within seconds everything would be smothered by the wreckage of 231 Madison Avenue.

He ran, and the contents of the Apex's penthouse rained and rolled left to right around him. Red-streaked paintings, cutlery, chairs, potted plants, cushions. A pillow hit him in the face. A toaster hurtled by like an artillery shell. Fifty degrees and Wren ran the last few yards on the windows themselves as New York opened like a chasm below. Hellion screaming. His whole body burning. He raised the Benelli and fired the single trocar round into the east side window ahead, sending fracture patterns ripping out, then his shoulder hit, the glass burst like a hailstorm and he was through.

He somersaulted down alongside the cascading structure in a fall of glass. The world opened up and the morning sun speared into his eyes and the gray sky spun toward blue. 1,200 feet, maybe twelve seconds fall time, and he stiffened out his body like an airfoil to glide away away from the chaos of 231 Madison, soaring east above Billionaire's Row.

Maybe six seconds down at five hundred feet high, with

New York rushing up like a cannon ball, his right hand found the release strap and pulled. The chute shot out from his pack and snatched him out of freefall. Ten more seconds passed as his velocity cut out, then crosswinds slammed him into the side of another building, three seconds after which he dropped hard into oncoming traffic.

36

LITTLE BIRD

Wren's legs gave out on impact with the road and he slapped into a rag-doll roll, past a yellow cab veering away in a screech of brakes, limbs windmilling across the median until he flopped on his back before a steaming semi, parachute tugging tight at the harness across his chest.

He twisted the release and the chute whipped away. Charcoal clouds and gouts of black smoke swirled across the sky. The semi braked only yards from his face, and Hellion's voice came in static bursts in his ear. Horns honked until all the honking stopped and the car doors opened and the people stepped out to watch the top twenty floors of Madison 231 peel away like a piece of rotten fruit.

Flames stamped a ragged crown across the 73rd floor, just visible through the pumping smoke. The first chunks of falling debris hit the street below in what seemed like slow motion, sending pummeling vibrations through the blacktop. Wren tried to stand but the juddering earth wouldn't hold him. He watched as the top floors of Madison 231 tipped beyond its ability to hold, support trusses blown, separated from the concrete core, ripping clear housings and the glass façade until finally the whole thing fell.

Terrible seconds passed as the top twisted and disintegrated under its own weight, tumbling to the street. The impact began with a gut punch to the spine and kept on coming as a mushroom cloud of dust blasted out.

People screamed and coughed. People ran in the sudden gray pall. People cursed and engines revved. "Not again," someone cried. .

Wren tried again to get up but his arms couldn't lift him.

"…coming!" Hellion called in his ear.

The road skittered like a drum skin as Madison collapsed.

"Hey man, are you OK?" somebody asked, leaning over him through the rush of dust. "I think this guy came out of the building!"

Wren tried to say something but managed only a feeble cough.

Another face loomed close. "That's Christopher Wren! You say he was in the building?"

"I saw him parachute out of it!"

"That settles it."

There was the click of a hammer cocking, cutting through the voices and sirens and falling rubble. There was a gunfire report nearby.

"What the hell, are you crazy man? He's one of the good guys!"

"He's a damn terrorist, and if you don't get out of the way I'll blow your head off too."

The shouting rose. Bodies shifted in the blurry smoke. Wren couldn't keep track of the fight. Blows were thrown. He tried to say something but couldn't, tried to roll away but didn't even have the strength for that, until a second massive piece of the building landed and unleashed a sandstorm blast of grit that muffled everything.

Then there was a hand on his shoulder.

"He's here!"

Hands lifted him and he didn't fight. People carried him at a run through the thick smoke, making turns until flashing hazard lights appeared ahead, the back of a van opened up and Wren was bundled in.

"Hellion," he whispered, barely audible.

"They have you, Christopher," she answered, her voice coming clearer now. "We did it, Rogers has proof, now just stay alive!"

The van kicked into motion. Proof? He didn't understand. Hands moved across his body now, cutting away his strike suit, pushing intravenous feeds into his arms and pressing bright white gauze to his wounds. He blinked and re-opened his eyes standing over a pit in the desert.

They were all there. Galicia. Chrysogonus. Zachariah. Gabriel. Tomothy. Even little Grace.

"They aren't dead," came the deep voice behind him, one arm wrapped around Wren's shoulders. The Apex. "Merely in waiting."

"They're alive," he answered.

"I know, Sir," came the reply, dragging Wren back to the moment. It was a man he'd seen before, and a name burred into the front of his head. Jimenez? Gently prying Wren's fingers away. "We're stabilizing you, sir, you've lost too much blood, if we don't-"

"If we don't have the faith to follow in their example, then what are we?" asked the Apex, standing now on the fake town's Main Street with little Pequeño 3 at his side, looking out over the one thousand spreading back. "My own children walked in the fire, for you! They are waiting now, for you to join their army!"

The people cheered.

"So many people," someone was muttering, and Wren

blinked, felt the sharp snip and pucker of needles punching through his skin, saw the gray face of a young man sitting with his head in his hands mumbling. Kato?

"He's conscious," somebody said. Wren saw Jimenez above him, and was that Miller? Bombs expert. Blood up to both of their elbows, curved needles in their fingers trailing blue surgical thread.

"Sir, we can't sedate you," Jimenez said, "your system's on the edge. You need to keep calm. Every movement's causing more damage."

More damage. The words echoed without meaning in his head.

"Ready to turn him," Miller barked.

"Turn," Jimenez answered, and abruptly they flipped Wren, throwing him face to face with-

"Every last one," said the Apex.

They were standing amidst the charred corpses of the dead, and the Apex was holding Pequeño 3 by the shoulders, gazing into his eyes. Smoke drifted between them. Pequeño 3 remembered little but the blue oases of his irises, brimming with joy.

"Have you ever seen something so beautiful?"

"Clear!" came the shout, and Wren gasped, chest convulsing as the yellow crash cart paddles pulled back, the shiver of a thousand volts working its way out to his extremities. "He's back."

"Stay with us, Sir," Jimenez shouted, leaning in. "That's an order."

Wren felt himself falling already.

"We're losing him again, prep for another-"

"Shall I tell you a secret?" whispered the Apex in his ear.

Pequeño 3 said nothing.

"There is no world beyond," the Apex said, voice straining with glee. "No holy army, no sacred mission.

They're just dead." He pointed. "That one, and that one, and that one. And do you know why?"

"He's back!" came the shout. Someone was shaking his arm, rubbing at his side. "This wound in his side's the real bleeder. Almost in his armpit, straight into the chest cavity. Looks like she stabbed him clean through, there's blood in his lung, we have to-"

They flipped him onto his other side, probed deeper at his chest, and again he saw gray-faced Kato, this time staring directly at him, wearing the same face as the misshapen victims behind the cage walls of the zoo.

Horror-struck. Wren's lips moved, forming soundless words the man needed to hear. "It's going to be OK."

They didn't register on Kato's face. It wasn't believable. Who was Wren to promise anyone anything…

"Because it feels good," the Apex crowed. "Because it feels good when they die, and what else is there in this shitty world than feeling good?"

He pulled away then, spread his arms and addressed the river of smoking dead stretching away. "Go forth, my army! Serve me well on the other side!"

He laughed. Pequeño 3 couldn't follow it and didn't move his head until the Apex reached down to angle his chin upward.

"Hey," he said, and winked. "Don't look so down in the dumps, son. You and I, we're the good guys here." Pequeño 3 said nothing. The Apex gently dabbed his nose. "Only tell them the truth, little bird. Open their eyes to the wonders we worked."

37

STRANGLEHOLD

Wren opened his eyes.

"He's awake," came a voice that sounded echoey and flat, like shouts heard underwater.

Everything hurt. Bars of light flared when he shifted his head. Memories came back in rags and tatters: floor 74 in flames with half his team down; the zoo, the green cells, the photograph, and then-

Galicia.

His mental checklist stuttered like a scratched record, playing and replaying snippets of his sister's appearance, her voice, the way she'd wielded that knife.

His sister was alive. She had been alive.

The memory brought the pain on harder. Aching in his shoulders. Throbbing in his hands. Galicia's work.

He blinked to clear the grit in his eyes and the face above him resolved; blond hair pulled back tight, bright green eyes, someone he hadn't expected to see at all.

"Rogers?"

His voice was barely a croak.

"In the flesh, Christopher," she replied. He blinked and the space around her took on shape and color: an apartment of

some kind, with the sense of other people in the room, though he couldn't lift his neck to see. To either side hung the plastic tubes of empty intravenous blood and plasma bags.

"I hopped a flight as soon as I could," she said. "Hellion sent me video of your strike. She said you were almost dead."

He tried to take that in. It felt like only minutes ago that he'd been in the zoo and-

"How long?" he asked. "You were in Cincinnati. That means…"

"Four hours, all in. I wanted to wake you sooner, but…" she trailed off, gesturing generally at him. The message was clear.

"I'm in bad shape."

"The worst I've ever seen. We're lucky you're a universal blood recipient, otherwise they'd never have kept you juiced, all the holes you had in you?" She gave a wan smile. "Add that to your prodigious lung capacity and one helluva thick head, it's still a miracle you survived the jump from an exploding skyscraper."

He tried to absorb that, then tried to push himself up but his body didn't respond.

"Why can't I get up?"

"You're restrained," Rogers said. "Chest straps. Also you're on a pretty hefty dose of morphine. Both for your own safety; you were thrashing around, shouting about the Apex, Galicia, the Pyramid."

That checked out. "So administer epinephrine." The word was hard to say. "Unbuckle me. I need to get moving."

She snorted. "You wouldn't last five minutes. Just about all your stuffing came out, Wren, and they barely got it back in. You're more stitches than man right now." She took a moment, as if considering how much to say, before plunging on. "That bitch sister of yours, Galicia? She punctured your shoulders, your hands and your left lung. That's bad. It also seems you took one shot in the back; if that had been a flush impact you'd be dead now. Plate armor, that thick skull and the blessed acute angle saved you. Look forward to pissing blood for a couple weeks." Another pause. "In short, I'm not letting you up just yet. "

Wren restrained a sharp retort. Maybe she was right. "OK. So what can I do?"

"Advise me. Things are going to hell in a handcart here, fast, and I don't know what to do."

"The firestorm?"

"Ongoing," Rogers said. "But pushed off the front pages by the terrorist bomb in a Manhattan skyscraper." She paused a moment to let that sink in. "57 dead so far, and that low number is thanks solely to Hellion sealing the surrounding roads via traffic signals and hacking about a dozen emergency warning speakers to get pedestrians off the streets. Nobody knows about that, though. Right now all the talking heads can talk about is you, Chris, and your 'pathology'. 'He was never a real American', they're saying, 'went extremist out in Afghanistan' and 'hates our way of life', you know how that goes? They're calling this a second 9/11, and with all the genuine footage they've got of you and your team fleeing the scene?" She gave him a look. "It's hard to disagree. If anything, their stranglehold on the news cycle just got tighter."

Wren took a labored breath and felt the left side of his chest catching. He'd hoped the skyscraper raid would provide the proof they'd needed, but...

Gray smoke streamed by the window behind her.

"We're still in Manhattan," he guessed.

"That's right," Rogers said, turning to glance out the window. "Madison 231 hasn't stopped burning yet. They can't put it out, apparently, its inside the steel core. Right now we're at an apartment McKenzie Slade keeps on 40th and 5th

Avenue." She took a breath. " They shut the bridges and tunnels almost instantly. They only let me into the city as I'm the one who caught you last time. I'm expressly tasked with bringing you in. You're on a high wire here, Wren. Lucky your team evacuated before the roadblocks went up, lucky Slade has this place, lucky she let us use it, lucky the smoke covered your escape from ground zero, lucky for lots of things."

Wren didn't feel lucky. He ran the simple calculation in his head, a strike at dawn plus four hours for her flight. "What is it, about eleven in the a.m.?"

"Ten of," Rogers answered. "Can you handle the rest of it?"

He tried for a grunt but didn't have the wind to land it. "It sounds like Keller's pinning the whole thing on us, painting me as the mastermind."

"Got it in one," Rogers said. "He's been out there decrying you since 231 fell. They've produced their own deepfake footage of what happened in the zoo. By their account, it looks like you entered the penthouse, executed the family inside, children included, set your bombs then blew the place up. It's a good deepfake; if I didn't know better, I'd believe it."

He cursed.

Rogers wasn't done. "Now the whole country's turning on you and your Foundation. There's nothing yet linking you to the firestorm, 23 dead women so far, but that can't be far behind." She paused a second. "There's already t-shirts selling out that show with your severed head. There's a playing card 'kill' deck of all the Foundation members, complete with photos, numbers, addresses, selling online right now for $2.31, a tribute to the fallen tower."

Another punch. "And David Keller's out there leading the charge."

Rogers nodded. "He's erecting a rally stage on the

National Mall right now, laying out his trademark red and blue mats. He didn't get the permit, but nobody cares. People are flooding to him, already in excess of ten thousand. Washington's going crazy. Emergency meetings everywhere, on top of the emergency meetings they were already having for the firestorm. Humphreys is incommunicado, so we're cut off there. Congress have been in a special session since before the dawn. It's all..." Rogers trailed off, losing steam. "It's all going to shit."

Wren took a tight breath, snagging his left lung. One hell of a situation report. It all spiraled in his head, merging with the chaos of the zoo. Now more than ever they needed to cut through the lies and break Keller's chokehold on the media.

"You have my bodycam footage of the strike. That's proof. Why don't we have that out there?"

Rogers said nothing and looked uncomfortably off to the side.

"What?"

Another figure appeared to his right; thin, all in black, with cutting eyes and a pursed sliver of lips. McKenzie Slade.

"Because it wasn't enough, Christopher," she said, words dropping like ten-pound bags of sand. "A half-cocked raid on an overbaked horror set, more grotesque than an R-rated movie? The reveal of your sister, shock, she's alive, when no one in the country even knew she existed, let alone cared she was dead?" She fixed him with a hard glare. "It adds up to nothing. Hot air. It's not proof of anything. You grabbed that photograph, but what does that mean? It only ties you closer to the Pyramid!"

Wren struggled to keep up, but couldn't argue with anything she was saying.

"The zoo," he managed. "All those people-"

"Are gone," Slade finished. "Destroyed beyond all recognition in the blast. Your Apex had a plan for this eventuality, and he outplayed you. You want to break through the noise? Turn yourself in!"

She was angry. Maybe that made sense. He'd dragged her into something with enough momentum to crush her underfoot.

"So what will it take?" he asked. "What kind of proof?"

"Something that hits in the gut," Slade said sharply. "Keller's got the people high on hatred and fear, and facts about the family history of the Pyramid aren't going to cut it. Emotion sells, and he's got the dark side cornered. You'd have to go hope and change to stand a chance, but you just don't have the goods." A tight smile. "If you could lift the firestorm's boot heel off people's throats, then maybe they'll be able to listen about 231 Madison. Win them there, then maybe you can get into the weeds about your sister and the zoos and the links to Keller." She waved a hand dismissively. "But you don't have any of that. You don't know what the link is. You can't stop these women killing themselves. Hell, you didn't even know your own sister was alive!"

She panted a little. Wren felt he'd been punched in the face again. She was right.

Even now he was still living in the false reality the Apex had built. He'd never once considered that Galicia might be alive. That any of them might be, because if Galicia was alive, what did that mean about the rest of the Pequeños? About the Apex? About-

Something shook loose in Wren's head. He was back in the black-tiled corridor again, Galicia bleeding out on the floor, looking at the group photograph of the Pyramid with all the Pequeños lined up in a row, and-

"Where's the photograph?"

Rogers plucked it off a nearby table. "Here. There's no help in it, though. Hellion and B4cksl4cker have run it through a dozen facial analyses already."

Wren squinted but couldn't pick out the details clearly. "Can you at least unstrap my hands?"

"Are you done yelling and thrashing?"

He glared back at her. "Let's find out."

She made a face and worked the Velcro strap on his left wrist. His arm came free and he lifted it; the whole hand was wrapped up like a baseball glove. He managed to pincer the crumpled photo and held it close to his face.

Apex at the center. Seven Pequeños on the right at the front, standing in order of age. There was Galicia. The resemblance was apparent, from sixteen to middle age she hadn't changed that much. And standing next to her…

His mouth went dry. His pulse rocketed. His gaze flickered between Slade and Rogers. Dark hair, light hair. Wide cheekbones, oval face. Everything else could change, but you couldn't fake the eyes.

He couldn't believe it. He had to.

He held out the photograph, thumb clamped tight under a sullen teenaged boy with fierce blue eyes. "Who do you see here?"

"Some punk cultist," Rogers said. "He looks pissed off."

"He always was. I think he still is. His name's Chrysogonus. He's my older brother, and I always thought he died with the others in the pit, but now I see I was wrong."

"So what?" taunted Slade. "I already said who cares about the Pyramid family history?"

Wren met her gaze undaunted. "This is American history. You're looking at President-elect David Keller."

38

GASLIGHT

A stunned silence fell. Slade and Rogers looked at each other then back at Wren.

"You're sure?" Rogers asked.

"One hundred percent. I'd recognize those eyes anywhere. David Keller is my dead brother Chrysogonus."

Rogers gazed at him, maybe weighing his opinion against Hellion and B4cksl4cker's facial analysis algorithms, then turned again to Slade. "Is that good enough to break through?"

Slade's thin lips pursed to the side. "If it's true? Not on its own. But if you can also stop the firestorm?" She chewed on it. "Maybe. One thing everyone knows about David Keller, he was adopted. There are no hard records on his early childhood, beyond his US birth certificate. Linking him to the Pyramid like this'll look like a smear, but it'll play to the conspiracy folks and the Wren supporters, plus your hacker team could make it stick on social media. If…"

Wren stopped listening.

Everything was playing out before him now like pieces on a chessboard, a grand multi-decade gambit slotting into place and bringing the country to the brink of checkmate.

Everything Jamal Jalim had said. The zoo. Chrysogonus. Keller. A pit full of dead brothers and sisters who had never really died. Galicia had said it herself; their deaths had served as leverage to push the rest of the Pyramid over the edge.

His breathing grew shallow.

It was the same trick the Apex was pulling right now on these women, updated for a new age and a new technology. He just needed to figure out how. If he could expedite their belief via some perceived, remote sacrifice, then maybe he could...

"I think we're close to breaking the firestorm," Rogers said.

Wren looked up, then remembered that Hellion had said Rogers had proof. "How? What did you find?"

Rogers offered a small smile. "It's good, Chris. It's part of why I woke you up."

"What is it?"

"You remember John Day, Rachel Day's husband? You remember he said he saw her using a 'ghost' phone that night in their bedroom, when she was looking at flames on, in their bedroom."

"Of course," Wren said. "Wait, you found it?"

Her smile spread. "I found it; in her bag at the Mall of America. It was badly charred, but data techs have managed to scrape some information off it. It's given us some ham radio frequencies to search for, plus one video data file, possibly the very one John Day was talking about on that night. Hellion and B4cksl4cker helped decrypt it. It's a doozy."

Wren stared at her. This could be the breakthrough they'd been waiting for. "Let's see it."

Rogers raised a tablet and tapped to play.

The screen filled with flames. Through them, Wren picked out what looked to be a bedroom. There was a double bed in the center of the frame, ivy-green wallpaper in back, twin side tables with lamps, and upon the bed kneeled a man on fire.

Wren flinched.

"Audio," Rogers said, and tapped the screen. The volume unmuted and screams played through the speakers. The man thrashed on the sheets and burned alive, his skin blackening, his face blurring as it lost all definition. Around him the bed burned, and the side tables and the wall. It looked at once totally fake and entirely real; the colors too saturated, the movements too choreographed, but utterly fluid and bloodcurdling.

The video ended when the man collapsed.

"Play it back," Wren said.

Rogers ran it back to the start. It began with flames, but at this point the figure hadn't blurred down to nothing. "Pause it."

Rogers paused it. Wren peered closer. The figure in the center was a man in his mid-forties, hairline receding; a figure Wren recognized. The breath stopped in his throat.

"That's John Day," he said.

"Exactly what I thought," Rogers said.

Wren didn't know what to think and looked up at her. "You think this is what Rachel was looking at, that night? He obviously didn't burn, so the Apex deepfaked her husband's face onto footage of someone burning alive?"

"If it's a deepfake, a computer construction alone, Hellion and B4cksl4cker say it's like nothing else they've seen. Really incredible work."

Wren stared into the flames. So this is what Rachel Day had seen. It felt like the key to her radicalization, but Wren wasn't sure how. A body on a bed. A figure burning alive. A personalized message relayed through a personalized screen.

Then it hit.

"I know how he's making them burn," he said.

Both women turned to face him.

Wren took a breath and felt the ache in his sides as the pieces slammed into position like falling rubble. "This whole thing is a giant gaslight operation."

"It's what?" Rogers asked.

"Gaslighting," Wren said. "You know what that means? Making someone believe reality's not real. But on an industrial scale, with unprecedented real-time technology. Convincing these women every person they love is secretly suffering the worst pain imaginable. That's what this video showed to Rachel Day, right? Her husband dying the worst death possible. Add to that the Apex's core ideology; that everyone's souls are literally in hell, they need to be saved, and there's only one way to do it? That'd make her kill herself to do it."

Slade stared. "To do what?"

"To go to hell first and set her husband free."

There was a brief silence, broken by Rogers. "Sounds like the usual Pyramid BS. So OK, let's say you're right. He shows videos like this to all the women, makes them believe their loved ones are not sleeping peacefully, their souls are actually roasting endlessly. Maybe that would make them burn themselves. But how would he do it? Hellion said this imagery is way beyond deepfake technology. It's perfect."

Wren didn't know how to explain it; he didn't even know if it was possible. "Is Hellion on the line?"

"I am monitoring," came Hellion's laconic accent from Rogers' phone.

Rogers held the phone up as Wren aligned the pieces of his theory like feather flights along an arrow's shaft. It linked the zoo to the firestorm and beyond.

"The green cells in the zoo, Hellion. Picture this. If I

wanted to transpose imagery from one setting to another, like special effects in a movie, how would I do it?"

"Transposition of imagery?" Hellion asked, playing along. "Hmm, yes, this is standard process. Film this imagery on uniform background color, one that is bright and unusual, and ensure no actor wears this color. Software then cuts out this background color, overlays the captured images on top of a different background, and-"

"An unusual color," Wren interrupted. "Like bright green?"

There was silence for a second. Wren felt pennies dropping all around him.

"Yes," Hellion confirmed. "Green screen is commonly used. You are suggesting the green cells in horror skyscraper were-"

"Were individual film studios," Wren sped on, his thick tongue barely keeping up with his mind. "Transposing footage of pain. So imagine that every time Rachel Day pointed her 'ghost' phone at someone she loved, not just John Day but anyone, maybe her kids, her mother, whoever, it automatically overlaid a person suffering genuine torture in one of the zoo's green cells." He thought back to his brief time in the zoo. "There was a ruined bed in the cell I saw. Scorched, bloody, matted. So when Rachel points her phone, they grab a victim and set to work, burning them, lashing them, stabbing them, whatever it takes, then they cut out the green and overlay the image on top of reality, and the only part they swap out is the face. Is that possible, Hellion?"

"Yes, certainly."

Wren raced on. "It makes Rachel Day's ghost phone into some kind of," he snatched a tight breath, searching for the right word, "window into hell. A nightmarish version of reality, of her husband screaming in agony and written over with flames."

Rogers' eyes narrowed. "Pretty deep, Wren."

"It even explains the barber shop moment," Wren sped on, thinking back to Rogers' live reenactments. "When Day pointed her ghost phone at the barber shop window, she wasn't filming the interior; she was looking through the hell window at her own reflection. What she saw was her own body in flames, screaming. That's what made her sick and terrified."

Nobody said anything. After a moment, Rogers cursed.

"Is that even possible, Hellion?" she asked. "In real time?"

"Certainly it is possible," Hellion answered. "I am thinking. For best realism, the torturer should place his camera on a, what is the word, B4cksl4cker? Automatic rotating device?"

"Gimbal," he said.

"Yes, gimbal! Synchronized to this ghost phone or hell window. So, as Rachel Day is moving her 'window', changing angle, height, position, then gimbal-mount camera in zoo will shift and track perfectly. This will add to realism. It will appear seamless."

Slade held up a hand. "Hang on. This is a huge jump. We don't even know how the Apex, your father, got these phones into the hands of these women. We don't know why they'd believe anything they see through them. And what's even more confounding, even if everything you're saying is possible, why would the Apex go to all this trouble with the zoo and green screens and film crews and torturers, when they could just use full deepfakes?"

"Excellent question," Hellion said. "Yes. But this is computer processing issue, McKenzie Slade. True deepfake video requires many steps of facial rendering, for layering shadows, light, texture. It takes much time, and to produce one in real time? It will look like bad video game. You will not accept it is real."

"I don't accept it now," Slade said, teeth gritted. "It's all too complicated. Imagine the real husband moves the wrong way at the wrong moment, throws his arm up maybe, the illusion cracks!"

"There need be no crack," Hellion countered. "It is simple matter to force a torture victim's arm up. Magic figures wearing green suits step in, lift the arm, it goes up. They are invisible. Delay of one second perhaps."

Slade snorted. "But these operators won't even be able to see what's happening. How will they sync up? You're talking about-"

"McKenzie Slade," Hellion said with finality. "This is simple matter. Weather people on television have been doing this for many years. How do they see rain and wind on display behind them? Do you think perhaps they feel a little cold on their lower cheeks when it blows?"

That shut everyone up.

"It does leave questions, though," Rogers allowed. "Say we accept that's all possible, even likely. How did the Apex get the phone into Rachel Day's hand? How did he make her believe what she saw on it? I've dug into her life like a committed stalker, accounted for near every minute she had alone, and I don't see him anywhere. Not even a shadow."

"Who cares right now?" Wren answered. "Maybe he hired actors, framed some complicated tableaux, faked up a whole reality for her to wander into and made her believe reality wasn't real? Or maybe she just found the phone on the sidewalk and radicalized herself? Wouldn't you, if it started showing you everyone you loved burning?" He took a sharp breath. "The fact remains, they have the phones, and we need to block whatever signal's feeding out to them." Wren took a breath, taking another leap forward. "I saw maybe eight cells in Madison, but if we're really looking at a firestorm of a thousand women, he'd need more to serve the capacity. That means more zoos, more victims, more green cells on standby at all times. If there are more zoos, we have to find them and shut them down immediately. Rogers, you said we have the ham radio frequency, can you spin up-"

"Christopher!"

It was McKenzie Slade, a sudden shout, and Wren looked over to her. She was holding her phone up for him to see, her face draining white.

He focused on the screen. A news site. There was a photo and a bold headline. The photo showed a man in a suit being led out of the White House grounds, a black bag over his head. He read the text.

CIA DIRECTOR GERALD HUMPHREYS ARRESTED FOR TREASON

39

LIES

There was another slack-jawed silence. Wren felt like he was trapped in the end game gambit of some long-choreographed drama.

"They must've linked him to the SWAT team you just used," Rogers said rapidly, working her phone hard with her thumbs. "We got them on his orders, though we thought we'd buried it through enough layers of bureaucracy that it'd take longer to track back. That means they can link him to me, maybe to Slade, to the exfiltration vehicle, to you." She looked at the windows. "To this place."

Slade frowned. Maybe the first time Wren had seen her disdain break since Redhook. "This apartment is owned by multiple shell companies; they might buy us some time, but they won't hold up for long against the State Department."

The rest went unspoken. Doors blown in. Bullets fired before questions were asked. America's number one terrorist executed in his Manhattan lair.

Wren dropped the photograph and reached over to release the Velcro cuff on his right wrist. Rogers made feeble noises to slow him but didn't get in the way. His whole body bloomed with fresh pains as he twisted. Tightness in his shoulders, agony down his back, flashing lights across his vision. The cuff came off.

"Christopher," Rogers said.

"We have to move," he answered, leaning forward to free his ankles, but was stopped cold as the stitches under his left arm yanked like a row of fishhooks.

"Let me," Rogers said, and stripped the ankle cuffs. Wren swayed his legs out and let Rogers help him to a sitting position, and for the first time saw the space around him properly.

It wasn't furnished like an apartment, as he'd presumed. Instead it was filled with large cardboard boxes. It took him a second to put the pieces together, then he turned to Slade.

"Contraband?"

She stared back at him, contemptuous again now. "How did you think I kept multiple apartments in Manhattan on a consulting detective's salary?"

Truth was, he'd never thought about it. It didn't matter and he didn't care. Drug gangs were chaff in the wind next to this.

"Mafia," he guessed, building out a fuller picture. "Hence your connection with the foreman." She said nothing. "I'm guessing you're their point person for import/export? That means you've got a hook-up at the ports too."

Slade said nothing. Wren shuffled off the edge of the bed and set his feet on the floor. His legs shuddered, but there was no good waiting any longer. Rogers tucked herself under his arm and helped him to stand. He tried to take his own weight but sagged onto her; a good thing she was a weightlifter. She flexed and pushed him back to standing.

"That's how you knew where the kids were in the containers back in Redhook," Wren guessed. "You told me it was my fault we lost the middlemen dons, that we almost lost the kids until some immigrant stevedore came through for you, but it wasn't my fault at all, was it?"

Slade's stare became black ice. "You don't know me, Christopher Wren."

That said it all. Another false reality fell like scales from his eyes; gaslighting he'd swallowed for so long. "I know enough, McKenzie. Those guys I killed, they were mafia, but not as high up as you said. I'm guessing you made a deal with the dons: corner me into killing a couple of low level guys, and they'd give up the kids in exchange for their own skins? In return you got the reputation as a genius consultant detective, plus a pay-off, and you use that new reputation to grease the wheels on future drug deals."

Her lips pursed tight. "Don't even think about judging me."

He aimed for a snort, maybe got halfway there before his lung tightened up. For ten years she'd been branding him as reckless when she'd really just set him up. If he had the wind, he'd laugh. "Yeah. So here's what happens next, McKenzie. You're going to tap every mob contact you've got and you're going to get us out of New York right now."

His legs firmed up a little under him.

"That's not possible," Slade countered. "Everything's locked down, there isn't-"

"There is," Wren insisted. He stumbled with Rogers around the edge of the makeshift gurney, and saw that it was just blood-soaked boxes padded by plastic packets filled with white powder. Around the base of the boxes lay a halo of cast off gauze still bright with arterial blood. Three of his SWAT team members stood by the walls: Jimenez and Miller watching him; Kato staring out the window.

He refocused on Slade. "Now, McKenzie. Either you burn all your contacts to get us out, or we wait for Keller's people to storm in bullet first, bring your drug empire crashing down, make an orphan of your daughter and a pincushion out of me." He sucked in a breath. "So what's it going to be?"

Her jaw worked hard under tight skin. "I'll make some calls."

"Make them fast. I've got a few I need to make too." He felt a sharp chill and looked down, noticing that a piece of gauze had dropped away from his stomach, leaving him naked. He focused on Rogers. "I'll need a phone. First though, can we get me some pants?"

40

GIRL POWER

P ants came first, a paint-splattered designer pair of skinny jeans Jimenez had already picked up from a nearby boutique, then someone slotted an earpiece into his ear. While Rogers worked to get him dressed and Slade made angry calls in the background, Wren brought Hellion and B4cksl4cker onto a private line.

"I did not say this yet, but we are glad you are alive, Christopher," Hellion said in his ear. "I have many excellent jokes about falling buildings, and-"

"We need to stop the next burning and break the firestorm," Wren interrupted, no interest in jokes. "So tell me about the ghost phones. You were co-opting civilian infrastructure to nail down some radio frequencies, to pinpoint locations. Did you find anything?"

"We have co-opted several ham radio transmitter/receiver arrays," Hellion answered, switching tracks easily. "This gives us partial coverage of the country. The signal of a radio receiver is very faint, but there are oscillations. If we have the frequency, we believe we can begin to triangulate every woman who is using one of these ghost phones."

"Excellent," Wren said, then looked down to Rogers, who

was struggling to push his left foot through the tight cuff of the skinny jeans. He tried to help but was no use at all, his muscles feeling like linguini. "So we need the frequency. Have any other witnesses recollected seeing these phones?"

"Some," Rogers allowed, looking up as she ruffled the pants up his calf. "We've had a few hits in other locations, one in Idaho, a close friend saw the woman there looking at a strange phone a few days before she burned." She tugged the jeans over his ankle with a snap, causing Wren to wince. "A couple others mentioned red screens like John Day saw." She was absorbed for a moment in pulling the pants up over his knee, and shot a wicked glance to Jimenez. "Why are these pants so damn tight?"

Jimenez shrugged. "It's the fashion."

"Dumb fashion," Rogers muttered to herself. "Or your legs are too fat."

Wren ignored the slight. "Hellion, can you use any of those instances to home in on a frequency?"

"Working," Hellion answered. "B4cksl4cker, we will need your botnet ready to crunch several quadrillion data points on these sightings. Is this possible, or is it too tight, like Christopher's pants?"

"Standing by," B4cksl4cker said. "Like very stiff pair of pants."

Wren didn't acknowledge any of that. "Good. Get it done."

Rogers abruptly pulled the jeans all the way up hard, slamming into his crotch, and Wren sucked in another sharp breath.

Hellion's keys flew. Wren went to button the pants up but couldn't achieve a thing with his bandage-gloved hands, so Rogers did that for him too.

"They're coming now!" Slade said abruptly, dropping a phone from her ear, eyes wide. "It seems Keller cut through my protections like soft cheese. A SWAT team will be here in minutes, acting on shoot-to-kill orders from DOJ, and that's the last warning we'll get. I've got a contact coming in for you, Wren, standard mule vehicle, but it's going to be difficult. You need to get to street level right now."

Wren took a step forward without thinking, and his leg gave out. Rogers just barely caught him and hoisted him back up.

"Careful, Christopher," she cautioned, hooking a hard arm around his chest. "We go together. We're in this together."

His head spun and he felt suddenly dizzy and breathless. "Lead the way," he wheezed.

"You got that right," Rogers said, and took a step.

"You should go faster," came Hellion's voice.

"His pants are very tight," B4cksl4cker offered.

"Shut up," said Rogers, voice tightening as she took the strain of Wren's weight.

"And us?" came a voice from the side. Jimenez.

"Can your transport accommodate them, McKenzie?" Rogers asked.

"No."

They reached the door.

"Then run," Rogers said. "If they catch you, they will kill you. I'm sorry. Thank you for what you've done. If we can fix this, we'll fix things for you too. If we can't…"

She left that hanging as they passed out into the corridor, Wren's feet carrying barely a quarter of his weight. Rogers punched the elevator button.

"They're dead whatever happens now," Slade said, following on behind. "I'm dead. I should never have-"

"Then you better hope we bring Keller down," Rogers countered, and turned to look into her eyes. "You lying bitch."

Slade's eyes flared. "I didn't-"

"You lied about Wren," Rogers said, deadly cold now. "I

grant you that he can be an idiot and he's definitely reckless, but he'd never put children in danger the way you accused him of. That much I know." Wren tried to say something but everything was blurring silver now, and he couldn't quite figure out how to open his mouth. "You rode him to money and then cast him aside when you couldn't face what you'd done," Rogers piled on. "Now just pray your mob contacts come through. If they don't, you better believe I'm coming right back up here for you."

The elevator chimed, the doors spread open, and Slade's face rinsed white as milk.

"You wouldn't-"

"You didn't deserve him as a partner," Rogers said, then stepped into the elevator and the door closed.

Wren hung off her side, barely holding his head up off his chest, gasping.

"The hell is the matter with you?" Rogers demanded as the carriage started down.

He was laughing, or coming close, but he didn't want to say as much. "That was badass," he managed. "My knight in-
"

"Shove your knight," Rogers spat. "That was me being nice. The woman's a bitch and I told her so." A moment passed. "I've been working on my bad cop."

He laughed some more. The elevator passed the tenth floor.

"Christopher," came Hellion's voice, "I know this is bad time, but what shall we do about Chrysogonus/Keller connection?"

It was right on the tip of his tongue but he couldn't get it to come out.

"Sync them up," Rogers said in his place. "Facial analysis to the photograph. Prep a million memes, videos, gifs, whatever you can to spread the word about who Keller really is and what he's done. The zoo, the cells, the ghost phones, all his bag of tricks. The instant we break the firestorm, we want this bastard tied to that bastard and both strung up on a viral pike. You feel me?"

Wren gasped more laughter.

"I like this new Agent Sally very much," Hellion said. "Girl power."

"Shut it," snapped Rogers, and the elevator hit ground floor. The car doors slid open. Standing in front of them was a cop with his gun raised.

41

STREET LEVEL

Not SWAT. An NYPD beat cop, Wren figured, mid-twenties. He'd probably heard the warning go out, most likely was cautioned to stay away but had come in regardless looking to make a name for himself.

"Hands up," the guy said.

"So shoot," Rogers said, cool as a Western gunslinger and started walking.

"I'm serious," the cop barked.

"Son, I don't care if you're standing on your head," Rogers answered. "Shoot if you have to or get out of the way. We've got a country to save."

He stared but made no move to block their progress across the foyer. It was cheaper-looking than 231 Madison, with ceramic tile instead of marble, stainless steel on the walls instead of verdigris copper. A guy behind reception stared wide-eyed, phone in his hand.

"Is it true, what they're saying about him?" the cop called after them. "That he's a terrorist? He blew up that building?"

"He was in the building when it blew up," Rogers answered over her shoulder, already halfway toward the doors. "They tried to kill him and they failed."

Through the doors they emerged onto the street, where people stood in pockets with their phones up, filming something to the left. Wren craned his neck over Rogers' shoulder and saw the pillar of smoke rising from midtown Manhattan in bulbous gulps. 231 Madison, still burning.

"Where's our pickup?" Rogers asked.

Vehicles deadlocked the four-lane avenue, many with their drivers missing. There was no way out except on foot. Overhead helicopters buzzed. A little engine revved closer and Rogers turned, swinging Wren with her; there was a moped coming up on the sidewalk, looked like a pizza delivery guy.

He pulled up in front of them, hit the brake and dismounted then held the key out to Rogers. "Get to Coney Island," he said, voice muffled through his helmet. "They'll be waiting."

He walked off. Rogers was left staring after him, at the moped.

"OK," she said, and flung one leg over the seat.

"Shotgun," Wren managed.

Rogers laughed. "You better hold on tight."

"I'll try."

She settled and he slotted in behind her, bandaged hands across her belly, then Rogers gunned the moped and peeled out straight south on the sidewalk, forcing pedestrians into doorways and flattened against windows.

Wren swayed against her back, only half-conscious of the world whipping by as the jolts and jerks pushed him into a state of agony and confusion.

"Hang on!" Rogers cautioned as they swerved around the bumper of a police car. In their wake the cops scrambled out and leveled their pistols. Gunfire rang out behind them.

"Christopher, Agent Sally," came B4cksl4cker's bass voice as they whistled through crowds at thirty miles an hour, "this is not best time, but I am afraid your country is beginning a coup."

"What?" Wren asked.

"Yes, is happening now," B4cksl4cker said. "I know you are on pizza bike. Here, I will read these headlines. Breaking news. President impeached and removed from office."

"Not possible," Rogers answered. "That's gotta be fake."

"Not fake," B4cksl4cker said. "Verified. I will read." He took a breath, and Rogers gunned the moped up to fifty down an avenue of gridlocked cars. "At 11:00am EST an impeachment vote was called in a rare sitting of both Houses of Congress. The vote carried near unanimously to remove not only the President, but in a rare and stunning rebuke, the President's entire administration."

Wren couldn't believe what he was hearing, but B4cksl4cker just kept on going.

"This is an unprecedented development. Early reports indicate Congress have been in discussions since midnight on how best to respond to the 'firestorm' currently sweeping the country.

"Speculation suggests the President's direct connection to ousted CIA Director Gerald Humphreys and wildcard agent-turned-terrorist Christopher Wren led to this wide-ranging Presidential impeachment.

"This story is breaking."

Wren reeled. If anything, it helped push down the fog in his head.

"Whole administration impeached?" Rogers shouted. "Can they even do that?"

"Looks like they just have," Wren answered.

"There is footage now," came B4cksl4cker's voice. "It is your Speaker of the House. Here, I will play audio."

Wren's earpiece briefly crackled, then there was the

recognizable drawl of the Speaker's voice, confirming everything.

"Tell me this is a deepfake," Wren muttered. "B4cksl4cker. Tell me this is more gaslighting."

"I have eyes-on verification," came his Armenian bass. "Your President has been deposed. Your Secret Service agents are already removing her and her family from White House."

The Speaker of the House kept talking, and Wren listened rapt as Rogers raced through a New York that was suddenly quiet. No horns, no people pushing back, everyone looking at their phones or listening to the radio, only the sound of police helicopters and sirens closing in.

"There can be no doubt that our President was complicit in the felling of Madison 231," the Speaker said. "Investigations are commencing immediately, though what matters most in this moment is the question of succession."

Wren saw it coming before she could say it.

"To ensure clear leadership, Congress has determined that the inauguration of President David Keller be brought forward and held in two hours and thirty-seven minutes time, on the National Mall at 2 p.m. this afternoon." She paused, and Rogers shot across a Fifth Street intersection that was filled with cars but eerily silent, every face lit by the light from their phones.

"I ask that the American people remain calm in this troubled time, and have faith in the spirit, if not the letter, of our Founders' intentions. We have a President-elect. We will have a new President this day. Thank you."

Journalists cried out questions. The Speaker did not answer them.

Wren didn't know what to say. Two hours and forty-seven minutes? The gameboard had just shifted completely.

"We did this," Rogers shouted, saying exactly what he was thinking. Wren glimpsed the Hudson Bay ahead and caught flashes of the Statue of Liberty, her back turned on Manhattan. "This is our fault."

Less than three hours. It couldn't be enough. It squeezed enough adrenaline into his body to push back the fog.

"Get us a charter jet to Washington," Wren called into the wind, putting just enough gas behind the words to be heard.

"Done," said B4cksl4cker. "I will arrange private jets at every nearby airport. Now reach one of them!"

Coney Island opened before them. The esplanade, the sea front, the tourist throngs standing motionless in front of coffee shops, frozen in the moment. Up ahead a speedboat raced across the Bay, firing up a comet trail of white breakers, the only vehicle moving on all the water.

"I think that's for us," Wren said.

42

SPEEDBOAT

The speedboat raced up, tracked by helicopters blaring out warnings over bullhorns. Wren and Rogers stood under the canvas cover of Pier 11, him hanging from her side, slapped by cold foam off the wind-tossed East River, shadowed now by twin mafioso in dark suits and shades like CIA bagmen.

The speedboat swirled up to thud broadside against the pier. A beautiful Cigarette AMG Electric Drive, sleek as a .22 Long Rifle caliber shell, fast enough to give a helicopter a run for its money.

Wren leaned forward and Rogers took a step toward it, but one of the mafioso stepped up and put a hand on his chest.

"Not for you," the guy said. As tall as Wren and broader still, he made for an impassable obstacle.

Wren tried for anger but came up empty, not nearly enough to bull through whatever this was. Maybe a last moment exploitation from Slade? If she'd sold them out then it was over already.

"What do you mean?" Rogers asked tightly, and Wren felt her coiling toward action.

"Wait one moment," the guy said, as behind him two figures moved. It took Wren a second to register what he was seeing. One was a big guy hunched over, dressed in the same skinny jeans and rumpled jean jacket Wren wore, with a sturdy blonde holding him up. At first he thought he was seeing double, then it registered.

"Decoys," he muttered.

The mafioso stood motionless as the would-be Wren and Rogers boarded the speedboat, until there was a strange bubbling sound.

"Now," the guy said, and pointed. Wren and Rogers went as directed to a spot directly in front of the Cigarette's trocar-sharp prow, where something like the flat lead-bottomed hull of a fifteen-footer yacht was rising up from underwater, breaking through the choppy waves. Wren stared, trying to figure out what this was. A sunken ship floating to the surface? A hidden escalator into some underwater hell?

Then there was a metallic clinking sound, a hatch in the top of the flat hull opened up and a face appeared within, one hand beckoning.

Wren laughed.

"Narco-submarine," he muttered.

"What the hell?" Rogers countered.

He'd come across them once or twice before, working on logistics with the Qotl cartel to smuggle heroin and cocaine up through the Gulf of Mexico to make landfall in New Orleans. Often powerless and rudderless, they were basically airtight shipping containers sunk some thirty feet underwater, tugged into port by innocent-looking fishing vessels and capable of carrying some eight tons of illegal narcotics.

"It's a drug sub," Wren said. "Invisible from the air. Let's not keep them waiting."

Rogers gave him a look then moved to the edge, where a ladder awaited. With the big guy's help they got Wren down and ushered him through the hatch into the hull of the sub. It was dark but for a halogen light up by the prow, a raw iron ceiling barely four foot high and half filled with stacked drug packets.

The guy inside the sub smiled and nodded at them like an amiable old Geppetto. "That's right, lie down," he said, with a faint Italian burr beneath his Brooklyn accent. "There are no seat belts but we won't be going so fast."

Wren grunted and lay down. His specialty right about now, though it only took seconds for the cold, hard metal of the hull to start his battered back crying out. Rogers lay down next to him.

"They could sink us without a moment's thought," she said quietly. "Game over, America."

Wren was feeling curiously light-headed and found this comment hilarious.

"I don't know what you're chuckling about," Rogers muttered.

The smiley old guy pulled the hatch shut and rotated the locking wheel, closing off their view of Pier 11's canvas roofing,

"Won't be a jiffy," he said, looking pleasedto have company. "I don't often ferry civilian passengers."

Wren couldn't stop himself from laughing. The old man beamed, seeming to enjoy the irony, and bustled to the front of sub where he sat down at the controls and called, "Hold on!"

The sub's engine fired. It sounded like a dishwasher revving up to spin, but powerful enough to glide the sub gently into motion.

"Hold on tight!" Wren cautioned, as the sub pulled away at what could only be a stately two or three knots.

Rogers ignored him, and soon enough the humor bled

from the situation. Wren's teeth chattered as the chill of the East River set in, soon becoming whole body shudders.

"Here," Rogers said, and pulled off her jacket, which she laid over Wren. He switched his gaze to her, lying on her side in the low space and looking down at him with something like concern, maybe even affection.

He took a breath and steadied himself. "We need a backup plan."

"Completely agreed. So what is it?"

He thought for a moment, but there was really no good answer. "Something ugly."

Rogers' face creased, then paled as she realized what he was suggesting. "No."

"Yes," Wren insisted, figuring the logistics as he went along. "We'll need a team, well-armed on the National Mall. We're going to assassinate the President."

43

DEHAVILLAND

An hour later Wren sat strapped into a faux leather seat in the shaking fuselage of a DeHavilland Turbo Beaver Seaplane, trying to push through the pain of the propeller's vibrations as they shot up his spine.

"There is no way we can traffik you through an airport," Hellion had said in his ear, as soon as the drug-sub came up in the Redhook Channel just past Governors Island in the Upper Bay. "This sea plane will be faithful steed."

He'd been in no position to argue. Rogers had helped him out of the sub and into the DeHavilland, floating out in the middle of nowhere. It was a narrow cabin with two rows of seats, far from the luxury of his Cessna C4, with no air steward up front to brew him an Americano.

"Will it get us there in time?" he'd asked.

"Yes," B4cksl4cker said. "Top speed 150 miles per hour. She is beautiful creature. You will arrive with one hour to spare."

Wren had grunted. An hour to land, transfer, get into position.

At least they'd made progress hunting the zoos.

Thirty minutes into the flight, swinging out over the coast to avoid breaking too many airspace zoning codes, Hellion told him about the zoo they'd tracked to a Des Moines skyscraper, run by an aged-up version of his brother Zachariah-Of-The-Marshes, and another in Orlando within sight of Disneyland, run by a similarly altered version of Gabriel-In-Extremis.

Looking at a map on a tablet held by Rogers, Wren felt the chess board beginning to resolve.

"How did you find them?"

"Frequency uncovered from Sally Rogers' ghost phone. It is shortwave amplitude modulation, ranging 157 to 158 kilohertz. This frequency can reach long distance as skywave, bounced off ionosphere. It can go anywhere, Christopher. These two locations are broadcasting."

Wren grunted and looked at the pictures of his two brothers. Caught in reflections for CCTV, seen from above. Their whole lives stretched out behind them, reaching directly to a point in the desert where little Pequeño 3 thought they'd all died.

Zachariah had always been aloof. He looked it now, wearing wireframe spectacles, a trim silver goatee beard, slim and waistcoated in the latest fashion. Gabriel had run thick, becoming a shaggy bear of a man. He'd always shared his rations with Wren and chucked him under the chin when he felt down. His brothers, become monstrous.

"And where is that frequency being picked up?" he asked, bundling a welter of emotions away.

"This is harder. Hellion and I have stolen access to more receivers, such as radio telescopes, radar facilities and national defense listening posts to build a picture. It is now emerging. I think our meme assault is forcing doubt."

Wren blinked. "What meme assault?"

"Oh yes," B4cksl4cker said cheerfully. "I forgot, you were

in water. Much of your day has been spent in water or in mud, has it not?"

"B4cksl4cker!"

"Sorry, Christopher. Hellion's jokes are bad influence on me. Hellion and I decided to start breaking firestorm now. Why not, yes? Sow doubt, seed uncertainty. We have bankrolled one Ukrainian virality factory, and so far they have released three hundred memes, just as you suggested. These are funny pictures, doctored video, all revealing some or many aspects of David Keller's past, his father's vision, purpose of zoos, green cells, red fire ghost phones. There is so much material! We could manufacture amusing gifs like this for months!"

Wren put one bandage-gloved hand to his head. Amusing gifs? They'd just completely undercut him. He'd wanted to reveal all that at once. Power the revelation with the assassination of David Keller. Now Hellion and B4cksl4cker had taken the impact of that announcement off the table.

New players on the chess board.

"What is the matter?" B4cksl4cker asked.

Wren took a breath, trying to get perspective. Maybe this could be spun positively. Maybe this was even better, preparing the ground for what was to come. They were the Internet experts, after all.

"You say it's having an effect?"

"Yes! In very many cases we have gone viral. There are people wanting to believe you, Christopher. In your Foundation. Many who do not like Keller. Genuine footage of your zoo assault is trending. Pickup on shortwave spectrum is rising too, and we take this to be the Apex's women across your country, activating their ghost phones to seek reassurance. The zoos must currently be working at capacity to feed them visions of torture."

That was something. "And you're tracking these pickups, correct? Any way to know who's next?"

A beat passed. "This is difficult, but we believe there is one way. We are putting drones over these women who are tuning in, notifying Foundation affiliates nearby, and…"

Wren almost missed it. "Foundation affiliates?"

"Ah yes," said B4cksl4cker, followed by an uncomfortable pause. "Affiliates." Wren waited for him to say more, but he didn't.

"What do you mean, affiliates?"

"This is Theodore Smithely III's latest Foundation initiative," B4cksl4cker said weakly. "I actually am not supposed to tell you this."

If Wren's hand hadn't already been to his head, he would have put it there. More new players? "Not supposed to tell me what?"

"Really it is just one large mailing list right now," B4cksl4cker said, wheedling slightly. "Single list of all those interested in joining your Foundation."

"A list of affiliates, what does that even mean? You don't just 'join' the Foundation like it's some fan club, B4cksl4cker!" The silence deepened. Wren didn't like it and gravitated to the question that mattered most. "How big is this list?"

"It is modest size, Christopher. Very small."

"How small?"

"We have two hundred thousand on our most engaged list," B4cksl4cker gulped out. "With several million warm leads."

For a moment Wren just stared out of the window. The gray Atlantic lay frozen below like gray poupon mustard, carved into intricate ruffles. He felt blindsided, the chess board flipping again. He leaned into it angry.

"How long has this been going on?"

"Some time," said B4cksl4cker.

"Some time? And you've got two hundred thousand 'engaged', whatever that means? Several million? Last I heard, Foundation expansion was set to be slow and steady. At no stage did I approve expanding that to millions!"

"Technically, your approval was not needed," Hellion joined in sharply. "You are figurehead, Christopher, not CEO. You are driving and drinking every night in motels, yes, feeling sorry for self? This is not the action of CEO."

Blindsided again. Not wrong, though.

"My drinking aside, it's an unacceptable risk," he said, settling on the moral high road. "When I formed the Foundation, it was not as some kind of commercial outreach movement! You're talking about leads like this is a marketing effort, and-"

"It is marketing effort," Hellion interrupted firmly. "Everything we do is marketing now, Christopher. Memes are marketing. Beating back your father is marketing. It is necessary-"

"Not like this!" he snapped. "It's irresponsible when we're facing such a real risk. What's the joining incentive, do they get a lapel badge, a hat with some stupid logo on it? The whole thing is-"

"Necessary," Hellion finished. "Christopher, I understand you are cautious of growth. You doubt Theodore III. But these people have wanted to help us for long time. Do you remember who brought down Saints? Across your country, Christopher, regular people moved to protect schools and churches. They put their lives at risk then, and they did not even know you! Now they do, and they want to be part of your Foundation, and your fears of somehow becoming evil cult leader like your father should not prevent them finding this as place to unite!"

She breathed heavily. Wren's mouth opened, closed.

"Hellion is passionate about this," B4cksl4cker said unnecessarily.

Wren clawed for something to hold onto. These were the deepest cuts yet. "I am not like my father, and I'm not a cult leader." He paused, mind whirring. "I'm not afraid of becoming like him, either, but neither am I a politician, a salesman, or anyone's damn mascot. You should not have-"

"This is not your choice," Hellion barked. "It has happened and it is best. You are currently sole public figure fighting this Apex, so you are our most powerful weapon against him. American President has been impeached. Gerald Humphreys is in black site. You are last man standing, and that is your brand, Christopher. Stop complaining about fan club you have built and get used to leading it."

He almost laughed.

"Besides, we will need these people now," Hellion pressed. "You should be grateful for Theodore's planning. Do you think I can summon gig workers on darknet right now, to risk their lives bringing down women who wish to burn themselves alive, in midst of national lockdown? No, I cannot do this. No amount of money could. But Foundation faithful? Warm leads in our outer ring, hoping to join what you have built? Yes, this they will do."

Wren closed his eyes, trying to swallow the anger and the new reality. This wasn't just new pieces on the chessboard, this was a whole new board, and he wasn't sure if it was a good thing or not. Personality cults were dangerous things to play with. He didn't want millions of people hanging on his every word.

"I can't be responsible for all those people. I can't-"

"If it helps at all," Hellion easily overrode him, "every new joiner is immediately told in onboarding email that you are leader-in-absentia, figurehead only, and that Foundation is managed by elected Board, with Theodore as current elected chair. Not you. Does this make you feel better?"

It didn't, but now wasn't the time to belabor the point. He flipped the switch in his head. "OK then."

"OK?"

"OK." The new gears spun in his head. "We'll come back to this. In the meantime, we do what we have to do. Put all the Foundation 'fans' on alert. Use them to stop burnings if they can, but there must be no violence, no law-breaking unless it's absolutely necessary to save life. Our goal is to bring the temperature down, not pump it up. If they break these rules, they're out forever. Make that clear."

"As crystal. Now, that is everything. No more secrets, Christopher. Teddy ordered this kept from you, but Teddy is not our actual, actual leader. You are." A brief pause. "Even if in-absentia." Another pause. "If you wish to take away our coins, we will understand."

Wren snorted. The infernal coin system rearing itas head again. It was never meant to be so complicated

"We'll talk," he said, then looked over at Rogers. She was shouting on speaker phone, flicking through screens on her phone too fast for him to track. Maybe arranging his shooters on the National Mall or coordinating the hunt for the next woman to burn.

"Who are our shooters on the National Mall?" he asked Hellion. "Are they core members or," he didn't want to say it but couldn't think of a better word ,"new initiates?"

Hellion's fingers flew noisily over the keys. "At most recent count, one hundred and thirty-three Foundation members both core and fringe will be on Keller's red and blue mats at National Mall. I do not have exact breakdown. All are armed. All have orders to assault stage and kill David Keller on your signal."

Wren's heart skipped a beat. One hundred and thirty-three? A far bigger conspiracy than JFK. On the news they were calling him a terrorist, likening him to bin Laden, and this would just prove it.

So be it.

"Good," he said. "Have them ready. And there's one more thing you can do for me."

"Yes?"

Wren sat up straight. His ribs, shoulders and back throbbed. The double vision had faded a little but the dizziness was still there. Time to embrace it all.

"I need you to place a call for me. He'll be busy, but I want you to keep trying until he answers."

"Of course. To whom?"

"David Keller. I need to speak with my brother."

44

WASHINGTON

The phone rang. The plane flew. They snipped the tail off Delaware, shot low over Chesapeake Bay, crossed a bulge of Maryland at Port Tobacco until they hit the Potomac River, where wideband frequency radio warnings of a fifteen-mile Temporary Flight Restriction around the inauguration forced them down for a water landing just west of Fort Washington.

The DeHavilland thumped as they hit the river, bounced, hit again and entered a juddering deceleration, sending shockwaves of pain up Wren's spine. His vision muddied and his hearing fogged.

"Coast Guard are inbound," Hellion said in a soupy voice in his ear. "You have ten minutes."

The pilot up ahead was shouting and flailing now, objecting to the way they'd used him, until Rogers pulled a gun. "Tell them we held you at gunpoint," she said calmly.

"You are holding me at gunpoint!" the pilot shouted.

"There you go," Rogers said, and disappeared out of the fuselage. Wren slumped at the cab's edge, feet dangling over the choppy Potomac waters as Rogers waved to something too far off for Wren to pick out.

He sucked air. The sound of an engine drew in. Wren's vision grayed as a speedboat rushed closer.

"You have seven minutes until Coast Guard reach you."

The boat's white gunwale pulled up and Rogers guided him onto the deck, then they took off. The wooziness only got worse as they thudded over low breakers, each punching up into Wren's spine. He bit his lip as the veil of unconsciousness crept closer, clinging to the simple sound of a phone ringing in his ear.

Hellion calling David Keller.

"Hang in there, Christopher," Rogers said.

"Thirty minutes until inauguration," Hellion said in his ear. "You are clear to Jones Point, but it's-"

He must have passed out, because the next thing he knew Rogers was supporting him into an SUV.

"Get your head together," she said as the vehicle took off. "We need you on overwatch, Boss. I'll go operational."

The words fuzzed in his head until the agony relented slightly and his vision resolved. No more crashing waves helped. He look out the window to see political pennants streaming by, held by people in their thousands.

KELLER 4 AMERICA read one.

EXECUTE CHRIS-TRAITOR WREN said another.

"Your vehicle has diplomatic precedence," Hellion buzzed in his ear. "You do not know how many strings I have pulled to get you this fast pass to the center."

"How long was I out?" he asked.

"Hard to say," Rogers answered without looking up from her phone. "Since the plane? Forty minutes, give or take."

"Where are we?"

"Ten minutes out from the Mall. The stage is filling up with dignitaries."

"Who?"

Rogers looked up from her phone. "I'd guess it's Keller's

future Cabinet, plus half the Senate, the House Speaker and select Congresspeople, some corporate leaders, the VP's wife, their kids. No sign of the Apex yet. The audience-"

"He's not there?"

"I'm scrolling the major news sites, but there's no sign of him. Looks like he's sitting this one out, hand all the glory to your brother."

Wren didn't buy it. The Apex had never handed the glory to anyone else unless it furthered his plans.

"And the firestorm?"

Rogers flashed a brief smile. "Good news there, Boss; looks like your hackers blocked the burn orders. They're overdue their last burn by forty minutes, and they're claiming responsibility in your name everywhere we can. Some good press for the Foundation, but it's not going to be enough to stop the inauguration now."

His mouth went dry. They'd finally stopped the firestorm and broken the stranglehold, but too late.

"Are you all right now?" Rogers asked. "You went gray for a while. I wasn't sure you'd be with us for the endgame."

"I'm here. Wouldn't miss it for the world. Thank you, Sally."

Her green eyes quirked. "For what?"

"For all this. Trusting me, basically."

She smiled. "The jury's out on that yet, Boss. And technically you've been unconscious, trusting me. But back on point, are we still set on the original plan?"

"Let me see the lay of the land."

Rogers held up a tablet showing an aerial shot of the National Mall. Wren picked out an enormous crowd spreading away from the Washington Monument toward the United States Capitol. Tens if not hundreds of thousands of people packed onto Keller's trademark red and blue mats.

Wren grimaced at the checkerboard sight. The Apex was

always thinking about the visuals, the marketing, always one step ahead. With something so simple as colored mats he created a powerful visual uniting the two political parties, reinforcing his appeal to some united vision of the future.

"Can we see the stage?"

Rogers swiped a few times, and another aerial feed showed the wide D-shaped stage closer up, itself striped with the same red and blue mats as the Mall. Already it was nearly filled with power players. In back of them were twin big screens to the right and left, framing the shot of the US Capitol dome beyond.

"Where's Keller?"

"In the wings, as far as we can tell. He was last out on stage an hour ago."

Wren caught a whip of movement through the truck's tinted windows. "14th Street Bridge?" he asked.

"That's right. We should be there in seven minutes. Wren, I need to know if we're sticking with the plan."

The 'plan'. She didn't want to say 'assassination' and he couldn't blame her. Chess moves raced through his head. The phone kept ringing.

"Fifteen minutes until Keller takes the stage," Hellion said in his ear.

"Our people are out there," Rogers pressed. "They're all armed, and I don't need to tell you how illegal that is. What's the plan, Chris?"

"Where are our people positioned?"

She swiped back to the first aerial view of the Mall, then hit a button which dropped dozens of tiny digital pins. "These are our people."

Wren scanned the distribution; they were clustered primarily right before the stage, though there were others spread back throughout the crowd too.

"What are these ones doing?" Wren asked, pointing.

"Standing ready."

Wren considered. This was the exact kind of terror threat he'd spent a lifetime protecting against.

"We go with the plan. In the event primary shooters miss, they should all go on the hunt for him." He drew a long oval around the Mall and Capitol building. ""This is our cordon, and nothing gets out. Agreed?"

Rogers looked at him. Now they were all becoming traitors. "Agreed."

"What about the stage; does it have plexiglass protectors?"

"It does," Rogers said, and drew three lines at the front of the stage. "Bulletproof on these angles. There are gaps we can use if he strides around, which he always does. We're putting our best shooters in the best positions. Give the order and we'll have a dozen firing at once."

Wren liked the sound of that.

"Ten minutes until he speaks," Hellion said.

Wren looked out the window; they were pulling up Jefferson Drive now, southwest alongside the National Mall. The crowd was everywhere, spilling off the mats all the way to the block concrete of the Smithsonian Air and Space Museum, all cheering for their new President.

The truck pulled up on the side. Wren could just see through the American elms to the video screens above the stage.

"And this is where I leave you," Rogers said. "No way you're coming with me. Here, take this." She handed him the tablet.

"Where are you going?"

She gave him a look. "Who do you think our best shot at Keller is, Chris? Some Foundation fringe militiaman who's been to the shooting range twice in his life, or me, a Quantico-trained field agent?"

That made Wren's stomach sink. "I didn't…" he began but trailed off. Of course that's why they were here. He would do it himself, if there was any chance he could train in a rifle.

Rogers smiled, then unexpectedly reached out to touch his cheek.

"Chris," she said. "Don't worry. I'll get him."

For a long moment he just looked at her, seeing all the ways she'd changed and grown. He'd betrayed her and she'd learned from that. He'd bent the rules and she'd learned from that too. Now he could only hope it wouldn't damn her.

Still, it made him proud.

"Stay safe," he managed.

Her eyes danced with amusement, like she saw right through to what he was feeling. But what was he feeling?

"And you, Boss," she said, then pushed open the door, pulled a long bag out of the open back and melted into the crowd.

Wren was left sitting clutching the tablet.

"I'm going to cry here," came Hellion's voice in his head. "That was beautiful."

"Shut up," Wren muttered.

"And you handled it so well."

He took a breath. Get things back on track. "Track her on this screen, please."

"Yes, Boss," said Hellion.

He winced. She was never going to let that go now. Worst case scenario, she'd turn it into a ring tone. Still, a new pin blipped into being at the edge of the crowd, brighter than the rest and moving toward the front.

"In other news," Hellion went on, "it looks like we have an answer."

"What do you mean?"

"I mean your brother. It seems he is willing to talk."

Wren realized that the constant ringing in his ear had

finally stopped. Asking for that call felt like a lifetime ago. Now his vision tunneled tighter and his breathing shortened as a fresh adrenaline boost came on. He was going to need it.

"Put him on."

45

CHRYSOGONUS

T he line clicked. There was a second of nothingness; Wren cupped one bandaged hand over his ear and strained to hear over the clamor of the crowd.

"Am I speaking with Christopher Wren?"

David Keller. He had the same casual but professorial tone, with hints of both his midwest Arkansas upbringing and his East Coast education; the perfect amalgam of America's twin populations. This was the same Keller whom Wren had hung up on a day earlier, had threatened, had watched ascend to the stage claiming Wren himself as a hero, but he wasn't only that.

He was also Wren's brother.

"I think we both know that's not the name you want to call me," Wren said.

A moment passed. Wren's breath came in short pulls, zinging in his chest. His heart was a drumbeat. The cries of the crowd disappeared as a black wall came down, and he was back with his brother in the dark of the Pequeño dormitory, outsized and outmatched, with nothing to do but take whatever punishment Chrysogonus-With-Bared-Arm decided to hand out.

Except he wasn't that little boy anymore.

"What should I call you then?" asked Keller.

"Take your pick," Wren said, his voice rough and guttural. "Your campaign's been calling me America's worst terrorist. Your organization calls me the ungrateful son. Your sister Galicia called me little brother, your father named me Pequeño 3, and for you I'll answer to them all."

Another moment passed, then Keller laughed. It was musical, attractive, well-practiced and a clear evolution of Chrysogonus' sadistic laughter, when he'd beaten Tomothy or Gabriel or Wren himself with a spiny ocotillo neck, twisted their arms so far the sinews squeaked, dunked them in a rain barrel for minutes at a time.

"Shall we go with little brother, then?" Keller offered, his voice twinkling with amusement. "It's only taken you twenty-seven years. No one ever called you fast on the uptake, brother dear."

"I had a standing start."

Keller laughed again. "And what a life you've made of it. Oh, my brother, it is an unexpected pleasure to stop pretending. Why don't you say my name, for old time's sake."

Wren felt his hot breath drawing close, remembering the long punishments, the pain, the hand clamping around his throat in the dead of night. "Chrysogonus."

"Again," Keller commanded, "with a little more reverence this time. I'm about to become President."

Wren gulped down the old fear and ignored his stampeding heart. His goal here was to press Keller into some accidental revelation, some misstep before a bullet took him out for good.

"It'll be short-lived. You're not cut out for management."

More laughter. "So the upstart speaks. Trying to bait me, little brother?"

"Like an animal to rotten meat," Wren went on. "Galicia

244

took that bait like a harpy. She spilled everything. But then you always were Daddy's second choice, weren't you? Galicia was smarter. Aden had more substance, and Gabriel had our father's charm. Now you're just living in his shadow and building your fortune in his name. Do you honestly think you'd have amounted to anything without him?"

"On the attack, then?" Keller mused. "But you don't know a thing about who I am, little boy. About what I've become. It has been the honor of my life to serve our father's will, to trap you like a bug under glass. You'll find no self-doubt here."

Not deep enough. Wren had to go harder.

"You're wrong. I remember how you used to be. You were cruel, a bully, but you weren't insane, not until he broke your mind, Chrysogonus. Was it through the zoos; is that where he used to take you? He used them to mold you into what he wanted, just like he did with all these women. He made you his slave."

"And I serve at his will," Keller said brightly. "Little brother, really. You can do better. We have moments yet, take your best shot."

Wren's mind raced. What else? "Galicia mentioned you, at the end. Said she was glad it came at my hand, not yours. I think there's nobody she hated more. All the ways you-"

"Galicia pitied you," Keller interrupted, his tone sharp. "From the start we always pitied you. You were born a runt and never grew out of the mindset. Small. Weak. Incapable of seeing past the world as it was, the sickness inherent in all things, all people, even in your precious Galicia."

Strike. Wren pushed the blade deeper, remembering stray glances, how Galicia had never come in for the same punishment as the others, how he'd listened to her at times. "I see you, Chrysogonus. I know why you beat me so badly; you were jealous of our sister's love."

Keller scoffed. "I had her respect. Far worthier than the

pity inherent in whatever 'love' she felt for you. Do you know, we used to laugh about the car crash you've made of your life? Tell me now, 'Christopher', how are your family? Are they still in hiding from you?" He laughed. "What a joke you became to us. Always striving to be like the rest of these idiot people, trying to bleach the stain of the Pyramid from your skin like that poor fool Richard Acker, and turning on your own family in the process. If only you could see yourself the way we do."

"Tell me who 'we' is, Chrysogonus," Wren countered hard. "Galicia's dead and it's only a matter of time before I gut Gabriel, Zachariah, Aden and the Apex himself. They can all whisper what a fool I am as they die."

Keller chuckled. "You were always entertaining. So let me try one on you, 'Christopher'. This may cut deep, so ready yourself." He took a breath. "You never earned a Pyramid name, did you? To the rest of us you were always just Pequeño 3. But after the Pyramid ended you were given the choice of a new name. And what name did you take?" Keller paused, sounding delighted. "Only the name that aped everything you'd seen before of power. But that was my name, little boy! Chrysogonus. Christopher. When I first heard that I laughed myself silly."

Wren gritted his teeth. That was something he'd never once considered. "I left off the 'With-Bared-Arm' though, didn't I?"

"Always some smart-alec response. You never knew your place. But if that doesn't cut through, then look at your last name. 'Wren'. You may have forgotten but I never have. The pet name our father gave you was a childish affectation no other was cursed with, a form of pity that even now you cling to like a five-year-old child hungering for the hand that smacks, desperate for some sign of love."

Wren sucked air through his teeth. "What are you babbling about?"

"How little you know, Pequeño child," Keller crooned. "You were so frail as a baby. Bird-boned, they said. Your infant days in the cages were spent in such helpless bleating, you sounded like a cactus wren. The call of a runt for its mother. Our father called you 'little bird' ever since, and still does." He paused, clearly savoring every moment. "Did you hang on to that tiniest taste of affection, Pequeño 3, all these years? His little bird. His little cactus wren." He sighed like he was reliving a happy old memory. "I honestly never expected you would so immortalize that memento, but I was delighted when you did. Christopher Wren. I underestimated how needy you truly were."

It was too much to take in. "That's a lie," Wren blurted.

"Is it? Think back, little bird. I was eight years your senior. Think back to the cages, with your little beak pushed against the bars."

Half-glimpsed memories billowed at that, a wellspring in black and white like pictures of dead Victorians in some mortuary book. He glimpsed memories he'd long-repressed, his own tiny arms straining at the bars of the cages with his father's beautiful face leaning close, whispering the slightest comforts.

"My little bird. My cactus wren. Sing sweetly for me."

Wren tried to push the image away but once it was there it stuck, along with everything that came with it. His name had been the first real choice he'd made, a year out of the Pyramid and free to define himself however he'd wished. He'd always thought he'd chosen a path in a completely fresh direction, a path that was solely his own, one he could walk and become his own kind of man. Christopher Wren, one of the greatest architects in history; so he would become a great architect too, of people, of systems.

Except he hadn't.

"Are you reeling?" Keller asked, sounding excited. "Is your world turning upside down? Are you beginning to see how well we laughed?"

Wren had nothing. "It's just a name."

Keller laughed, though now the polish was off and it sounded raw and sadistic, like the Chrysogonus of old. "Oh, little brother, the things you come out with. I'll say this, it's been my pleasure to face off with you this past year. Never mind that I'm about to become President, while you're hated as the worst terrorist of our modern age. The truth is you could never win, because at heart you are frail still. When I hear that mock bass voice, when I see you out calming the masses or jumping out of falling buildings, all I picture is the little cactus wren warbling his song into the night, at our father's command."

Wren squeezed his bandaged fists so hard his hands grew hot. "You were in those cages too, Chrysogonus. I bet you warbled pretty good."

"Yes indeed!" Keller cheered. "Though you never saw that, did you? You never heard it, so you couldn't know how it changed me. I became something better, little wren. Something stronger, whereas you let it make you weaker still. You've embraced your frailty like a nice warm blanket, and ultimately it's what will smother you."

Wren felt himself sinking. He had to break through before the opportunity was lost. "I've got memes on the Internet right now tearing you down. You know we broke your firestorm? We have your zoos in our sights and strike teams are lining up to crack them. Gabriel, Zachariah, Aden, we'll get them all. Once footage of that goes live you won't last as President more than a week. The truth emerges, Chrysogonus, like it always did. You can bury bodies in the desert, but the bones will out. The Pyramid burns, and now we all know why."

"We do, and it burns so sweetly doesn't it?" he countered joyfully. "That's the one thing you'll never understand, because we have seen things you never could." Keller's tone turned darker. "Don't you know that's why our father let you survive, at the end of the Pyramid? Because he pitied you too much."

"He's a sadist," Wren shot back. "He wanted me to suffer."

"And pain is a doorway, little wren, through which men see their fate. I see mine. I've seen it for decades now, whereas I don't think you've ever known what your future will be. Too afraid to truly live in the dark. Too broken to live in the light. I pity you even now, still that helpless bird singing in your cage. The day will come soon, though, and I know you'll think of me then. I only wish I could be there to see it."

"Planning a trip?"

"Further than you could possibly imagine, little brother. Draw a little closer and find out. Now, my fate calls. Walk in the fire."

The phone line cut.

Wren was left dizzy.

Memories swamped his numb head: the image of an infant wailing in his cage; the Apex watching on; his brothers and sisters dead in their pit, but not dead. His thoughts spiraled and he couldn't make sense of anythijng.

Ahead the crowd crescendoed. Keller had just taken the stage. He appeared on the jumbo screens over their outstretched hands, larger than life and twice as handsome, his deep voice already rising.

Wren tried to focus on what he was saying but failed.

Little bird, he'd said. Little wren.

"Hellion," he said, pushing through with raw force of will.

"Yes, Christopher."

"Tell our people to get ready."

"They're in position. At your command."

Wren opened his mouth to give it. Kill Chrysogonus. Bring this travesty to an end. Use Rogers for the task she'd committed to, even if it meant she'd be first to bear the counter strike, but then the words froze on his tongue. Keller's words spun back through his head, homing in on one thing that didn't fit.

Planning a trip.

Further than he could ever imagine.

Then he saw it all. Order resolved out of chaos with the felling hand of inevitability. The Apex's greatest magic trick, stretched out to the grandest scale possible.

Keller's voice surged across the crowd, but all Wren heard was the desperate thump of his own pulse. Sweat poured down his face. Any moment now.

"Hellion, get me in every Foundation member's head right now!"

An instant passed as keys flew on some distant keyboard. "Done."

"This is Christopher Wren," he said. "Draw your weapons!"

46

WALK IN THE FIRE

The crowd roared as Keller drove them higher, leaning out like a ship's figurehead at the very fore of the stage, shielded by thick plexiglass screens with his arms spread wide, the great and good clustered tight behind him.

"I built myself from nothing," he boomed. "The sun did not shine upon my birth. I started out a lowly orphan but under Lady Liberty's loving eye I rose to wealth. All things are possible, my friends! Hope is our strength. Wisdom is our armor. Who would have believed that this poor orphan would one day rise to become your next President of these United States?"

The people became furious noise.

"But that dream is dying. We are under assault by an unstoppable darkness. Even the bright torch of Lady Liberty cannot beat back this ocean's tides as it circles the world to beat against our shores. It despises our way of life. It abhors our success. It looks upon our works with envious eyes and seeks to drag us into its own filth."

They roared. Wren opened the SUV's door and stumbled out on numb feet.

"I promised you a better day, and that day has finally come," Keller called. "It begins here and now, as we open our eyes and welcome the truth. The time for childish things is past. The time for truth is here."

"Fire your weapons in the air right now," Wren shouted into the ears of his Foundation members. "Get these people out of here!"

"What is happening?" Hellion asked.

"Fire, fire, fire!" Wren shouted, so loud his lungs convulsed and set him into hacking coughs as his brother approached climax; arms flung up, voice thundering.

"You have been lied to all your lives," Keller cried, "told you can be happy, whole, safe and complete, but this is not true. You feel this in your bones. Everything is getting worse. Everything is sinking. The truth is, you have already lost everything, and you don't even know it because they won't let you see."

The people answered with tumultuous roars even as gunfire broke out across the crowd. "You are not happy," Keller shouted. "You are not safe. You are not free. You are nothing but slaves, burning alive in a hell of your own making, and there is just one way to escape that pain and fight back."

"Fire, fire," Wren called, staggering onward. "Rogers, get the hell out of there!"

"Fear is a portal!" came Keller's overwhelming voice, amplified by every loudspeaker in the park, and the people responded with a call and response they didn't understand, that could only lead in one terrible direction.

"Fear is a portal!" they roared back.

"Pain is a doorway," Chrysogonus boomed, and they answered him with rage and glee.

"Pain is a doorway!"

"Walk in the fire!"

Before they could answer, Keller flung his head back, his arms wide and was suddenly engulfed by a jet of flame from below.

Wren blinked, hardly believing what he was seeing.

Keller was swallowed whole in the surging jet, even as dozens more jets ripped out across the stage. There had to be at least forty gas burners all rigged to blow like fireworks under the boards. Now the jumbo screens filled with a real-life vision of hell, an inferno climbing high enough to be seen above the heads of the crowd.

Wren's mouth ran dry. People screamed.

Keller held court at the center of the firestorm, arms raised in beatification while the senators, congresspeople, judges and billionaires behind him spun into fiery cocoons that screamed, ran and rolled through the blaze.

This was it. A nuclear bomb dropped into the American psyche. The Apex's greatest trick on the grandest stage possible.

"Get off the mats!" Wren shouted, voice hoarse and barely audible over the screams as he stumbled closer to the crush of bodies. "Rogers!"

On the screen, the human torch that was David Keller strode to the edge of the stage and flung himself off. He hit the masses below as they tried to flee, and the fireball blew out across them instantly. Flames devoured everyone and everything in their path, so powerful Wren felt the blast of heat where he stood.

"It's the mats, get off the mats!" he roared, remembering the way those red and blue mats had looked, a patchwork stretching the entire length of the National Mall. They had to be soaked in kerosene; no odor, no tell-tale giveaways, now uniting Keller's crowds in the greatest firestorm of all.

"Rogers!"

"-unning!" came her answer in his ear, broken by static and gunfire as the first wave of the crowd blew out toward Wren like a human storm surge. A thickset man in a green bubble jacket led the pack, red cheeks and arms pumping. A woman carrying two small crying boys raced behind him. A man in a purple t-shirt fell and was trampled underfoot. The tide barely split before they reached Wren, crashing off his truck and down either side.

One of the big guy's wild elbows struck Wren in the temple and rocked him, then the constant stream of people thudding off his broad chest tipped him off-balance. He fell against the side of the truck and just caught himself on the door frame, feeling stitches tearing.

"Find Rogers, Hellion!" he shouted, as he pulled himself onto the truck's roof and watched the firestorm race back along the Mall like a napalm strike. Great swathes of the crowd were swallowed in flames that spewed out foul black smoke. Wren fought to keep his feet under him as the people kept hammering off the vehicle, gazing as if hypnotized into the fiery hurricane's heart; the Apex's vision of hell on Earth, realized again.

Dark silhouettes ran and fell through the endless blaze. Screams became the only sound.

"Rogers!" Wren boomed, and leaped off the roof and plowed back into the crowd. This time he got knocked down to the ground by a man with fire in his hair. He hit the grass and was instantly trampled underfoot, feet stamping on his chest, his arms, his outstretched legs, tearing more stitches and opening old wounds.

"Get up, Christopher!" Hellion blared.

"Get Rogers out!" was all he could shout as feet beat down, too weak to fend them off, already gagging on the smoke and the airless, acrid vacuum that the mass kerosene ignition left behind. A knee hit him in the forehead as he tried to rise, a foot jabbed him in the ribs, then someone tumbled across him, followed by another and another, too fast for any of them to get up. In seconds he was heaped beneath a scratching, clawing pile as the terrified throng fled for their lives.

"Hellion!" he cried.

"I'm trying," she shouted back. "B4cksl4cker!"

"Boost- … signal," came B4cksl4cker's bass voice. "Stealing …- ccess. Christopher, stay with us!"

He couldn't move, couldn't even breathe. He was a little bird in his cage again, bleating through the bars for help.

"- is she?" shouted B4cksl4cker.

Wren tried to shout again but got only a mouthful of smoke; buried alive again beneath a mound of burning bodies, ash sucking into his lungs, his vision spinning rapidly to black…

Then a hand clamped onto his wrist. For a horrendous moment he felt sure it was Chrysogonus; ripping him from the safety of his bed, pulling him out for more punishment, and he yanked back with all his flagging strength. He didn't want to be his brother's plaything one more time.

But just like then, the arm was stronger than him, and he was ripped upward through bodies and into a gritty orange light, slumped on his knees atop the dead as flaming bodies ran on all sides, gazing dead-on into a shock-paled face.

"Let's get the hell out of here, Boss!" Rogers yelled.

He barely heard her. Her long hair was frayed and flying in the hot wind, soot was smeared on her cheeks and blood ran from a gouge down her scalp, but it was Sally Rogers.

Somehow, he found his feet.

"Hang in there," she shouted, battling a path through to the truck, where he slumped into the passenger seat and she took the wheel. "Hellion's got hospitals on standby. We're going to make it!"

We're going to make it.

The last thing Wren saw before darkness claimed him was the Apex standing beyond the bars of his very own cage, blue eyes gazing hungrily into his own, stroking his shivering skin and calling him his 'little bird'.

THE NEXT CHRIS WREN THRILLER

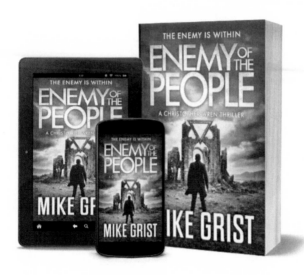

On the run. Hunted by all.

CIA black-ops legend Chris Wren is on the run. Hunted on all sides by the followers of 'X' - an Internet conspiracy theorist preaching hellfire and lies - he barely makes it out of Washington alive.

But X isn't done. As America tears itself apart and Congress scrambles for control, X releases an 'Enemy of the People' kill list. And number 1 on that list?

Chris Wren.

Now the whole country turns against him. Civilians on the street open fire. Wren's only hope is to team up with tough-as-nails agent Sally Rogers to hunt down and kill X, before the country burns itself alive.

The enemy is within. The cure is death.

AVAILABLE IN EBOOK, PAPERBACK & AUDIO

www.shotgunbooks.com

HAVE YOU READ EVERY CHRIS WREN THRILLER?

Saint Justice
They stole his truck. Big mistake.

No Mercy
Hackers came for his kids. There can be no mercy.

Make Them Pay
The latest reality TV show: execute the rich.

False Flag
They framed him for murder. He'll kill to clear his name.

Firestorm
Wren's father is back. The storm is coming.

Enemy of the People
Lies are drowning America. Can the country survive?

Backlash
He just wanted to go home. They got in the way...

Never Forgive
His home in ashes. Vengeance never forgives.

War of Choice
They came for his team. This time it's war.

Learn more at www.shotgunbooks.com

HAVE YOU READ EVERY GIRL 0 THRILLER?

Girl Zero

They stole her little sister. Now they'll pay.

Zero Day

The criminal world is out for revenge. So is she.

Learn more at www.shotgunbooks.com

HAVE YOU READ THE LAST MAYOR THRILLERS?

The Last Mayor series - Books 1-9

When the zombie apocalypse devastates the world overnight, Amo is the last man left alive.

Or is he?

Learn more at www.shotgunbooks.com

JOIN THE FOUNDATION!

Join the Mike Grist newsletter, and be first to hear when the next Chris Wren thriller is coming.

Also get exclusive stories, updates, learn more about the Foundation's coin system and see Wren's top-secret psych CIA profile - featuring a few hidden secrets about his 'Saint Justice' persona.

www.subscribepage.com/christopher-wren

ACKNOWLEDGEMENTS

Sincere thanks to Su, Pam Elmes, Monte Montana, Sue Martin, Julian White & Siobhan McKenna.

- Mike